A *Lady's* WAGER

Arlem Hawks
Josi S. Kilpack
Sarah M. Eden

Mirror Press

Copyright © 2023 Mirror Press
Print edition
All rights reserved

No part of this book may be reproduced or distributed in any form whatsoever without prior written permission of the publisher, except in the case of brief passages embodied in critical reviews and articles. These novels are works of fiction. The characters, names, incidents, places, and dialog are products of the authors' imaginations and are not to be construed as real.

Interior Design by Cora Johnson
Edited by Meghan Hoesch and Lorie Humpherys
Cover design by Rachael Anderson
Cover Image Credit: Nathalie Seiferth, Arcangel

Published by Mirror Press, LLC
A Lady's Wager is a Timeless Romance Anthology® book. Timeless Romance Anthology® is a registered trademark of Mirror Press, LLC.

ISBN: 978-1-952611-31-5

Timeless Georgian Collections
Her Country Gentleman
A Lady's Wager
A Midnight Masquerade

Timeless Regency Collections
Autumn Masquerade
A Midwinter Ball
Spring in Hyde Park
Summer House Party
A Country Christmas
A Season in London
A Holiday in Bath
Falling for a Duke
A Night in Grosvenor Square
Road to Gretna Green
Wedding Wagers
An Evening at Almack's
A Week in Brighton
To Love a Governess
Widows of Somerset
A Christmas Promise
A Seaside Summer
The Inns of Devonshire
To Kiss a Wallflower

Timeless Victorian Collections
Summer Holiday
A Grand Tour
The Orient Express
The Queen's Ball
A Note of Change
A Gentlewoman Scholar
An Autumn Kiss

Timeless Western Collections
Calico Ball
Mercer's Belles
Big Sky
A Wyoming Summer

TABLE OF CONTENTS

The Diamond of Bristol
by Arlem Hawks _____ 1

Women of a Certain Age
by Josi S. Kilpack _____ 119

A Most Unsuitable Suitor
by Sarah M. Eden _____ 215

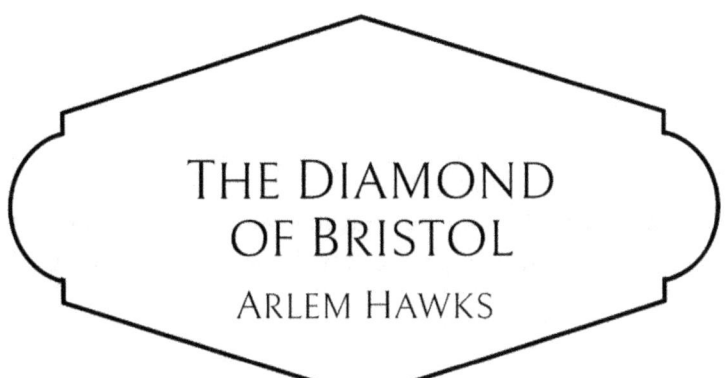

The Diamond of Bristol

Arlem Hawks

To the wonderful Chathams—
Thanks for accepting me (and all my questions) into your crew, even if I'm not good for much more than a ship's boy.

One

Bristol, England
18 January 1793

FOR A BRIEF MOMENT, CORAH Bradford considered letting her grandfather pack her off to London if it meant getting out of the clutches of Mr. Haltwhistle. The bachelor stood across from her as they awaited the start of the dance, his temples gleaming with sweat and shoulders dusted with powder that hadn't stuck to his oversaturated hair. While those could be forgiven, the hungry, self-satisfied glint in his gaze as he looked at her could not.

Corah swallowed, smoothing the silk of her gown. No one had made her favorably consider dirty, overcrowded London before making the acquaintance of this gentleman. The orchestra still fussed with their music in the balcony above the ballroom. She didn't know whether she wished them to hurry so this humiliation would pass more quickly or take their time and delay the lingering touches and leering grins her partner had manifested in the previous dance.

Either way, supper was soon expected. She had to stay with him through that to win her wager. She closed her eyes against the chill that oozed down her arms. Curse Melinda and her pride for getting them both into this.

Corah glanced down the set to her cousin, whose eyes were locked on a young man who was not her partner. The one Melinda was supposed to have secured as her partner for supper but clearly hadn't managed to. Was she even trying to hide her disappointment? If so, Melinda was failing miserably, but concealment had never been one of her talents.

The humiliation of failure seemed preferable to winning the wager just now. Mr. Haltwhistle cleared his throat and leaned forward, forcing Corah to return her attention to him. "Did your grandfather mention I called on him yesterday morning?"

"I don't believe so." She didn't know that her family had any connection to the Haltwhistles at all. Living across the river from Bristol had sheltered them a little from the city's society. A blessing, if it meant fewer acquaintances like the gentleman before her.

"He seemed rather eager for us to meet."

She drew in a breath to reply but held it when she couldn't think of something to say. Grandfather threw young men at her rather frequently. If this was his latest attempt, he must be scraping the bottom of the barrel that was Bristolian society. If he scraped the barrel clean, it was off to London for Corah.

Off to London. Mr. Haltwhistle said something else, but she didn't hear him. Candle wax dripped to the floor between them. The tiny flames above created a coverlet of heat that made her knees want to buckle. The thought of London, of leaving home, of securing a match to some gentleman far from Bristol and rarely returning . . . Her stomach twisted.

Suddenly, supper sounded unbearable. She attempted a smile at Mr. Haltwhistle's enquiring look, the muscles of her face tight and unwilling. With him as her supper partner, she wouldn't be able to eat a bite. The urge to excuse herself and drag Melinda and Aunt Mary back to the house nearly overwhelmed her.

A smug smile up the line of dancers kept her rooted to the ballroom floor. Miss Whiting, in her crimson gown and bright rouge, must have smelled impending victory. The young woman, a niece to the owner of the assembly rooms, prided herself in controlling the assembly ball wagers. Secure the supper dance with a man selected at random from the list of guests or subject yourself to public humiliation—that was Miss Whiting's rule. Corah had never participated in these stupid games, not in three years out in Society, but Melinda had begged her to play along to gain the favor of Miss Whiting and her friends.

This would be Corah's first and last wager. And she would win—not to claim the prize of arriving with the Whitings in their carriage at the next assembly, but to be able to wipe that sneer from Miss Whiting's face.

"Perhaps, Miss Bradford, you would enjoy a ride around Kirkby Park tomorrow? I have just procured a delightful little phaeton I think you should particularly enjoy." Mr. Haltwhistle's brow, dusted with white hair powder, lifted saucily.

"I . . . " Grandfather would not approve of the phaeton, even if he approved of the gentleman.

"I would be very pleased to explore your grandfather's estate." Mr. Haltwhistle reached across the gap and seized her fingers. She recoiled, but he held firm. "I hear it is a rather lovely property."

Eyes had turned toward them, and still he clasped her

hand across the aisle. There, in the middle of the ballroom for all to see. He might as well have proposed to her in this horribly public setting. The orchestra continued their leisurely preparation for the next song. Corah prayed they would hurry. Miss Whiting's grin had only deepened.

"Unhand her, you blithering, addlepated son of a blunderbuss." The sharp voice rang in her ear as an arm appeared from behind her, taking her wrist in a firm but gentle grip. A blue silk sleeve marked it the arm of a gentleman.

Mr. Haltwhistle dropped her hand, nostrils flaring. "How dare you, sir. You have no right to insult me with such vulgarity. Who do you think you are?"

A musky scent, caught in the hazy heat of the room, enveloped her as Corah looked up at the welcome intruder. He was young, perhaps a few years older than her twenty-one. His unpowdered hair was tied back in a neat but simple queue with a black ribbon.

"Richard Bradford, and as her brother, I have every right," the gentleman said, the shadow of a smirk on his lips.

Corah stiffened, his hand still about her wrist. This man was certainly not her fourteen-year-old brother. Though with hair nearly the same shade of brown as hers, one could possibly mistake them for brother and sister.

Mr. Haltwhistle's gaze narrowed. How much did he know about her family?

The violin's bow skipped across the opening chords, and couples up and down the line bowed. Those closest sent eagerly curious glances toward the trio's altercation.

"If you would excuse us." The imposter wrapped her hand around his arm and steered her away from the dance. Mr. Haltwhistle's clipped footsteps followed them out.

"Now see here, Mr. Bradford . . . " The violin's crescendo drowned out Mr. Haltwhistle's whining voice.

They rushed from the ballroom into the corridor, and Corah tripped over her shoes as she studied the young man's profile. A strong jaw and angled brow would have given him a gravity both worrisome and enticing except for the little grin he could not keep hidden. To be swept off the dance floor by a mysterious stranger was the stuff of romance novels, and she couldn't help the erratic pattering of her heart. Disturbances like this didn't happen in reality.

The young man glanced at her with deep blue eyes and winked as though they were friends sharing a joke. Who was this? She loosened her hold on his arm. If word of this incident returned to Grandfather, she could only imagine his frustration.

"Halt, sir! Or I shall call you out for your nefarious slander," Mr. Haltwhistle shouted.

The stranger stopped as Corah's hand fell to her side. The two men stood toe to toe, Mr. Haltwhistle breathing heavily like a bull ready to charge, and the newcomer completely unaffected.

Mr. Haltwhistle folded his arms. "I thought you were at sea, Mr. Bradford."

"My ship was paid off and I am on leave until my next commission."

Corah looked between them, chest tightening. Though fewer people occupied the corridor, the three of them still drew attention. Marriageable women should not draw attention. Not like this. Grandfather had reminded her of that on too many occasions.

"Which ship?" Mr. Haltwhistle's tone had taken on a skeptic tautness.

"I am most recently of the *St. George*, but I am to join HMS *Adamant* in a few weeks."

Her brother had just transferred from the *St. George* to

the *Adamant*. Corah inched back. Mr. Haltwhistle was right—who did this newcomer think he was? And how did he know so much about Richard?

Mr. Haltwhistle sniffed. "I find it difficult to believe the Royal Navy would stoop to commissioning so offensive a whelp as you."

"Offensive whelp?" The stranger snorted. "I see you forgot your wit at home this evening."

Mr. Haltwhistle drew himself up to his full height. "I thought your family of better breeding than this. How can you bear him, Miss Bradford?"

"She can stand me much easier than she can stand a sweat-drenched, leering cad like you, of that I am certain."

Corah bit her lips against the bark of laughter that nearly burst from her. Such directness. And truth.

Mr. Haltwhistle's face flamed, his eyes widening into an unbecoming blend of horror and rage. He sputtered. "I demand a public apology for these offenses."

The stranger shrugged. "You'll be dead before you get one."

"Portland Square. Tomorrow morning," Mr. Haltwhistle hissed.

A duel. Her heart jumped to her throat. "This is madness."

"I'll be there," the newcomer said with a smirk.

Mr. Haltwhistle turned on his heel and stomped away to the faint announcement that supper was served. Corah clapped her hand to her forehead. What had just happened?

"You'll have to—" the young man began, but she overrode him, an unintended shrillness in her voice.

"Have you lost your mind completely?"

Derrick Owens couldn't help a chuckle at Miss Bradford's bewilderment. She'd paled but for the light brush of rouge on her cheeks and lips, a stark contrast from the flush that had graced her skin in the ballroom. Those hazel eyes caught him as securely as a gale pinning a ship against leeward shore.

Bradford had mentioned her kindness, her excitement, her intelligence, but he had failed to mention how attractive his sister was. Though one could hardly expect more from a new midshipman.

"My mind is steady as ever," he said, hauling his smile back in. It wouldn't do for her to think he was mocking her.

"A duel?" She lowered her voice, arms rigid at her sides. "Over a woman you hardly know? We haven't even been introduced."

"You seemed distressed by that overdressed louse." He shrugged. "I couldn't stand by and watch one of Bradford's relations get harassed by such—"

"How do you know my brother?" she demanded. "How do you know *me*?"

Scenes of dark lower decks splashed with orange lantern light played through his mind. Swapping jokes with the young gentlemen—Bradford, Addison, Brenton, and all the other mids—in evening hours when responsibilities had eased and the sun had drawn most of the worries of the day down with it. Bradford liked talking about his family. And not having one of his own, Derrick liked listening.

"He was one of the midshipmen under my watch aboard the *St. George*."

Her face softened, recognition lighting her features. "You're Lieutenant Owens."

"At your service." He bowed. "I take it he's mentioned me in his letters."

"Each time he writes. He says you make him send letters."

She laughed softly, then quickly sobered. "But that doesn't give you reason to enter into a duel over my dancing with Mr. Haltwhistle."

He raised his hands. "There will be no duel, never you fear."

She gestured the direction Mr. Haltwhistle had gone. "I heard him call you out."

"I wouldn't trust that man to know how to handle a pistol. Or a sword, for that matter." He'd faced a healthy share of peacocks like Haltwhistle, too full of pride and confidence in their own abilities to see their incompetence. "The ones without knowledge of weapons can be more dangerous than the ones who know what they're doing. I intend to avoid dueling that overly powdered baboon at all costs."

Her lips pressed together in a way that clearly read she didn't trust his words. "You are quite . . . unique in your insults."

"Why offend someone if you cannot have some fun with it?" He offered her his arm. They'd be late to supper and cause another scene. While he didn't mind, something told him he'd drawn too much attention to Miss Bradford for her comfort that night. "Shall we go in?"

"You won't duel him, then?"

He grinned at the concern in her eyes. Usually, the only concern he received was from friends of his late parents. People who had no sway over him but wished they did when they pressed him for details about his life. "I will not."

"Do you promise?"

She looked so much like her brother, especially when he was seriously attending to his duties. Their brows pinched in the same way when troubled, and their eyes narrowed as though the stress of it pained them. He wanted to reach out and smooth the worry away. Which would be a terrible idea, as they'd only just met.

"I promise, on my honor as an officer of the navy. I shall not engage that—"

"'Blithering, addlepated son of a blunderbuss?'" she finished. She slipped her hand back around his arm.

"That's one of my better ones, if I do say so myself."

Her lips turned upward. The warm light of the corridor's chandeliers twinkled in the little jewel she wore about her neck and washed over the silk ribbons woven into her softly powdered hair. "I see you are like Richard in that you both enjoy hearing yourselves speak."

Indeed, though he would keep quiet to listen to her. "I cannot refute it, I am afraid." Could he maneuver them to a table with silent supper partners? Or perhaps louder neighbors would be better, as it would award them more privacy. He matched her unhurried pace as he led her to the refreshment room. After hearing so many stories about this young woman, to the point it seemed he knew her before they'd met, standing beside her felt surreal.

Miss Bradford balked at the entrance. She scanned the guests already seated, then her shoulders sank.

"Is something the matter?" he asked, placing his free hand over hers. Was it because they were conversing without proper introduction? "I'll tell them we were introduced."

She shook her head, the little curls of her coiffure swaying. "It isn't that."

"What is it, then? Allow me to assist you." It was the least he could do for the sister of his very young comrade.

"You cannot turn back time, and therefore, there is no way to amend it." She sighed. "I have only lost a ridiculous wager, and I fear there will be rather humiliating consequences."

"Shall I have words with the bettor on your behalf?"

"Heavens. Please do nothing of the sort," she said quickly.

"I shall draw up my best insults for him."

Her lips twitched. "I'm certain you would." She did not say it with frustration or condescension. The friendly tease in her tone lit something inside him he hadn't felt in ages. Perhaps, for once, he could enjoy himself in this place he'd chosen to occupy between assignments. He wouldn't go so far as to wonder if he could call it home, but for this moment in the company of a fetching young woman, he could pretend that home was not an unreachable dream.

Corah kept her face impassive during Melinda's lament. Her cousin threw her arms around the bedpost and laid her head against the carved wood in the image of a hopeless Andromeda.

"How can it be we both lost our wagers?"

Corah removed the last pin from her hair and massaged her aching scalp. They'd returned so late, she hadn't bothered to ring for Jemima, the maid she and Melinda shared. "I told you the wagers were ridiculous."

Melinda's mouth turned down into a pout. "You sound as though you don't care about singing 'Little Bingo' at the crack of dawn before everyone in Portland Square." The last came out in a squeak as she no doubt imagined Society matrons and gentlemen alike poking their heads out of windows, nightcaps and all, to investigate the early crooning. "Why does it have to be Portland Square?" she whimpered.

Corah took up her brush and began the task of preparing her hair for bed, brushing with methodical strokes. "Because that is where Alexandra Whiting lives. She wouldn't be bothered with rising that early to make sure her victims perform their punishment properly."

"Victims!" Melinda sank onto the bed, her dark eyes wide. "Miss Whiting is not so much a villain as that."

The powder from Corah's hair came out on the brush and the cloak she wore over her dressing gown, her hair becoming more of its true brown with each stroke. It really was a very similar color to Lieutenant Owens's hair, wasn't it?

"We agreed to something," Melinda went on, "and we did not achieve it. It is an act of honor to keep our word."

"Honor is ridiculous." Duels. Wagers. What people wouldn't do in the name of honor, no matter how stupid the activity. Her stomach clenched again at the thought of Lieutenant Owens dueling Mr. Haltwhistle. What if he'd only agreed not to fight him to pacify her but truly intended to carry on with it? He was a navy man, after all. Richard was always mentioning various duels between officers in his letters.

"Then you don't intend to follow through with the punishment?" Melinda cried. "Corah, you must. Miss Whiting will shun us both if you don't, and if she shuns us, then the rest of Bristol society will too."

Corah worked the brush toward the top of her head. As magical as it was to see a refined figure materializing in the mirror when Jemima readied her for a ball, there was something equally marvelous about removing all the layers and becoming plain, ordinary Corah again. Not trying to impress anyone, not trying to catch a gentleman's eye.

"I will be in London soon, so I suppose that is not my problem," she said. The brush finally swept smoothly through her hair, and she returned it to the dressing table. She purposely did not meet Melinda's eye in the mirror.

"You cannot be so cruel as to leave me here to suffer the disgrace alone, Corie." Her cousin still used the childhood nickname, even after all these years. "Do you really think

Grandfather will send you to London?"

Corah bit her lips as she sectioned her long tresses. The powder hadn't entirely left her hair—keeping it clean and dry until the next washing day—but now it only muted her natural color slightly. "He hasn't said for certain since Christmas. But he told me all of last year that if I didn't find a man to marry before the Season, it was off to London for me. Clearly, I do not have a man. And Parliament is already in session, so Society has started its migration from country to Town."

Melinda leaned back on her elbows, brow furrowed. "I wonder if Mama and I will go with you."

Corah certainly hoped so, but there was the potential for Grandfather to not agree to pay for a Season for Melinda with her being only eighteen. He'd only pay for such an expense if he thought her ready for a match. "Don't let my fears of London keep you from getting excited about the prospect." Corah slowly plaited her hair.

"But London is where Bristol girls go and never return. That's what you said."

"So they do," Corah said. "Look at my mother. And your mother. And our aunts. Spread all across the country because of whom they married." Her hair formed into a thick rope, and she pulled it over one shoulder to finish the plait.

"Mama only returned because of Papa's death." The melancholy in Melinda's voice made Corah's eyes smart. They'd lost their fathers and come to live with Grandfather within a year of each other—Corah with her youngest brother and sister, Melinda with her mother. They'd both had to grow up too fast, but Melinda maintained an air of innocence Corah envied.

No need to worry her any further. Corah plucked up a ribbon and fastened the end of her hair. "Most of them are, or were, very content in their situations. So I suppose we should not pity them. Who is to say you and I would not also find happy situations?"

"Who was that gentleman you were stuck with at supper?" Melinda asked. "Someone said he stole you from the dance floor."

So she hadn't seen it. Good. Perhaps Grandfather wouldn't catch word. Corah set herself to removing her cloak and tidying the dressing table. "Oh, he was just a lieutenant who served with Richard. He thought I seemed distressed, though he was very much mistaken." He'd read the situation too clearly. Was it strictly Mr. Haltwhistle's overly eager expression that had caused Lieutenant Owens to step in? He couldn't have seen her face from behind. Unless he'd been watching since the start of the first dance.

"He was quite attentive to you, though I am sorry you were stuck with Mr. and Mrs. Johnson as your table mates."

Corah swallowed, willing her cheeks not to turn pink. She'd almost forgotten they had shared a table with the silent old couple. Lieutenant Owens had filled her ears with farfetched tales he'd collected from the Mediterranean, the Caribbean, and the South China Seas. When they'd exhausted those topics, he had thrown them into a discussion solely about her. In fact, they'd hardly talked about him the whole of supper.

"Why did he not ask you to dance afterward?" Melinda asked. "I know it isn't the thing, but surely he wanted to."

Corah closed the table's drawer and sat back. "He said he had to leave." Like an apparition from a dream, he'd melted into the crowd and vanished, leaving her to find Aunt Mary and Melinda.

"A handsome and mysterious lieutenant, returned from the wars at sea to win your hand." Melinda sighed.

Corah pushed herself to her feet. "Oh, Melinda, don't be

ridiculous." But a grin spread across her face. "We aren't even at war."

Her cousin giggled. "That is the only thing you disagree with. You want the lieutenant to win your hand, don't you?" She seized a pillow and tossed it at Corah, who stumbled backward as it hit her shoulder.

"I doubt I will even see him again," Corah said through her own laughter as Melinda hurled another pillow.

"But you can dream!"

Corah snatched up one of the pillows from the floor. Grandfather would be horrified to see them like this. "We should be getting to bed. We only have a few hours before we have to pay for the awful wagers." She threw it at Melinda, who dodged and collapsed on the bed.

Melinda closed her eyes as the laughter subsided. "Perhaps you won't have to go to London after all."

Corah paused as she wound up to throw another pillow. If that was the reward, she would beg the lieutenant's attention at all costs. If only it were that simple, to find a man she enjoyed speaking with who would live out his days in Bristol. Somehow Lieutenant Owens did not seem the type to be tied down.

 Two

DERRICK STROLLED DOWN THE LANE, casually glancing toward the green from under the brim of his cocked hat. His hostess hadn't been awake when he left that morning, probably for the better. Mrs. Stewart, his late grandmother's friend, would have tried to convince him to stay away. So would Miss Bradford, if she could see him now. But he wasn't about to miss the amusement.

Not far ahead, under a little cluster of trees on the corner of the street, two figures stood in the early morning light. Their breath drifted up in puffs of white. This park in the middle of a square of townhouses was rather small and public for a duel, but he didn't expect a man like Haltwhistle to have a good mind for such things as choosing dueling locations.

As he approached the two men, he took up whistling a tune that had been a favorite of *St. George*'s crew. Something rough and roaring at which his present company would turn up their noses.

One of the men rushed toward him, the frozen grass crackling under his shoes. "You are late."

It was time for the games to begin. Derrick pretended to

startle, grabbing the forward corner of his hat. "I beg your pardon."

"You are late, Bradford," Haltwhistle snapped. "I'd almost given you up for a coward."

Derrick grabbed at his cravat, mimicking a lady clutching at her pearls. "Forgive my ignorance, but do I know you? I believe you've mistaken me for someone else."

"Last night at the assembly rooms." Haltwhistle folded his arms. "I had engaged your sister to dance, and your brazen insolence made a mockery of me in front of all Bristol."

With a glance around the deserted street, Derrick retreated a step. "My good fellow, you insist you know me, and yet I do not have a sister. Nor a brother, for that matter."

Haltwhistle's jaw tightened. "I am talking of your sister, Miss Corah Bradford."

"*My* sister?" Derrick conjured a bewildered look. "Of course Miss Bradford is not my sister."

"Stop this nonsense, Bradford!" Haltwhistle snatched the hat off Derrick's head. "You see? You are the very man who insulted me last night. I demand justice."

It took all of Derrick's might not to snicker at Haltwhistle's antics. How did the man think he'd respond? *Oh, yes, good sir. I see now. I am the man.* Lunacy. But laughter would ruin his ruse.

"My name is not Bradford, and I will thank you to return my hat." He grabbed it back and clamped it on his head. "You would do well to keep your dirty hands off my person."

Haltwhistle shook his fists like a child. "You are a liar and a coward!"

"If I were a lesser man, I would call you out to duel this moment," Derrick said with a sniff, straightening the lapels of his greatcoat. He leaned around Haltwhistle to address the second man. "I am very sorry, are you this gentleman's friend?

I do believe he is unwell and ought to be returned home immediately."

The man shifted uncomfortably. "Haltwhistle, do you think—"

"Do not try to fool me." Haltwhistle's voice had gone shrill. How could this jarring a sound be so satisfying? "I know what I saw. I know what you said. You will face me like a gentleman, or I will see the name of Richard Bradford dragged through the muck of Society."

"Richard Bradford." Derrick stroked his chin. "You mean Mr. Colston's young grandson? The midshipman in the navy? That would be rather heartless of you."

"I think you have the wrong man," the friend said uncertainly.

Haltwhistle shook his head and seized Derrick by the sleeves. "You will not escape this."

"Unhand me, you libidinous tub of guts." He brought his arms up between Haltwhistle's, then whipped them to the side, breaking the other man's grip. "You would do well to keep your insanity to yourself. I take my leave, and it is in your best interest not to follow."

He turned on his heel to the sound of Haltwhistle's incoherent raging while his friend tried to pacify him with assurance that he must have been drunk and not remembered the real story from last night. With his back squarely to them, Derrick allowed himself a sly grin. The navy had a system that naturally rooted out many half-intelligent and self-important fops, but he'd found ways to cross words with more than one numbskull throughout his career in the navy. He couldn't explain the pleasure it brought him.

As he made his way around the square, he caught a flash of color on the otherwise muted landscape. Two bright red cloaks huddled together near the empty fountain at the center of the park. A bit early for ladies to be out walking, especially in January with the sun not quite up.

One of them stepped onto the lip of the fountain. She wobbled, catching on to an upper decoration for balance. The other looked around the square and covered her face with her hands. The first said something to her, then straightened as best she could on the unsteady perch and began to sing. Derrick paused his walk and bent closer to listen.

"*The farmer's dog leapt o'er the stile. His name was Little Bingo.*"

What in the name of Momus was this? With a glance over his shoulder to ensure Haltwhistle had gone, Derrick abandoned the path, making for the clear tones of silly music spouting from the fountain. Whatever it was, he wasn't about to miss it.

Corah drew in a breath. Almost done with this absurd payment and then she would be free of Alexandra Whiting. The capped head poking out an upper window of a townhouse was most certainly Miss Whiting, and Corah could only imagine the gleeful sneer.

"*J-I-N-G-O* !" Corah sang, anticipation of the end increasing her volume. "*I think it is, by jingo.*"

Thunderous clapping from behind made her yelp and shrink back. The thin ledge of the fountain did not agree with her shoes. Her heel slipped off the stone and she teetered, waving her arms wildly until someone caught her by the arm and waist. Blue eyes twinkling with mischief filled her vision as she grasped his strong shoulders to balance herself.

"Never have I heard so stirring a rendition of 'Little

Bingo,'" Lieutenant Owens said, his hold on her waist steady in a strangely comforting way. "May I help you down from your stage?"

No, she would rather he didn't and instead let her fall back into the basin and down the empty drain to wallow in her humiliation. Despite the biting cold, her whole body seemed on fire. Of all people, why would he be walking about this early in the morning? And in Portland Square? She didn't resist as he took her hand and guided her back to the ground.

The duel! Mr. Haltwhistle had named Portland Square. She whirled on him, icy dread rushing through her. "You gave your word." How could he lie so brazenly to her last night? Had they already fought? She scanned him from head to toe. He looked unharmed and in good humor. Too good of humor by the brightness of his face and the carefree tilt of his felt hat. She looked him over once more to be certain, but most of him was covered by the heavy wool of his greatcoat. Winter clothing wasn't supposed to flatter anyone, but somehow his did.

She blinked. And what of Mr. Haltwhistle? Richard's talk of the lieutenant didn't lead her to believe him capable of missing with pistol or sword. Much as she disliked Mr. Haltwhistle as a companion, she didn't wish him harm.

Lieutenant Owens held up a hand. "I have kept my word, Miss Bradford."

The tension inside her eased. "You have?" Praise the heavens.

"Everything was settled without violence, rest assured." He nodded toward Melinda. "As we have already been introduced, might you present to me your companion?"

Introduced. They hadn't been, but she couldn't admit to that. "This is my cousin, Melinda Lee."

He bowed. "And will you be favoring me and the rest of Portland Square with a performance as well, Miss Lee?"

How much of her song had he heard? Curse Miss Whiting with more pimples than she had mouches to cover them with, and may they appear just in time for the next assembly.

Melinda turned several shades of green.

"You'd best get it over with before more people wake," Corah said. A few early walkers had appeared in the streets around the square.

"Of course you are right, but I . . . " Her eyes enlarged and she covered her mouth with a hand. "I'm going to be sick," she squeaked, dashing for the other side of the fountain.

"Melinda," Corah cried as the sound of her cousin retching filled their ears. She hurried to Melinda's side.

The poor girl shuddered, huddling by the side of the fountain. "I can't do it! I can't."

"Then by all means don't." Corah crouched beside her, rubbing her back. "It was a stupid wager. This is not worth your health, love." It wasn't worth anything, in truth. She'd have dismissed the offer without another thought if Melinda hadn't begged her to participate.

"But Miss Whiting will shun me," Melinda wailed. "I can never show my face at assemblies again."

How fortunate Miss Whiting was not in Society yet when Corah was eighteen. Even then, she didn't think she'd have fallen for the allure of friends in high places. What's more, the Whitings were hardly the wealthiest family in Bristol and only had acclaim because they owned and controlled the assembly rooms. "What a silly thing to think. Miss Whiting is not the goddess of Bristol society."

"I might as well accept my spinsterhood now."

Heavens above. Corah handed her a handkerchief to wipe her mouth. Why did Melinda go into these states where no one could reason with her? "Let's get you home."

"Do you live nearby?" The concern in Lieutenant

Owens's voice warmed Corah from within. When had he followed her around the fountain?

"No, we live in Yanley, near Long Ashton." Not far by coach, but a long walk. "Our carriage is just down the street."

"Allow me to assist you to the carriage." He extended a hand toward Melinda.

Her cousin shrank back. "Oh, Lieutenant Owens! No. How humiliating for you to see this." She hid her face behind her hands again.

"Never mind that. I've seen much worse." He took both young ladies by one elbow and helped them to their feet. "The navy has a way of making it so very little upsets you. Which direction did you leave your carriage?" He released Melinda's arm but held on to Corah's elbow as though he'd forgotten to remove his hand.

"If I leave without singing, it will be the end of me," Melinda said miserably, leaning against Corah's side. The sudden weight pushed Corah firmly against Lieutenant Owens, who didn't seem to mind holding them both upright.

"What did you do to warrant such grave punishment?" the lieutenant asked.

Nothing she wanted to admit to him. She nudged Melinda back and scooted away from Lieutenant Owens's warmth. That musky cologne cutting through the cold air set her insides flipping in odd ways.

"It is your choice, Melinda," she said. Her cousin's terrified, red-rimmed eyes made her heart ache. Perhaps . . .

Corah pursed her lips. Miss Whiting was too far from them to be able to tell the difference. She groaned inwardly. Why did she always do these things for her family? It all came from loving them too much. "Very well. I will do it for you."

Melinda clutched her sleeve. "But she will know it isn't me."

"Only if she has a spyglass. Lieutenant, will you help her to our carriage? It is just there." Corah gestured in the opposite direction of the Whitings' residence to where the coach waited. She hardened her expression, preparing to force herself into another mortifying spectacle.

Melinda threw her arms around Corah. "You are the very best of cousins. How shall I ever—"

"Please get back to the carriage," Corah said more gruffly than she intended. "I wish to leave the moment I am finished." She flexed her fingers. A few more minutes of singing. She could survive this.

"Come, Miss Lee." The lieutenant offered her his arm, which the girl eagerly took. For a moment an unfamiliar sensation arose in Corah's chest. They looked well together, Lieutenant Owens kindly smiling down and Melinda's upturned face perfectly pink from the chill. Why did she not like the sight? Then he turned his gaze to Corah, brows lifted expectantly.

"Go, then." She waved them toward the coach.

"I thought to stay for your encore, and then we may all walk back together."

She ground her teeth, planting her fists on her hips. "If I have to do this twice, I shall not have an audience." Well, not him as an audience.

"I will be sorely disappointed to miss it." He cocked his head. "I get so few opportunities to hear voices as fine as yours."

Shameless flattery. She wouldn't give in. "I'll call you out myself if you stay," she said, wagging a finger at him.

His lips twitched as if he enjoyed the mental picture that painted, but he bowed his head in defeat and turned. Corah stayed in place until he and Melinda had made it a good distance across the park. She caught every time he covertly tried to glance over his shoulder. The scoundrel. Had Richard mentioned what a rascal he was? She supposed while aboard ship, he had less opportunity for jokes.

Satisfied they were a safe distance away, Corah regained her position on the fountain and filled her lungs to begin. "*The farmer's dog leapt o'er the stile . . .* " But the lieutenant's laughing eyes and the happiness they brought would not leave her mind. Nor would the fact that Melinda was enjoying several minutes alone with him. The longer she sang, the more she thought he might as well have stayed. Somehow she didn't mind the thought of him listening as much as she insisted.

Three

CORAH SAT NEAR THE FIRE in the library, *A Sicilian Romance* sitting forgotten in her lap as her attention wandered. Nearly a week had passed since Lieutenant Owens deposited them in their carriage at Portland Square and sent them back to Kirkby Park. She'd tried to discover more about him as she accompanied her aunt on visits, but few of their friends and acquaintances knew much.

The flames crackled in the hearth, and she mindlessly thumbed the pages of her novel. She had hoped to meet him again, perhaps in town or at one of the homes they visited. No luck, though someone mentioned he was staying at the home of Mrs. Stewart, a widow who had been a dear friend of his late grandmother. That was all they could give her.

The door creaked open, and Grandfather entered. He wore his thick white hair in a queue with the sides curled in straight, horizontal lines. The image of classicism.

"Good morning, my dear." He closed the door behind him. "How do you fare?"

Corah sat up, closing the book and tucking it between her

and the couch. Grandfather didn't approve of romance novels. "Quite well, thank you." Though she would be better if she could find out more about Lieutenant Owens. Would Richard's letters give her more? She would have to dig them out to see.

"I had something I wished to speak with you about." He sat on the other side of the couch and folded his hands.

"Of course." Aunt Mary didn't know Mrs. Stewart as more than a passing acquaintance, but she might be persuaded to pay a visit. It seemed the old woman was the only one in Bristol who knew the history of Lieutenant Owens.

"It is about London."

Corah froze. She'd awaited this conversation for weeks. "What about London?"

Grandfather didn't look at her for a moment, as though trying to choose his words. "I think it is time."

She didn't have to ask what he meant by that. Her mouth went dry, and she tried to swallow. They'd go to London, find a husband among the hundreds of single gentlemen, and then she'd be banished from Bristol for always. She couldn't find a reason not to like every one of them. If only she had found a good enough reason to like someone in Bristol.

"I hope to leave the first week of March. That will give us ample time to order you new clothes before Easter."

Just more than a month away. The book dug into her side, rigid and unmoving compared to the softness of the couch around it.

"Unless by some miracle we can find you a match before then." He sighed. "However, I think we both know there is no one in Bristol to suit your fancy." He patted the couch in a steady rhythm, eyes still lowered in thought. "But you cannot spend your whole life playing about with your cousin. If Bristol will not do, we must try our luck in London."

Corah nodded. How else could she respond? Grandfather was right. She had exhausted her possibilities here.

"I don't blame you," he said, a hint of regret in his voice. And was that sorrow hidden there in the wrinkles around his eyes? "I will not push you the way I did my daughters." His voice broke and he covered it with clearing his throat. More than one of her five aunts had landed in unhappy situations. Though he didn't say it, she knew that guilt was filling his mind. "I want you to at least like the man. Enjoy his company. Have hope for respect and amicable companionship. Perhaps even love."

"Yes, Grandfather." Her hands trembled. She blinked, then blinked again, willing tears not to fall from her burning eyes. London would not be as terrible as she feared. She had to believe that.

Grandfather took her hand and gave it a squeeze. He rarely did that. He preferred to show his affection through praise, which he would give in very serious tones. So serious it sometimes worried Melinda. "We tried our best, my dear. When the usual venues do not produce the desired results, one must look elsewhere. You still have time, but we cannot wait until time is out to pursue our prize."

"I think it a good plan." How she wished she meant it.

Grandfather nodded, face still troubled. He knew she was trying to be brave. "I will leave you to your reading, then." He rose and adjusted his coat. "Do spend a moment or two in something more intellectual, if you have the time."

Corah smiled in spite of herself. Of course he'd spied what she was reading. Before he could quit the room, she hurriedly asked, "Is Melinda coming?"

Grandfather paused, and Corah's heart sank. "She will have her opportunity another year when she has matured. This Season will be all for you. We cannot have Mary distracted with keeping her out of trouble."

It wasn't as if she'd be alone in London, but somehow going without Melinda felt wrong. They'd hardly been apart since they came to live in Bristol. Aunt Mary couldn't play the part of her daughter, with the late-night giggles and matchless support.

He rested a hand on the door. "You and Melinda are off to the Whitings' this morning, are you not?"

"Yes." She hadn't managed to convince Melinda to give up.

"I'll accompany you. I have a few things to seek out in town. Perhaps we can stop by the bookshop." He'd taken her there often just after Papa died and they were forced to sell the house. The bookshops of Bristol became their special outing whenever Grandfather could see her spirits were low. She nodded, forcing a smile.

When he'd gone, Corah returned to staring at the fire. Its warmth seemed far away, too far to reach. What she wouldn't give for someone to lean into just then, to tell her everything would work out for the best. She couldn't go to Melinda. Her cousin would dissolve into tears at the announcement of their impending separation. Aunt Mary was in town. Her sister, Helen, and youngest brother, James, were too young to understand. Her oldest brother, John, was away at school. Richard was at sea. No one left to confide in.

Corah finally pulled her novel out again and ran her finger over the decoration on the cover. What she wouldn't give to lean on the strong shoulder of Lieutenant Owens again, his fine wool coat warming her and musky cologne calming her nerves.

Her finger halted. She gulped. Why would she want that? She hardly knew the man. She shook the thoughts from her mind. Ridiculous. The fear of London had clearly muddled her thoughts.

Derrick settled into the offered chair at The Ship and glanced out the coffeehouse's window. The St. Mary Redcliffe church loomed across the street, a grey Gothic structure with half a spire. A single bell pealed as the clock struck nine.

The small coffeehouse buzzed with the morning chatter of merchants on their way to offices and gentlemen escaping tedious breakfast conversation at home. Derrick reached for a newspaper that had been left on his table. The *London Packet*, dated the twenty-third of January. Yesterday. Perhaps a paper named after a ship would have some navy news. Anything that would get him off half pay and back in full service instead of wandering around the country paying visits to friends.

He drummed his fingers on the table. This venture to Bristol hadn't been entirely dull. In the two weeks he'd been there, he'd already avoided a duel and enjoyed a private performance by a rather fetching young lady in the middle of a park. Mrs. Stewart hoped he'd stay for many weeks, no doubt to try to match him with all the girls she kept inviting to her home.

Why was it older women enjoyed trying to make matches? It wasn't as though he were a catch. A lieutenant of a little means all sitting in London banks, but no home and no living family to speak of. Raised by a well-connected grandmother who had died a few years previous while he was at sea, he was not the sort of young man gentry families clamored to secure for their daughters.

"Owens, isn't it?" A young light-haired gentleman stopped beside his table and nodded a greeting. "We met at the assembly. Do you mind if I share your table?"

Derrick rose. So much for a quiet morning at the coffeehouse. "Good morning, Mr. Whiting. But of course. Please sit." They shook hands and Derrick found his chair again.

"I could hardly stand to be at home this morning," Whiting said. "My sister is up to her wagers again, and all the young ladies in Bristol are descending."

"Wagers?" Derrick glanced back at the paper. Perhaps if he had something to say about Miss Bradford, but news of any other young lady was of no interest.

"Stupid games," Whiting grumbled. "She assigns them the name of a man they've never met, and they have to be introduced and get him to engage them for the supper dance. If they manage it, our family has the misfortune of carting them to the next assembly. If they don't, public humiliation for the poor girls."

Miss Bradford's sunrise singing and Miss Lee's wailing about potential ostracizing flashed through Derrick's mind. "How ridiculous," he said. Miss Bradford participated in these? She seemed a wise sort of lady, not one that would take part in activities with more risk than gain.

A serving maid brought them both cups of coffee, and Derrick thanked her. What was this downturn in his mood? Disappointment that Miss Bradford hadn't quite been who he assumed? He glanced back at the newssheet, now partly covered by their cups. A line of blackletter text caught his eye: Death of the French king.

He sat forward. They'd killed him? He scanned the lengthy article detailing the gruesome event, which was filled with English and monarchist rhetoric he didn't think the French would agree with. They'd killed him. He hadn't thought they'd reach that point.

Whiting continued to grumble about his sister's games as

Derrick searched. There had to be something about the navy in here. An event of such worldwide importance wouldn't go unanswered by King George, and depending on the severity of the response, that meant a chance of a lieutenant of little means getting called up to service.

"You should beware," Whiting said. "I think your name was in the mix for next week's assembly."

Derrick blinked, lifting his gaze. His brain had fuzzed in his pursuit of news. "My name?"

"Your hostess told my mother and sister you planned to attend. Someone will have their cap set at you at the assembly."

This hardly mattered right now. Not with kingdoms at stake. "Mrs. Stewart said I'd be there?" Of course he'd planned to go, mostly to catch another few minutes with Miss Bradford. Now he wasn't so certain he wanted to risk that, if he'd be avoiding another young lady the whole night. Perhaps he'd just served in the navy too long, but being someone else's prize did not suit his fancy.

"Even if she hadn't, Alexandra would have found you out. She likes finding the gentlemen no one knows for her games."

"How interesting." A game of cat and mouse could be amusing. In other circumstances. Would he be called up soon enough to evade the sport? He could only hope. "I'll be on my guard."

While Whiting complained about his sister, Derrick pulled the newspaper until it slipped out from under the other man's coffee cup. The article took up the entire sheet. He ran a finger over the lines of print.

Finally he spotted it. Whitehall—the Admiralty's headquarters. There had been a council at Lord Grenville's office. And a meeting of the Admiralty. The third-rate HMS *Illustrious* had been commissioned, along with two frigates.

Derrick stood, his chair's legs grating against the floor. This was it! What he'd waited for. They were outfitting ships and sending them off.

"Something the matter, Owens?"

"Urgent business I must attend to." He folded the newspaper and shoved it into his back coat pocket. He'd be off to London before the week was done. Of course, it would take time before all the orders were worked through, but he would be ready and waiting the moment the Admiralty sent him their commands. Derrick gestured to the unfinished cup. "Tell them to put this on my tab, would you? I'm very sorry to leave so suddenly. Good day to you." He wouldn't miss the man's prattling.

He rushed out into the winter sun, greatcoat draped over one arm. Shoving his hat onto his head, he hurried past the oddly shaped shot tower beside the coffeehouse. He needed pen and ink. Blast, he'd take a pencil. Anything to write with so he could send a letter to one of his former captains immediately. Wasn't there a bookseller at the end of this street?

In his musings he nearly bowled over an old gentleman and two young ladies descending from their carriage. He skittered to the side before he could hit them, mumbling, "Terribly sorry. Do excuse me," and nearly turned without another thought—until he locked gazes with a pair of hazel eyes. A melancholy cloudiness in their depths brightened as she took him in.

"Lieutenant Owens!"

His breath hitched for an unguarded second. He swept off his hat. "Miss Bradford. How lovely to see you this morning."

"Where are you off to in so great a hurry?" The pale green gown under her crimson cloak set off her skin in a rather enchanting way that morning. Or perhaps it was the soft winter light.

Where was he off to? His mind had gone blank. Somewhere important. "The . . . the bookseller, I believe."

One corner of her pink lips curled upward. "You believe?"

His face heated. "I am. Yes, I am most certainly going to the bookseller's." The old gentleman accompanying her watched him with narrowed eyes.

"Allow me to introduce my grandfather, Robert Colston."

The man clutched his hand with such strength, Derrick feared he'd crush it. It took all Derrick's fortitude not to wince.

"This is the lieutenant from the *St. George* you were introduced to at the ball?" Mr. Colston asked.

Miss Bradford cleared her throat with a swift glance at Derrick. "Yes, it is."

The man grunted a barely intelligible greeting, looking Derrick over with more severity than a captain inspecting his crew before welcoming an admiral aboard.

"I suppose we can all go in together, then," Miss Bradford said, slipping a hand around his arm. She cocked her head with an enquiring look.

"It would be a pleasure, of course." The mounting agitation from reading the newspaper deflated as he led her into the shop. He couldn't very well write his letter with her about. Not with this unusual fog clouding his brain.

"I've been wondering when I'd see you again," Miss Bradford said quietly. "Have you been hiding?"

He laughed. Suddenly, his task didn't seem quite as urgent as it had in the coffeehouse. "I try not to be predictable." The letter could wait. The mail wouldn't leave Bristol until tomorrow, and no war had been declared yet, after all.

There would be plenty of ships. What was a little delay if it meant a few moments in Miss Bradford's cheery company?

Corah and Melinda waved to their grandfather from the steps of the Whitings' townhouse. When the coach rolled away, Melinda leaned in. "Lieutenant Owens is rather charming, isn't he?"

Corah ignored the knowing tone. "It is a comfort to know Richard has such kind officers watching over him." She quickly tapped on the door, willing the footman to hurry in his door-opening duties. The flutter inside of her that hadn't receded since their meeting with the lieutenant in the streets threatened to creep into her voice. She would not let on to Melinda that it had affected her.

"He was joking and flattering you the entire time we were at the bookshop. Quite the flirt, if you ask me. And you should have seen Grandfather watching you."

"He was not flirting with . . . " Corah gulped. "Grandfather was watching us?"

"I never know what Grandfather is thinking, but he was certainly thinking something about the two of you." Melinda sighed. "If only he did not scowl so much."

Corah seized her arm, ready to pull more from her cousin, but the Whitings' footman finally opened the door and ushered them in. She let go and followed her cousin inside. What had Grandfather been thinking? That she'd rejected the notion of marrying every eligible gentleman in Bristol and its surrounding towns only to fall for a lieutenant she hardly knew?

She halted as she pulled off her mitts. No, she hadn't

fallen for Lieutenant Owens. She'd met him three times. One couldn't fall in love after three meetings. She handed her mitts, cloak, and bonnet to the footman, then reached up to make sure her hair was in place. It wasn't as if she didn't know him. Richard had served under him for three years, almost since he started his time in the navy. She knew Lieutenant Owens to be a good and honorable man and that he preferred to spend his time in company of the ship's boys and midshipmen when they were in port rather than dallying about on land. That had to count for something.

She followed Melinda into the sitting room where several young ladies had already gathered. Though she knew them all, she would not count a single one of them as a friend. She kept to quieter circles.

"Miss Bradford, I daresay you are blushing."

Corah's head snapped up as Miss Whiting swept toward them. "It is rather warm in here compared to outside." She curtsied in greeting. What were the odds of this visit to the Whitings' lasting a short while? She suspected not high.

"A great many gentlemen have arrived and made known their intentions to attend next week's assembly," Miss Whiting said, her brow arched saucily. "Shall we make some wagers?"

Laughing glances found their way in Corah and Melinda's direction as well as toward the few others who had lost their wagers. Corah folded her arms. This might be some people's ideal method for finding a husband, but it was not Corah's style. She and Grandfather both wished she knew what her style was. Or perhaps these girls were simply trying to have some fun at what could sometimes be a stale gathering. This was not her sort of fun either.

"Miss Bradford, shall we start with you?"

Corah groaned inwardly. "Why not?"

They all took their seats on the sofa and armchairs like obedient children in the schoolroom. Corah attempted to keep her expression neutral so she wouldn't look like a prisoner awaiting punishment. No one could be as terrible as Mr. Haltwhistle. She prayed for someone dull, quiet, and easy to engage. Once they restored their honor, as her cousin put it, by winning wagers, Corah would never play these games again. Beside her, Melinda looked ready to lose her breakfast. Poor girl. Why did she insist on this if it terrified her so? She patted Melinda's hand and changed her prayer for two dull, quiet, and easily engaged gentlemen.

Miss Whiting grandly shook the jar where she kept the names written on little scraps of paper. "Who will the gods of assembly balls choose, Miss Bradford?"

If the gods of assembly balls were the ones who chose, Corah was fairly sure they were also the gods of pranks and foolery.

Miss Whiting reached into the jar and slowly pulled out a slip of paper to a chorus of giggles. Corah nearly rose and snatched it from her to read it herself. Must she do this so dramatically? Miss Whiting examined the slip and gave a slight scowl. "This is a gentleman I am unfamiliar with. My brother suggested this name. You will have to enlighten us after your victory. *If* there is one."

Just say who it is. Corah gave a tight smile. "Someone new. How fortunate am I."

"Your gentleman is . . . " Someone whispered in the long pause.

Corah ground her teeth and closed her eyes. This would be the very last time she ever kept company with Miss Whiting, no matter how much Melinda begged. Pleasing her cousin was not worth her sanity. At least when she went to London, she would leave this all behind.

"Mr. Derrick Owens."

Her eyes flew open. Melinda gasped and started to blurt something, but Corah silenced her with a nudge to the ribs.

"Is he not the old bachelor who recently moved into Queen Square?" Corah asked quickly. That was Mr. Owston, and Grandfather had already suggested she consider him for marriage. It hadn't taken long for Corah to make a decision on that, as he was opposite of Lieutenant Owens in every way. "I don't think we have been introduced." That part wasn't a lie.

Looks of recognition circled the group, and Miss Whiting's eyes caught a wicked glint. "I think you are right, Miss Bradford. How well you know our society. I wish you the best of luck, and I do hope he is an easier catch than Mr. Haltwhistle proved."

Corah gave a nervous laugh, but not for the reasons the rest of the young ladies thought. "I could certainly use an easier target."

Derrick Owens. He wasn't an easy target by any means, but the thought of finding a way to get him to engage her for the supper dance made her heart scamper about her chest. He'd been so attentive the last time, so protective of his comrade's sister. What's more, they could finally be properly introduced and fix the lie she'd told Grandfather.

She didn't listen to the rest of the names, only nodding and mindlessly murmuring in reaction to the announcements. Memories of his warm, uninhibited smile took up the better part of her thoughts.

And deep in the recesses of her mind, an idea—one she refused to fully acknowledge—blinked to life. Perhaps she wouldn't have to go to London to find a husband at all.

Four

THE SUN HAD NEARLY TOUCHED the horizon when Derrick and Mrs. Stewart set off to honor their dinner invitation. Somehow she'd secured an invitation nearly every night since his arrival. It made him miss the familiarity of wardroom dinners aboard the *St. George*, even if the food was gravely inferior.

"Remind me, who are we to thank for their generosity in inviting us this evening?" he asked. With any luck, he'd receive an answer from Captain McRae in a few days and not have to worry about social engagements anymore. Or perhaps Captain Lennox. Lennox resided just across the Bristol Channel in Newport. Derrick had decided to stay in Bristol until he received word, as it would be easier for someone to locate him if he stayed in one place. And if he could hardly bear Bristol's society, London would suit even less.

His hostess adjusted the carriage blankets around her. "Mr. Colston and his family. His wife died several years ago, and his widowed daughter keeps house for him. Her daughter lives there as well, along with several other grandchildren who lost their parents too early."

Derrick nodded. This wouldn't be as terrible as he thought. An old man and his daughter were hardly something to worry about. Unless the daughter was a young widow. Blast. He tapped his fingers against his leg. She most certainly was a young widow or Mrs. Stewart would not have been so keen for him to accompany her. The sly devil. No wonder she and Grandmother had been such fast friends. He could only imagine the trouble they'd caused in their younger days.

"Mr. Colston mentioned he met you the other day. He seemed impressed. At least as impressed as I've ever known Mr. Colston to be."

Derrick squinted. "Where did we meet?" He'd done an abominable job of remembering the people he'd met in Bristol. When one lived in a new city every month, renting cramped rooms by himself or relying on the invitations of friends, one met too many people to bother keeping them straight. There was one young lady he was certain not to forget, however—the one he'd caught singing silly songs at the crack of dawn in a park. Not only did she have the nerve to keep her word with the wager, but he'd discovered at their last encounter she was exceedingly well-read. Better than he was. She'd recommended a whole list of books to him he'd never have time to read. Though he might find a few to take with him on his next voyage.

"He mentioned he saw you at Haysom's. The bookseller's."

Derrick straightened. The Bradfords' grandfather. Of course. After three years of hearing young Bradford talk about the family, how had he forgotten? "He has two lovely granddaughters, does he not?"

"He has two fine granddaughters, indeed." She said it artfully, as though trying not to let on that his interest pleased her. "A man could not go wrong in securing the hand of either young lady. Though I have heard the elder, Miss Bradford, is quite pernickety when it comes to gentlemen. A man might have better luck with the younger granddaughter, Miss Lee."

Some men didn't mind a challenge. "Pernickety?"

Mrs. Stewart leaned closer as though they weren't the only two in the carriage. "Her grandfather has discussed drawing up marriage contracts with several young gentlemen since she entered Society, but he hasn't gone through with a single one. He gives reasonable excuses, of course. Still, rumors have abounded that it is not he but she who opposes the matches."

"Does she not wish to marry?" All the more reason for him to spend time with her while in Bristol. A lady who wanted nothing but friendship was just his sort of woman.

"No one knows, but it's a logical explanation. A girl with a face like hers should have had an offer by eighteen." Mrs. Stewart shook her head. "If he'd taken her to London three years ago as I suggested, they would have found someone to fit even *her* standards."

"Most assuredly." Part of him appreciated that Mr. Colston hadn't taken her to the London marriage mart.

It appeared he wasn't the only one caught by surprise. When they arrived at Kirkby Park's drawing room, Miss Bradford shot out of her chair, gloves clutched in one hand. "I thought you meant the Stewarts from Long Ashton were coming to dinner," she said.

"I believe I said Mrs. Stewart," Mr. Colston said, bowing to their guests.

Miss Bradford extended her hand, and Derrick couldn't explain his eagerness at taking it. The smoothness of her skin washed over the roughness of his, weathered from a lifetime exposed to the elements. He bowed deeply, but when he raised his head, it was her grandfather's skeptical stare that caught his attention. Derrick quickly dropped her hand and greeted Miss Lee, feeling Mr. Colston's eyes on him with every move he made.

When the butler announced dinner, Derrick came to the horrible conclusion that he and Mr. Colston were the only men in attendance at this dinner. No doubt their host would take an old-fashioned approach to sitting at table, with the women all on one side and men on the other. All excitement that had mounted in their carriage ride dissipated. If the table was too long, he'd be having a private conversation with the disapproving grandfather rather than a pleasant one with the amiable granddaughter. As he held out his arm to escort Mrs. Lee into the dining room, his stomach sank. He might as well be retaking his lieutenant exam for all the joy this dinner would bring.

Corah pulled back as Melinda's fan cut off her view of Lieutenant Owens, stopping them before they followed the rest of the company out of the drawing room. "What are you doing?" She tried to push the fan out of her face, but Melinda leaned in.

"He has his eye on you," she hissed. "You cannot tell me otherwise."

"How am I to know that?" Corah whispered, fighting a smile. Surely it was only because of their connection with her brother and the fact that he'd conversed with her more than the other members of their party, Mrs. Stewart excluded. But the way he bowed so elegantly over her hand, as though she were some grand lady deserving of his respect . . .

That was enough to make any girl hope he'd taken an interest in her.

"He hardly looks at anyone else when you are around."

Corah huffed. "You've seen us together twice."

"*Three* times before tonight. And if you do not have him secured before you are off to London, I shall give you all my pin money."

Corah shook her head. If Melinda had any pin money left. "We should follow the others, or Grandfather will not be pleased."

Melinda frowned. "I can already see the lieutenant's feelings. But what are yours? Do you like him?"

"This is hardly a discreet position to have this conversation," Corah said with a laugh, pulling her cousin's fan down and moving toward the door through which the others had disappeared. How was she to answer? "There are very few people I dislike." She greatly enjoyed his company on the few occasions they'd met. The way his coat hugged his shoulders always caught her attention for longer than it should have. And when he grinned, her chest seemed to expand in an odd bubbly sensation that made it difficult not to laugh.

"You know what I meant, Corie," Melinda grumbled. Corah refused to give her anything more.

In the dining room, two chairs remained vacant—one between Grandfather and Mrs. Stewart, and the other between Aunt Mary and Lieutenant Owens. She glanced at her cousin. Someone had to choose a chair. Melinda sighed as she closed her fan and pocketed it, then trudged to the seat near Grandfather, throwing Corah a long-suffering look.

How fortunate Grandfather had instructed the servants to shorten the table so there was not a gap between gentlemen and ladies. The lieutenant pulled out the chair for her as she rounded the table and slid it under her as she sat. Did his hands linger on her chair? Had his gaze remained a moment longer than usual? Confound it. Melinda's conversation was playing games with her head. Or perhaps it was the scent of dinner wafting up from the dishes before them.

"Have you begun *Celestina*?" Lieutenant Owens asked, quiet enough to not draw the rest of the table into the conversation.

He'd remembered her novel. "I've finished the first volume and begun the second."

"And how do you like it?" His voice carried a tone of genuine interest that warmed her through.

"Mrs. Smith is a rather sentimental writer." She scooped up her spoon to dip into the soup lest she fall too far behind the rest of the company. "I've enjoyed it. I suppose I can't help but hope for an orphan to succeed." She inwardly winced. Was that venturing too close to her past for polite conversation?

A faraway look clouded Lieutenant Owens's features. "I share the sentiment. If orphans can persevere in novels, perhaps we as real orphans can." Somewhere in those deep eyes, she thought she caught a glimpse of little Derrick Owens, practically alone in the world.

"Do you remember your parents?" she asked, even quieter than they were speaking before. She had no desire for the others to join this conversation. No one else had lost both parents in childhood, and for some reason, she wanted to protect this moment with him.

"Not very much." He cleared his throat and returned to his food. "But I do remember the books. Both my parents loved to read. You would have loved the library. At least I think you would have, according to what I've been told about it."

"What happened to the books?"

He shrugged. "Many of them stayed with the house. My father didn't own it. Others were given away or sold. I didn't have much use for them, young as I was. Now I wish they'd been kept."

What a shame. She hoped whomever she found to marry had an extensive library. She could imagine cuddling her children near the fire as she read them *Aesop's Fables*, their father reading his own book nearby, watching them with clear blue eyes. Her cheeks heated and she swallowed. How had Lieutenant Owens made his way into her daydream?

"What would you do with them while at sea?" she asked quickly.

"Perhaps I'd give them to you for safekeeping." He winked, sending her thoughts spinning all over again. "And you? Do you remember your parents well?"

She nodded. "I was fourteen. They died within a year of each other. I remember them quite well. Better than my younger brothers and sister do."

"I think I had the easier time of it," he said, twirling his spoon around his soup but not eating. "I did not know what I lacked."

She placed a hand on the table between them. "But we had family members galore to support us. You had almost no one."

"My grandmother, until I went to sea," he said. "Then I suppose the officers and mids became my family." It sounded so lonely.

"Where is your home, then?" Across the table from Lieutenant Owens, Melinda pointed downward with her spoon. What could she mean by that?

"Wherever I can find a place that suits me and won't get me run out the door." He stared at her hand, and for a moment she wished he'd take it in his again as he had when he greeted her, just so she could feel the tingling run through her fingers and up her arm.

"How sad to not have a home," she said. "I would have been lost without Kirkby Park and Bristol."

"Perhaps someday someone will convince me to find one." His voice had lowered, slowed. "Until then, I shall have to keep searching."

"Corah, dear," Aunt Mary said. "Is there something wrong with your soup?"

Corah straightened. When had she leaned toward the lieutenant? "Not at all."

"You've hardly touched it."

Her face must have gone a similar shade to the wine sauce in the nearby dish. So that's what Melinda had meant by her gesture. Corah mumbled her pardons and hurried to finish so the footman could clear away bowls. Every time she looked up, someone watched either her or the lieutenant. Mercy. Now they'd all come to the wrong conclusions.

When she met her grandfather's stern gaze, a rare flash of satisfaction glistened in his eyes. Rather than deepen her embarrassment, it made her pause. Would he nudge her toward Lieutenant Owens if he thought the man had caught her interest? For once she did not mind the notion. And if he approved, dared she hope it would mean staying in Bristol and not going to London? She caught the lieutenant studying her with a grin. Could there be any drawbacks to this unexpected situation?

Five

"You were rather friendly with Miss Bradford last night," Mrs. Stewart said at breakfast.

Derrick choked on the bite of ham he'd been attempting to enjoy and reached for his glass. She'd noticed? Of course she had. Nothing slipped past Mrs. Stewart's attention.

"Shall I expect an announcement in the papers?" she asked.

Derrick's insides twisted tighter than an anchor cable. A wedding. Is that what they expected? He'd known Miss Bradford just more than a week, not counting all he'd heard from her brother. It felt as though he'd known her for longer, but they couldn't understand that. Neither could they understand that once her grandfather learned his situation, Derrick wouldn't be permitted to walk through the door of Kirkby Park ever again.

"I think not," he said when he'd sufficiently recovered. Marriage. How could someone in his circumstances think of matrimony? Of course he had some funds. They wouldn't be destitute. But with war on the horizon and no home of his own, he couldn't begin to consider it.

"No?" Mrs. Stewart tilted her head. "The family seemed pleased at your interactions. To catch the eye of a girl who has turned down every other suitor . . . " She let the sentence trail off into a sip of tea.

"I cannot marry. Not now and possibly not ever." Derrick rose from the table, leaving his plate unfinished. It was as though a round shot had planted itself in his gut. "Please, Mrs. Stewart, do not encourage that line of thought with Mr. Colston or his family."

"Is it marriage you fear? Or something else entirely?" She spoke carefully. "Miss Bradford is the best of girls."

He knew it. Every time she smiled at him, every time her eyes lit up as she discussed her books, every time her hand reached his direction, his heart wanted to believe that maybe there was something more in his future than lonely cabins in dank lower decks. That maybe *she* was in his future.

But he couldn't be hers. Mrs. Stewart wouldn't understand that. No one would.

A footman entered with a tray of mail for his mistress, and Derrick hurried toward the door. His pulse raced, his head spun, and he needed fresh air.

"Wait, Derrick." Mrs. Stewart held up a folded piece of paper. "This is for you."

He stared at the square, stomach leaping to his throat. The sender hadn't noted his . . . or her . . . identity on it. He walked back, grumbling. Of course it wouldn't be from her. She was too proper for that.

Derrick tore it open, half expecting another invitation from Mr. Colston. The man needed more opportunity to make sure this lieutenant was worthy of his beloved granddaughter. Perhaps Derrick should save him the time and assure him this lieutenant was most certainly the most unworthy and fickle of buffoons.

Owens—

The girls picked their names. It appears Miss Bradford selected yours. I thought you'd like to know.

A few of us are playing billiards at Smyth's tomorrow afternoon. Consider this your invitation.

— J. Whiting

"What is it?" Mrs. Stewart asked. "You've gone rather grim."

Derrick rushed to fold the note. "I . . . " She'd picked his name. Another moment to enjoy her company. Her presence was a soothing balm to wounds he didn't realize he had, but even the best of medicines could prove toxic after a time. "I'm off to Newport in the morning to meet with one of my former captains." Surely Lennox had heard from his admiral father since the news of Louis XVI's death and would have some notion as to how many ships would be called into action. No one knew exactly what the volatile French government would do next, but England wouldn't sit idly by.

"Surely you'll be back," she said. "You've only just arrived."

Derrick blew out. Would he be back?

"Your grandmother tasked me with looking after you," she said, wagging a finger at him. "You haven't given me the chance."

He smiled weakly. He couldn't return to Bristol, not with his heart threatening mutiny. Neither could he disappoint her. "I'll try to return within the week." *Try* being the most important word in that statement.

Her eyebrow rose. It didn't take that long to travel to Newport, meet with one man, and come back. "Very well. I shall eagerly await your return."

As he quit the breakfast room, running through the list of things he'd have to see to before his departure tomorrow, he should have felt free. He could forget the weight of expectations, of a society too obsessed with making matches. He'd done it before—set the topgallants and sped away when it seemed some young woman or her mother intended to make a prize of him. Staying wasn't worth the risk of playing into their trap and getting forced into accepting a marriage he didn't want lest he ruin the girl.

Yes, leaving would be a relief. If only he wouldn't miss her company.

Corah had never marched into the assembly hall with so much enthusiasm before. The pale blue silk of her gown glistened in the candlelight as she paused by the mirror to be certain the rich crimson lip paint Jemima applied hadn't bled onto her teeth. With careful fingers, she laid the two thick curls hanging down from her coiffure over one shoulder.

"You've never cared so much about an assembly before," Melinda muttered as she also primped.

"I always wish to look presentable."

"Yes, but not so intensely as this." Melinda seized her elbow. "Admit it, Corie. You like him."

The little laugh that had lived inside her since Sunday's dinner, which she'd attempted to bottle up, would not be restrained. "Perhaps."

Melinda grinned, tugging on her sleeve. "I knew you did! I simply knew it!"

"Hush, Mel. No need to alert every guest." Corah gave a demure smile to the mirror. That would do.

Her cousin linked arms with her as they proceeded to the ballroom, leaving her aunt chatting with an acquaintance.

"How sly of you, not letting on that you knew him to Miss Whiting," Melinda whispered. "You're cheating."

The crush of people made it difficult to locate familiar faces. "I did not want to make any wagers in the first place," Corah said, going up on her toes to see through the forest of powdered heads. "I have no guilt." At the sight of Mr. Haltwhistle, she immediately lowered from her perch. She did not want an encore of the last assembly. "Do you see Mrs. Stewart? Perhaps he hasn't left her yet."

"Or he's escaped to the cardroom."

A logical suggestion. He'd hidden somewhere the entirety of the last assembly. Games wouldn't have started yet, as the minuet had not commenced, but he could be conversing with other gentlemen.

"Let us drift in the direction of the cardroom door," Melinda said. "We can peek in and see if we spot him or Mr. Grant." Melinda's target for the night.

On their way, a pair of gentlemen stopped them and engaged them for the dance following the opening minuet. Corah tried her best to look flattered, but she couldn't help her eyes racing about the room. Mrs. Stewart would be easier to spot. The lieutenant seemed to prefer darker, less flamboyant colors. Where was the woman?

The opening bars of a minuet drifted through the ballroom, and the cousins hurried to clear the dance floor. Miss Whiting was the lady dancing, of course. What use was owning assembly rooms if one didn't display their family to best advantage? Corah didn't watch the intricate steps the couple performed for all to see.

"Do not frown so," Melinda whispered. "Mama says it will become permanent. Like Grandfather."

Corah relaxed the muscles of her face with great effort. Where was he?

"There you are, girls." Aunt Mary appeared beside Melinda. "Miss Whiting is such a lovely dancer."

"I fear I am coveting her, Mama." Melinda leaned against her mother, who laughed and hugged her.

"You both dance as well as anyone, never fear."

As Corah circled her gaze around the room once more, she caught Aunt Mary watching her with a sad look. "What is it?" Corah's hand flew to her hair. Had she lost one of her feathers?

"I met Mrs. Stewart as I entered," her aunt said. Corah's heart leaped. "She said Lieutenant Owens was called away on business. Though she hopes he will return within the week."

"Oh." Called away? Her stomach plummeted like a stone in a pond. "I wonder what was so urgent."

"She did not say, but she seemed disgruntled."

Melinda took her hand. "Corie . . . "

Corah shook her head briskly, trying to dispel the sinking feeling inside. Lieutenant Owens was not the only man in Bristol. She could still enjoy the night, evading Mr. Haltwhistle and trying to find pleasure in dull conversation. Never mind the time she'd taken on her appearance or the daydreams of him taking her hand again. She'd liked assemblies before Lieutenant Owens.

Hadn't she?

Six

CORAH TRAILED HER FINGERS ALONG the window as drops splattered the diamond panes. The corridor, dark despite it still being afternoon, echoed with her footsteps. They must have removed the rugs for cleaning, leaving the passage more chill than usual. The February rain didn't help.

Where had James told her he'd set up the game? She thought her seven-year-old brother had said the sitting room, but he wasn't there when she looked. Grandfather was out on business, Aunt Mary and Melinda had paid a visit to the Whitings, and Helen was in bed with a cold. There was just she and James to keep each other company in this shadow-riddled house.

She paused by the last window at the end of the corridor and pressed her forehead against the frigid glass. More than a week had passed since the assembly ball, and she'd seen no sign of Lieutenant Owens. Just as well. Clearly, she'd become too attached. She smiled wryly. Of course the one time she had her interest piqued, the man didn't return the sentiments.

He wasn't a Bristol gentleman. She straightened and

rubbed her cold brow. Even if a match between them were probable, how could she agree to it? He'd drag her off to Portsmouth, London, Chatham. Somewhere she could see him the few times he came into port, but somewhere far from everyone she loved.

Perhaps it was fortunate he hadn't attended the assembly.

A voice from the library turned her head. "We were supposed to go looking for diamonds today. Do you know about Bristol diamonds? They aren't real diamonds, Corah says, but they look the same." There was James. She made her way toward the sound. No matter. The feelings for Lieutenant Owens would fade. London would prove a distraction, whether the thought of leaving terrified her or not.

"We spin the teetotum and move the token around the spaces?"

Corah halted in her tracks. That was too deep a voice to be James's.

"Yes, only we use buttons," James said. "I lost the tokens somewhere."

"That seems simple enough."

There was no mistaking the voice. Corah leaned around the doorframe, trying to stay in shadow. Lieutenant Owens sat on the couch. James had pulled a table and chair up before the fireplace, most likely by himself with how bunched the rug was. He knelt on the chair, placing buttons at the start.

"The Game of Human Life," the lieutenant read. "I don't think I'll do well at this game."

James huffed. "It's easy. Not like cards. You don't have to use your brains."

"That is a relief." Lieutenant Owens grinned, the firelight playing across the angles of his face. If only he was not so pleasing to look at. That would make it easier to get rid of these feelings.

"Corah!" James called. "We are ready to play!" She startled, drawing the lieutenant's notice. He took her in, expression warming. His study of her conjured an unfamiliar stirring within her.

"No need to shout, James. Helen is sleeping." She trudged into the library, arms folded protectively around her. No feelings. Why was he in the library playing with James?

"The game is set up. It's time to play." Her brother pointed to the buttons. "Lieutenant Owens is the anchor button. You can have the white one. And I'm the red one."

There wasn't anywhere else to sit except on the couch beside the lieutenant. Perhaps she should make certain Helen was comfortable instead. The temptation of a few minutes with Lieutenant Owens made her reject that idea too quickly. She needn't feel awkward. It wasn't as though he knew about the silly wager. Something she'd have to reconcile with Miss Whiting the next time they met.

He stood and bowed as though nothing had happened. She supposed nothing had for him. He'd traveled and returned without a thought of her. He couldn't have known her disappointment.

She lowered herself onto the couch. James extended the little top with numbers written on its sides. "Ladies first." Then he pointed to the writing scattered about the board. "Some of the squares you land on, you have to do what they say." He leaned toward Lieutenant Owens. "Corah reads them for me because I don't like to. She'd probably read them for you, if you want."

The lieutenant leaned in too, whispering loudly, "I think I would enjoy that as well."

"What brings you to Kirkby Park?" Corah asked, spinning the teetotum on the board. The path of squares each held a little picture of varying stages of life, from infant boy to aged man. The top landed on five, so she moved her button to the square marked Mischievous Boy. "My grandfather is out."

Lieutenant Owens rolled one and put the shiny gold button on Infant. "In truth, I . . . wasn't here to see him."

James giggled. "You are an infant, Lieutenant!" He rolled the teetotum for his turn.

"Just a social visit, then?" Corah asked lightly. He'd implied he was here to see her.

"To the only society I really care to have in Bristol." Lieutenant Owens kept his eyes on the game board when he said it.

The only society? What could that mean? She needed to take care. That phrase should not have bolstered her spirits as much as it did.

"Studious Boy," James cried. "Doesn't that mean I get to move forward, Corah?"

"Yes, all the way up to square forty-two. The Orator."

Her brother bounced in his seat, contentment at his significant advantage shining on his face.

"We cannot let him win, Miss Bradford." Though he wore a mask of cheerfulness, something stirred beneath the surface. Discomfort? Hesitancy? She couldn't say what. As the game progressed, it became clearer that Lieutenant Owens was hiding some thought, some emotion that would not let him rest. He kept glancing at her, his eyes lingering when she wasn't looking directly at him. She wished to ask him what was the matter, but not with James there. Her brother repeated anything and everything he heard.

"Five, six, seven. Ah, the Romance Writer," Lieutenant Owens said, examining the tiny picture of a man with paper and pen.

"You have to go back," James said. "Corah, where does it say that?"

She pointed to the instructions. "Back to square five, the Boy."

The lieutenant sighed dramatically. "Those fickle romance writers, always leading people astray."

"I happen to like them," Corah muttered, pushing the teetotum toward James for his turn.

"Romance is a thing of books, not for the real world," Lieutenant Owens said softly.

She opened her mouth for a biting retort but paused. He didn't have the usual teasing twinkle in his eyes, the one she'd admired even as he lied to Mr. Haltwhistle. She couldn't explain this strange gloominess. Perhaps he meant more than he said. "Why should it not be a thing of the real world?"

"It only complicates matters." Real frustration rang in his words.

She begged her heart to stop its premature skipping. At least his thoughts had turned to romance, even if it irked him. She couldn't know if it had anything to do with her, however.

"To those resisting, I can see how it would complicate their lives." She plucked up the numbered top and gave it a swifter spin than she had since the start of the game. "For those who embrace it, love only makes life more vibrant, more lovely."

The lieutenant steepled his fingers, tapping them against his lips. "But is that worth the price?"

"How is it not?" She moved her token, not caring where it landed. James would remind her if something was to happen. He'd memorized the game despite his refusal to read the instructions. "To spend each day living for another person, to let them know each part of you, to understand that they love you in spite of your faults just as you love them, to have a space of warmth and safety between you—surely that is something worth all the discomfort in the world."

The corner of his lip twitched upward. "This coming from the young lady who has rejected every man in Bristol."

She squared her shoulders. Whose turn was it? "Not every man." She hadn't rejected him.

The lieutenant spun the teetotum, then turned toward her, his knee brushing hers. "You don't think it slightly odd that such a romantic hasn't found her match?"

"Not at all." They simply hadn't been looking in the right places. Here she was, discussing this with the one man who had turned her head. She wanted to blush, to look away, but she stayed firm. "If I will settle for nothing less than a true love, surely that shows my unyielding belief in its power."

His face softened. Was that hope lighting his eyes or just the flames crackling in the hearth? The dizzying musk of his cologne muddled her thoughts, but one thing was clear. He was scared. She couldn't blame him. So was she. Living life practically alone for as long as he had would make it difficult to believe in love. Love meant grief eventually. How could she convince him it was worth it?

His gaze flicked to her lips and he swallowed. A thrill ran up her spine. Her breath caught in her chest. For a moment she allowed herself to hope.

"I win!"

"Did you, James?" She turned back to the table, where her brother tapped his button against the Immortal Man square. Had he cheated? He had a tendency to miscount on purpose.

"I did. See?" In his excitement, his button slipped from his hand and skittered off the table between Corah and Lieutenant Owens. "What did you end on? That's who you are, you know."

"I am the Friend of Man," she said, reading the square. Fitting. Always a friend, nothing more.

"And it would appear that I am the Lover." The lieutenant laughed as James's face scrunched.

"That is a terrible end, Lieutenant," James said. "We should play again." James jumped off his stool. "But this time I want to play with my green button. One moment." He ran for the door.

Corah shook her head and bent down to retrieve the button from the floor. Silly boy. At least it allowed her a few moments with the lieutenant.

Just as she located the button, his hand closed around hers. She froze, allowing him to pull her hand up from the floor and rest it, cradled in his own, on the couch. Her fingers seemed to melt, encircled by the warmth of his skin.

"How did you enjoy the assembly?" he asked.

Her brain couldn't come up with a lie. "You weren't there."

"I'm sorry." His brow furrowed. "I'm not so easily caught."

The wager. He knew? Heat crawled up her neck. She started to pull her hand away, but he wouldn't let her go.

"I didn't want to return to Bristol when I left," he said, running his thumb along her knuckles. Why did so small a gesture send such electricity through her entire being? "But then I couldn't stop thinking about a certain friend's sister. It made Newport rather dull."

"I thought you were away on business."

He squeezed her hand and she squeezed back, earning a faint grin. "So I was. There are many events afoot across the world. After a time I thought, with my future so uncertain, why not spend the time I have with the people . . . or person . . . whose company I enjoy most?"

He was leaving? Of course with the unrest in France and the king's execution, England would have to be on her guard. No one knew what the French would do. The light that had filled her soul on his guarded declaration waned.

"Do you expect to leave soon?" she asked.

"No one knows. But I should return to Mrs. Stewart's. I only wished for a few moments with you." He brought her hand up and brushed his lips against her fingers. She tried to breathe, to draw in every aspect of this delicious moment, but her lungs wouldn't cooperate. Then he winked. "Let us make the most of whatever time the Admiralty give us." He rose. "Give my regrets to young James. I suppose I shall have to content myself with remaining the Lover."

He left and she sank back against the couch. What had happened? He'd made his interest clear and in the next breath warned their time was short. She didn't know what she was to do with that information. No one had told her what a girl was supposed to do in such a situation as this.

She bounced off the couch. What a ninny. He liked her. He'd admitted it. And for the first time in her life, she could genuinely say she liked him as well. He was right. Whatever direction life decided to take, they must make the most of it. She hurried to the corridor in search of the housekeeper.

"Randalf? Mrs. Randalf?" Aunt Mary wouldn't mind if she had Mrs. Randalf send a couple extra invitations to their scheduled dinners, would she? Even if they were all directed to Mrs. Stewart and her guest? As the lieutenant said, they would need to take advantage of every possible moment.

Seven

"What a pity the assembly was canceled next week," Miss Whiting lamented. "Stupid business calling my uncle to London." All the girls in her sitting room nodded gravely. Corah agreed with them for once. She had hoped to dance with Lieutenant Owens after his absence at the last one. Who knew if he'd be in attendance at the next ball? She carefully avoided the subject of his departure when in his company, and he did the same.

"And we still have Miss Bradford's wager to settle."

Her wager? Corah sat forward. "I thought because he did not attend, I was not obligated to fulfill it." Never mind she wished she could.

"No, no, my dear." Miss Whiting waved her hand. "We shall think of something."

Corah pressed her lips together. "I really would rather not participate in another—"

"Would it be the same gentleman?" Melinda asked. "Mr. Owens?"

Corah shot her cousin a withering look. What did it matter? She didn't want another wager.

"Of course," Miss Whiting said in a condescending tone. "Miss Bradford has an obligation to fulfill."

The loudmouthed, overdressed boiled potato! She wondered what Lieutenant Owens would think of that insult. She should work on her insults before sharing. "I do not wish—"

"Perhaps Corah can engage him to take her on a ride," Melinda said innocently. "He has a lovely phaeton."

"Grandfather hates phaetons," Corah muttered through her teeth. The phaeton Lieutenant Owens had brought on his visits the last week was not even his. It belonged to Mrs. Stewart. And it was February. They'd be bundled up to their necks in blankets to avoid freezing. Although . . . that did not seem the worst thing, did it? Bundled up beside Lieutenant Owens for an hour or two while he joked and teased and perhaps gave another rare glimpse into his soul?

"Oh, come," Miss Whiting said, rising from her chair and clapping her hands. "Miss Lee has already earned her right to arrive with us at the next assembly ball. Surely you do not wish to be left out."

Of that, she certainly did wish to be left out. Corah sighed. "Very well. If you insist."

"I will ensure she does it," Melinda said with a conspiratorial raise of her brow. "I'll make sure Grandfather extends an invitation to Kirkby."

Corah laughed inwardly. She had already secured plenty of invitations for him and Mrs. Stewart. But the fact that Melinda had covered for her, even helped her, made her want to hug her cousin tightly.

When the other young ladies rose to inspect one of Miss Whiting's drawings, Melinda threw her a grin. "I had to repay you for the song."

"Wish me luck. I'm already dreading it." She tried to keep her face impassive, but a smile threatened.

Melinda elbowed her. "You've been spending too much time with the lieutenant. When did you become such a tease?" Then she rose to join the others, leaving Corah alone to revel in her good fortune. Perhaps she shouldn't criticize these wagers so much. In truth, they'd only given her more opportunity to admire the blue eyes and boyish grin of a certain handsome lieutenant.

Derrick lifted his fingers from the keys of the pianoforte, letting the final notes of the melody ring in the silence of the drawing room. Across from him, his hostess took another sip of her glass of port and nodded her head.

"It's a pity Miss Bradford wasn't here to listen to that." She twirled the deep red liquid in her glass. All propriety when in company, Mrs. Stewart had her quirks she let slip in the comfort of her home. Such as drinking port wine after dinner like a man but from the comfort of her sofa rather than the dining room table.

He laughed. "She'd have fun, for sure. I know her to have excellent skills in music." Not that he'd heard her sing anything except "Little Bingo." "I, on the other hand, am mediocre at best. And terribly in need of practice." Years of playing as a child at Grandmother's request had been difficult to continue at sea. Pianofortes weren't generally afforded space on ships of the line.

"Well, I liked it. And I have a feeling so would she."

Firelight painted the sheets of music on the instrument a golden orange, contrasting with the darkness of the rest of the room. With no visitors or invitations that evening, Mrs. Stewart hadn't bothered to light more candles.

"You like her."

Derrick lifted his head. "Like whom?" He'd hardly admitted as much to himself. Not in so direct a way. It should have been clear. She was all he could think about in Newport, no matter how hard he tried. He'd stayed away as long as he could, but like a compass's arrow always striving to point north, he could not turn his heart from pointing to her.

Mrs. Stewart raised a brow. "Do not fool with me."

He sighed and picked up his glass from the pianoforte. "France declared war on England last week. I'll be called up shortly." Days. Perhaps weeks.

"What has that to do with whether or not you like Miss Bradford?"

That had everything to do with it. Because the prospect of going to sea after months ashore should have excited him, but now it left his stomach sinking each time he heard a knock on the front door. "I don't have much time left in Bristol. What does it matter if I like her or not?"

Mrs. Stewart gave an unladylike snort. "And no one has ever formed an engagement before going to sea."

Derrick rose from the stool at the pianoforte and wandered toward the hearth, Miss Bradford's smile filling his vision in painful clarity. "And if I do not return for years? How can I ask her to wait that long? She needs stability. A home. Her grandfather will not be around forever, and she has a very young brother and sister to care for." Saying it aloud made the ache inside him pulse, thrumming through him until he could hardly focus on anything else.

"I am hearing that you do like her."

Exasperating woman. Derrick leaned his back against the wall beside the fireplace and threw up one arm. "Yes! Yes, I do like her. More than any girl I've had the pleasure of meeting. I've never allowed myself to think about a future with anyone else. Every time I think about what's to come . . . somehow she's always there, ready to tease me for my ridiculousness or offer a word of comfort." Derrick wasn't the romantic sort. Why had he started dreaming when he came to Bristol? Dreaming of quaint country houses with views of the ocean, filled with giggling little voices and the light in Corah Bradford's hazel eyes.

"Heaven have mercy, that's more than like." Mrs. Stewart set her glass on a side table. "I've watched you in the weeks since you returned from Newport. You both seem so happy when you're together and distracted when you aren't."

"I believe we have you to thank for all the opportunities of meeting." Despite the weight on his chest, Derrick grinned. "We've been together nearly every evening."

Mrs. Stewart waved a hand. "I cannot take all the credit. Mr. Colston has done his fair share."

Derrick had difficulty swallowing his sip of port. "Mr. Colston?" The man didn't seem to like him at all, rarely saying much and speaking with cool authority when he did. Mr. Colston must have received misinformation about Derrick's situation. Why would a gentleman of affluence want such a position for his beloved granddaughter?

"The young woman hasn't expressed interest in a single gentleman in three years. I can assure you, he is positively giddy that she has finally shown more than mere interest in someone. Especially someone with some wealth and a distinguished rank." She slowly rose from the sofa. "You do not give yourself enough credit, Derrick. You've more to recommend you than just a handsome face and a uniform."

He didn't know how to respond to that, but it added fuel to the fire of hope he'd tried to stamp out for weeks.

"If he has no qualms and neither does she, you'll find a way." She covered a yawn behind her hand. "I am off to bed, or I'll be dozing at Mr. Colston's table tomorrow night. Try not to let your thoughts keep you up too late."

Derrick couldn't promise that. One moment his heart soared higher than topgallants, and the next it pulled at him, heavy as ballast. He'd decided that afternoon of playing the Game of Human Life that they'd simply enjoy what time they had together. No thought of what would happen later. He'd overstepped the bounds of that decision.

He drained the last of the port, staring about the dark room. A reckless desire welled up, urging him to throw his worries to the wind and set a straight course for Corah. He wanted to let go, to let himself fall headfirst into loving her with all he had to give. But it couldn't be that easy. Life had never seen fit to bestow on him the simple path toward gaining the things he longed for.

Eight

MELINDA KNELT ON THE SEAT by the drawing room window, pressing her face against the glass. Beyond her, sun peeked through clouds that splattered the sky.

Corah tied the ribbons of her bonnet under her chin. The gorge could be chilly with breezes off the river, but she hoped the wool lining of her hat would protect her ears from the worst of it. "You seem excited for Gordon to bring the carriage around," she said. "You sent for it, did you not?"

"Yes, of course I did." Melinda did not move from her perch.

"I think we will need a bigger sack, Corah," James said, frowning at the little linen bag she'd given him. "We are going to find cartloads of diamonds."

She smiled. "I think we'll manage." Bristol diamonds weren't quite that plentiful. The crystals would sit on any flat surface in James's room for the next seven years until he saw fit to discard them, so she hoped they didn't find too many. Still, she'd promised to go search with him, and this warm late February day would be the best opportunity. Especially since she might be leaving for London within the month.

Her brother's hat had fallen to the floor, so she plucked it up and settled it onto his head again. Grandfather hadn't said anything about London since Lieutenant Owens started coming around more frequently. He didn't know the truth that the lieutenant would not be in Bristol much longer. Was it wrong of her to let him hope?

"Ah, there's the carriage." Melinda hopped up, beaming, and rushed for the door.

"You are entirely too anxious to get us out of the house," Corah said as James scampered after their cousin with equal energy. What could Melinda be playing at? Did she have a gentleman coming? What a silly idea. She wouldn't have been able to keep such a secret from anyone.

"Where's the carriage?" James asked as he bounded down the steps. "I don't see it."

Corah squinted as she followed. "Melinda, have you lost your . . ."

A phaeton pulled by a fine grey horse rolled toward them, not from the direction of the carriage house but the main road. The lone occupant wore a smart felt hat with black cockade.

Melinda giggled and hopped from one foot to the other. "You haven't fulfilled your wager yet, and Miss Whiting keeps asking me every time I see her."

Lieutenant Owens pulled back on the reins, slowing the phaeton. Corah tried to scowl at her cousin but failed miserably. "This is complete and utter cheating."

"It's just a stupid wager anyway. That's what you always say."

A day at Avon Gorge with the lieutenant all to herself. Well, the lieutenant and James. Had Grandfather agreed to such a young chaperone?

As though guessing her thoughts, Melinda leaned in and whispered, "Grandfather sent him the note, so it was half his idea."

"He hates phaetons. How did you manage to get him to agree to this?" Ever since a well-known poet died being thrown from a phaeton in Bath a few years previous, Grandfather had strongly disliked the vehicles. Not to mention Melinda was terrified of him. How had she found the courage to present this plan?

"I convinced him this was just the thing to secure the lieutenant's affections."

Corah frowned. "You are saying he cares for my marriage more than for my safety now?" He *was* desperate for her to find someone she liked.

Lieutenant Owens sprang from the phaeton before Melinda could respond. "Miss Bradford, I'm delighted to see you this morning." He couldn't be more delighted than she. With a nod to Melinda, he took Corah's hand and placed a quick kiss on her knuckles that sent all confusion at her grandfather's acceptance tumbling out of her head. "Are you ready?"

More than he knew. "I am always ready to find rocks with little boys." And gentlemen who teased like little boys.

"Little boys. Ha!" Lieutenant Owens put his hands on his hips, giving James a look of displeasure. "Did you hear what she called us?"

She hunched her shoulders. "Of course I didn't mean—"

"I think we shall have to prove our merit as men and diamond hunters this morning." He caught James under the arms and swung the slender seven-year-old toward the carriage. She blushed. The lieutenant hardly needed to prove his merit as a man. Richard had sung his praises in every letter—his bravery in battle, his kindness to the midshipmen, his joking to lift the morale of all the officers when times were bleak.

"Corah doesn't think we'll find many diamonds," James

said as the lieutenant helped him onto the seat on the back of the phaeton.

Lieutenant Owens planted his elbow on the seat and rested his chin on his hand, locking gazes with her brother. "Corah should not underestimate our capabilities, should she?"

A thrill coursed through her at the sound of her name on his lips. Melinda covered her mouth, eyes wide, and Corah willed her to control her emotions before he turned back around. He'd never used her given name, but then they'd always been in large company since the afternoon in the library.

He ruffled James's cap and turned. "Shall we?" He extended his hand toward her. She took it, and he handed her into the phaeton. "Good day to you, Miss Lee." When he'd settled in beside Corah and taken the reins, she had to keep her gloved hands clasped in her lap to prevent herself from looping her arm through his. She had to take care with James about.

Lieutenant Owens turned the phaeton around and set the horse off at a brisk pace toward the main road. Cool air kissed her cheeks as they quickly passed the bare trees lining the lane. James hummed a merry tune, legs swinging.

"So it is Corah now, is it?" She cocked her head.

A slow smile spread over his lips. "I am terribly sorry. I suppose I was so used to young Bradford calling you by your given name that when James did it, I slipped."

"I cannot say I mind." Had he called her that before? In his mind or to Richard?

His shoulder rested against hers. "If that is the case, do I have your permission to use it more often?"

"So long as Grandfather doesn't hear you." At least until he could be certain of a lasting relationship. She'd talked of marriage with Grandfather so many times in regard to various men. The idea seemed so foreign and yet so agreeable when applied to Lieutenant Owens.

"I suppose I can remember that," he said. He shifted until he sat snuggly against her and she couldn't help but take his arm. How she loved the feel of him beside her, the steadiness and calm he brought. Perhaps, with him at her side, she could face the world beyond Bristol. That was a new sentiment. She'd never wanted to leave since arriving seven years ago. Well, she still didn't want to, but the possibility did not seem as bleak as it once had.

She caught him staring at her. "Should you not be watching the road?"

"Quite right." His face snapped forward. "What a bother." He sighed. "I suppose I must console myself that I have achieved what half the gentlemen in the city have desired the last three years. Even if I cannot enjoy the view."

She tugged on his arm. "And what is that?"

His eyes twinkled. "A few hours practically alone with the loveliest woman in Bristol."

"I should have guessed your teasing would come with shameless flattery." But she could not help a grin.

"The troubling thing is I have that greasy old hog Haltwhistle to thank for our introduction."

Corah burst out laughing. The man's bulging, rage-filled eyes at Lieutenant Owens's interference would not be a sight soon forgotten. Well, Derrick's interference. If he wished to use her Christian name, surely she could use his. That would take some getting used to. He'd always been Lieutenant Owens in her mind.

James's head popped between theirs as he leaned over the back of their seat. "Who is a greasy old hog?"

"No one," she said. "Sit down so you don't fall."

Her brother grumbled about people not telling him anything and gave them a suspicious glare. That boy. She glanced at her hand holding firmly to the lieutenant's arm. James was certain to see or hear something that stuck in his mind on this outing. And she found that deep down, she had no desire to hide her interest. All of Bristol might suspect within the week if James opened his mouth. She squeezed Derrick's arm. Heaven help them.

The River Avon ran grey under the cloudy sky as they picked their way along its banks. Across the river, sheep grazed lazily in the downs, their coats thick and fluffy. The jagged cliff walls rose above them, providing shelter from the breeze that had hit them on the drive to the gorge. Derrick hadn't minded it, as the wind made Corah nestle closer against him.

"Be careful on the rocks, James," she said. The boy scrambled along the rough shore, hopping from boulders without a care while his sister stepped carefully, her redingote skirt gathered in one hand. A little ridge of rock jutted up in front of her, and she sighed as she started to climb up it.

Derrick hadn't realized she'd fallen behind. He trotted back and offered her his hand, which she took readily.

"You enjoy this too much," she said coyly.

"Of course I do." He didn't release her hand when she'd crossed the ridge, and she didn't pull away. Perhaps he should have been more careful, as the gorge was a popular place for gentry families visiting the area, but who knew how many more of these opportunities he'd have?

They walked along without conversation for a time, laughing at James's shouts that he had found a diamond, rapidly followed by shouts that he had changed his mind. How comfortable it felt being with her. How natural. She didn't mind telling him her thoughts or letting him see her emotions. Richard Bradford had mentioned several times his sister's ecstatic reaction when he arrived home after years at sea. What would it be like to have her welcome Derrick back from his voyages? He couldn't imagine a more wonderful sight.

On the river, a vessel—a pink, it seemed by the hull and rigging—sailed slowly toward the city, all sails unfurled to catch as much breeze as possible. A command, muffled by distance, echoed over the water. Little figures on the upper deck moved about in response.

"Does seeing ships make you miss your life at sea?" Corah asked.

It had. Before coming to Bristol. "That's the curse of the sailor. When you're at sea, all you can think about is coming back to land, and when you're on land, you want nothing more than to be at sea."

"What of your families? You don't wish to stay with them?"

Clearly, that wasn't the question she really wished to ask. What she wanted to know was if he desired to stay with her. His mouth went dry. How should he answer? He wanted to stay with her more than he could say. What good would that do either of them when he couldn't stay?

"Of course we do, but the sea is our livelihood," he said. "It's all we know. It's our home." The words came out tense, awkward. He didn't want to say them.

"Which is why it is so easy to leave." Her hand went loose in his, but he didn't let her go.

He stopped walking, pulling her to face him. "It's not easy for every man to leave. Especially when . . . " Dared he broach that subject? The gold in her hazel eyes shimmered in the uncertain light peeking through the clouds. He caught the long curl trailing down her back and brought it around to rest over her shoulder. Its rich brown stood out against the pale blue of her redingote. He'd always remember her like this, with her hair simple and unpowdered, clothing plain, and face full of longing. "Especially when he leaves someone dear to him."

"Are you one of those men?" she whispered.

He never imagined he would be, and yet here he was caught between the life he'd always lived and the future he wanted so desperately. Without thinking, he slid his hand about her waist and pulled her against him. She gave a little gasp, curling her fingers around the edges of his coat. Pulse racing, he pressed the side of his face to hers, drinking in the bright citrus of her perfume. He brushed his lips against her soft cheek and her grip on his coat tightened.

"Derrick, is this wise?" Her blissful voice contradicted her cautionary words.

He sighed, lips still against her skin. "I assume not. But I'm a terrible judge where wisdom should be involved."

"You made that quite clear on our first meeting," she said through a laugh. Then she tensed. "James . . . "

Derrick reluctantly released her. He couldn't bemoan her younger brothers—after all, young Bradford had practically introduced them, and James had given them a multitude of excuses to spend time nearly alone—but sometimes this littlest brother popped up at inconvenient moments.

James scampered toward them, showing no sign he'd witnessed what had transpired. He held up a brown stone a little larger than his fist. "I've found one, Corah!"

"Have you?" she asked breathlessly, reaching a hand up to the cheek where he'd kissed her.

"This is one. I know it." The boy shoved it in Derrick's direction. "Open it."

"Open it, *please*," his sister corrected.

"Please!"

Derrick chuckled, taking the stone and finding a large, flat rock to set it on. It seemed like too ordinary a thing to contain anything that resembled diamonds. He pounded it several times with another rock while James leaned ever closer to get a look. "Careful," Derrick said. "You don't want me to slip and hit your nose." With a crack, the rock fell apart, exposing glittering crystals with a yellow tint.

"Diamonds!" James cried.

Derrick picked up a small piece and held it up to the light. So unassuming a stone, and yet such beauty contained inside it.

"Look at that," Corah said, crouching beside the rock with her brother. "How lovely."

"We can buy a castle with this, I should think," the boy said. "Which castle shall we buy? Kirkby Park?"

She laughed. "I'm not sure one rock will be quite enough for a castle. Here, help me put the pieces in the bag."

Derrick ran his thumb over the hexagonal facets of the crystal. Two months ago he wouldn't have expected his stay in Bristol to be anything more than a visit to one of his grandmother's friends. He hadn't intended to find someone he'd struggle to leave. Of course he knew young Bradford was from Bristol and intended to make himself known to the family. Perhaps flirt a little with the older sister who could not be as wonderful as the midshipman made her out to be. But Richard Bradford hadn't exaggerated. There were diamonds in Bristol, and not in the gorge. He pocketed the piece of crystal. James wouldn't mind, would he?

The boy found a few more potential geodes before they returned, but only one turned out to have a little crystal inside. Even though he didn't find the loads of diamonds he'd intended, James chatted happily as the phaeton traveled back to Kirkby Park.

Corah sat close to Derrick, her face sometimes glowing and sometimes troubled. She didn't bring up his departure again, but the fact it stayed at the forefront of her mind was written on her features. Derrick banished the impending separation with difficulty. Memory of the feel of her cheek under his kiss kept him duly distracted, and even more so the wish that he'd had the chance to catch her lips as well.

Afternoon had faded to evening by the time he returned to Mrs. Stewart's house. He bounded up the steps and through the door, tossing his hat and cloak to the unprepared footman. Where were they to dine? He couldn't remember, but it wasn't with Mr. Colston's family. How was he to keep his focus on any of their company? He strode toward the stairs.

"Derrick?"

He pivoted toward the voice coming from the sitting room. "Did you have a pleasant day, Mrs. Stewart?" he asked. *He* certainly had.

"Perfectly wonted." She rose serenely from the sofa.

"What is on the schedule this evening?" He felt his pocket for the piece of crystal. Still there, just like the intoxicating sense of being with Corah that lingered about him.

"You received letters today," his hostess said, extending two paper rectangles, one sealed with a wafer and the other with wax. An anchor sat in the middle of the red wax.

Derrick's shoes felt nailed to the floor. The letters were upside down, their directions hidden, but he didn't need to see them. Distant thoughts battered his head, pounding like rock against rock until they burst into his mind. Part of him had hoped this wouldn't come, ridiculous as that was. He reached for the letters as slowly as if moving through an icy sea.

With unsteady fingers, he took the pages and turned

them over. The one sealed with a wafer had directions from Captain J. King in Deptford. King! The lucky devil. They'd been lieutenants together on the *Bountiful* before King was made post-captain. So he'd finally received a ship. Pride for his friend's success should have overwhelmed him, but the wax-sealed letter from the Admiralty at Whitehall weighed too heavily in his hand. Air fled from his lungs.

There was only one reason he'd get a letter from his newly commissioned friend and the Admiralty at the same time, and it meant this dream in Bristol had come to an end.

Nine

CORAH FLICKED HER CHEEK WITH the end of her quill as she watched the sun rise through the trees. She really ought to write to John at Oxford. It had been a few weeks since last she received word from him, and she'd failed to respond. He'd want to know Helen had recovered, among other things. The blank page before her didn't entice her to write as it usually did.

The door burst open, and she dropped the pen. Her cousin rushed in shrieking.

"Melinda!" Corah rose, a hand to her chest to still her pounding heart. "Mercy, what are you about?"

"Oh, good, you have already dressed," Melinda cried, still in a dressing gown and sleeping cap. She bounced over, smoothing down the white skirt of Corah's chemise dress. "It's perfect. You look so fine in this one."

"What has got into your head?" Corah swatted her hands away. "Why do I need to be dressed?" She wasn't usually dressed this early, but she hadn't been able to sleep and thought she might as well ring for Jemima.

Melinda pressed her fists to her cheeks as though trying to contain the peal of giggles erupting from her. "He's here."

She could only mean one person with this much giddiness. "Who is here?"

"The lieutenant, of course." She grabbed Corah by the arms and shook her. "And there is only one reason he could be here this early in the morning. He must have been absolutely mad last night after spending all day with you. Couldn't sleep a wink." She threw her arms around Corah, squeezing her so tightly that she couldn't breathe. "And now he knows he cannot live another day without you, so he has come to ask Grandfather for your hand, and—"

"Melinda, you'll smother me," Corah squeaked. Though she might have been out of breath from the idea of Derrick speaking to her grandfather.

Her cousin released her to hop up and down on the rug. "Miss Whiting said if a man comes to your house before breakfast, it can only mean an offer of marriage. That is the *only* thing."

Corah tried to bite down a smile, but the light in her chest would not be subdued. "That is not the only reason." But Miss Whiting did have a point. It was very early for a simple social call.

Melinda grasped Corah's hands. "Go. The footman was guiding him to the sitting room. If Grandfather hasn't taken him back to the study, you might have a moment to hear the news from him first. Oh, hurry! Hurry!"

She did not need to be told twice. Corah rushed to the door, attempting to rein in her excitement, with Melinda on her heels.

"And just wait 'til you see him," Melinda said. "He's in his navy coat, gold buttons and all."

Corah skidded to a halt, stomach plunging. She caught herself on the doorframe. His navy coat. They didn't usually wear their uniforms while on leave. He'd never worn his while in Bristol, at least not to her knowledge. She tried to find an excuse for why he'd wear it this morning, one that did not fill her with dread. She couldn't.

"If only all gentlemen wore navy coats," Melinda said, as though she hadn't realized they'd stopped. "The navy truly has the most handsome of men."

"Melinda, would you see if your mother has risen yet?" Corah could barely form the words. "You shouldn't be seen in this state."

"Of course, you are right. I'll fetch Mama and Jemima. Do not let him leave before I have time to congratulate you. Oh, Corie! Married at last." She continued her babbling as she skipped down the corridor toward Aunt Mary's room.

Corah turned and trudged to the stairs. Melinda could learn the sad truth later.

She hesitated at the entrance to the sitting room. Yesterday she'd feared his leaving, but now that it had arrived, she couldn't fathom it. She wrapped her arms around her stomach, steeling herself for the real news.

Derrick stood swiftly when she entered and the gravity in his eyes was evidence enough.

"You're leaving," she said, stopping just inside.

He nodded once.

She pressed her arms tighter against her stomach as the ache exploded inside her. All the worry she'd learned to cope with in regard to Richard came surging back in full force. War, illness, accident, shipwreck—there were hundreds of ways for a sailor to not return to his family. Now she had to fear for the lives of two of them.

"Corah, I'm sorry."

She shook her head, attempting to smile. "This is what you wanted. You needn't worry about me. I'll be safe at home." Heaven only knew where he would be. "When do you leave?"

"Practically this moment, but I had to see you before I caught the mail coach." He crossed the distance between them and gathered her in his arms. Her eyes burned as she laid her head against his white lapel. The gold buttons pressed against her ear, cold and unmoving. "I'll never forget these months with you," he whispered, voice taut.

She wound her arms around him in the warmth between his coat and waistcoat. They didn't have long if he was to make it to Bristol for the coach to London, but she wanted to memorize each second they had left together. These memories would have to sustain her. "I'll be here when you return." He had to return.

His embrace tightened and he nuzzled her cheek. She could feel him swallow under the neat black stock around his neck. "No, Corah. You cannot do that."

"Why not?" She nearly couldn't hear her own words.

"I don't want you to wait. It will be too long. There are too many uncertainties." His hold on her loosened and he stepped back. His bloodshot eyes wouldn't meet hers.

"I take no issue to waiting," she said, catching hold of his waistcoat and not letting him get too far.

"But everyone else in your life does." He smoothed her hair away from her face. "Including me."

"Why would you?" *Look at my eyes. You want this as much as I do.*

"Because like everyone else, I want you to be taken care of." His hands enclosed hers and slowly extracted them from his waistcoat. "You can't count on a man of the navy to support you. I may never return."

"Do not say that." Her eyes smarted. She caught his hands, tilting her head to try to get him to look her in the eye. "We have to believe, or we'll go mad." She'd fall to pieces if she didn't hold on to the hope that he'd return safe and sound.

"I do not want you to waste away pining for an undependable future," he said. "You must go to London and find a gentleman with a living who can give you security and a family. Why give up years of your life for someone who might leave you with nothing and no chance to move on?"

"Because it is you I want, Derrick."

His lips twitched, nearly forming a smile. He finally met her gaze and her heart clenched at the loneliness in the depths of his blue eyes. "I cannot give you a home in Bristol."

"I don't want a home in Bristol," she said, tears gathering behind her eyes. "I want a home with you." She meant it. For the first time in seven years, she didn't mind leaving the sanctuary of Kirkby Park. This place had helped her heal from the horrors of her parents' deaths, but she was ready to venture out into the world if it meant he could be hers.

"That can't be. We don't know how long the war will last." He retreated a step, pulling out of her reach. When she moved toward him again, he held up his hands, eyes clenched shut. "Please. I have a duty to my king and country." His desperate tone turned her as rigid as the gorge's cliffs. "I need to leave us behind."

Her breath came out in shudders she fought to control. "Very well."

"Farewell, Miss Bradford." He retrieved his hat from the sofa, head down.

She wrung her hands in front of her. Anything to keep the pain from spilling out in tears. She tried to speak. Her throat stung, and for a moment the words could not get through. He was leaving. And had no intention of returning. "I wish you fair winds and following seas, Lieutenant Owens," she finally said, voice raw.

He nodded, swallowing again, and made his way to the door. As he passed, he seized her hand and pressed a kiss to the tips of her fingers. After one last look, his eyes wet, he opened the door before the footman had a chance. Then he was gone.

Corah drifted to the window to watch Mrs. Stewart's coach roll away. A hot tear drizzled down her cheek. Her chin trembled. She clenched her jaw. She couldn't cry. If she started, she wouldn't have the strength to stop.

Large hands rested on her shoulders. That only made it more difficult to hold back the tears. She covered her mouth with a hand.

"I am sorry, my dear," Grandfather said, voice gruff.

A sob slipped through her fingers. She spun around and buried her face in Grandfather's shoulder. He held her without speaking as the emptiness drowned her.

Three weeks later

Derrick leaned against the frigate's rail as a jolly boat glided away from HMS *Swallow*. He glanced at his friend, who watched with brow furrowed. A little dark-haired girl and her mother waved their arms from the boat. The girl suddenly stopped and pointed toward them.

"Papa! Papa, come back!"

Captain King gripped the rail, his knuckles going white.

The girl struggled, trying to break free of Mrs. King's grasp. "No, I want Papa!"

"Listen to your mother," the captain murmured. Then he lifted his hand and shouted. "Farewell, Birdie!"

The child wailed, her sad sound fading into the clamor of the ships and dockyards around them. A steady stream of boats bobbed on the Thames moving toward the docks as ships readied to sail with the tide, and the captain's wife and child were soon lost from sight. Captain King turned, rubbing his brow. "It only gets harder, Owens."

That did not bode well for Derrick. His farewell at Kirkby Park had torn his heart out, leaving him a dull and lifeless shell. He couldn't imagine a more difficult parting.

"Just wait until you have a wife. It will not be so easy to leave."

"I do not believe I want one," Derrick said. It wasn't the truth, simply the pain talking. He'd tried to convince himself this path would hurt the least. It hadn't done the trick yet.

Captain King laughed. "There are more advantages than disadvantages, I assure you." He folded his arms. "Owens, you've seemed out of sorts since boarding. Of course I do not wish to pry, but a distracted first lieutenant is never a good omen."

Derrick shook his head and straightened. "There is nothing the matter with me." He needed to sink these memories of Corah into the murky waters of the Thames. He adjusted his hat.

"Are you leaving someone behind this time?" his friend asked.

Her laugh still echoed in his ears. His arms felt her wrapped in his embrace. And when he closed his eyes, there was her smile, illuminating the shadows of his mind. "No, I am not." He didn't sound convincing, even to himself.

King studied him but did not push the matter. "Pass the word for Mr. Hunter. Let's get this frigate under way."

The words shouldn't have disturbed him, not after three weeks without her. He glanced over his shoulder at the London banks. She should be there, somewhere in the heart of the city, dining and dancing and living a wonderful life. He whispered farewell in his mind, perhaps forever, then rushed from the quarterdeck to seek out the boatswain. Perhaps setting sail would bury this ache. As Corah said, he had to believe. He was already going mad.

Ten

Two weeks later

"ARE YOU READY FOR CHURCH?"

Corah looked up from her dressing table. The mirror held Aunt Mary's reflection, peeking through the doorway.

"Why did you not light any candles, love?" Her aunt moved into the dark room, footsteps barely louder than the rain pelting the windowpanes.

She had, but the candle went out and she hadn't bothered to send for a new one. "We were leaving soon," Corah said, rising from the chair. She stretched. How long had she sat there? Jemima had finished her hair more than an hour ago.

Aunt Mary held her at arm's length and examined her appearance. "A picture of spring. Just perfect for Easter services." She lifted Corah's chin. "The only thing missing is your smile."

Corah sighed. "I'm too tired to smile, Aunt."

"I know, dear girl." Aunt Mary hugged her. "When loved ones leave, they take a piece of your heart with them. You're never the same after that." Her aunt knew better than she. Her husband had died years ago.

Corah returned the hug. "I cannot push him from my mind, no matter how hard I try."

"Have you written to him?"

She pushed back, frowning. "Aunt!"

Aunt Mary fussed with the pendant tied around Corah's neck with ribbon. "Perhaps a month of separation has made him realize how much he misses you."

A clock chimed down the corridor. They'd be late for church if they didn't hurry. Grandfather must be pacing the front hall. Corah shook her head and made for the door. "He was right. We might not ever see each other again. The best we can do is forget anything happened." She'd repeated his words over and over, trying to find some comfort in their logic. For some reason, she struggled to believe them.

"Your grandfather and I simply want to see you happy, dearest. Whatever that means."

Corah hurried through the doorway. If only she knew what that meant for her. Happiness seemed a faraway memory. Nearly a month in Town hadn't taught her to dissolve this storm that had taken up residence in her heart. New gowns, fresh acquaintances, parties and dances galore—nothing had made her forget long enough. She'd die on the shelf, pining for a man who'd long since forgotten her. If he wasn't swallowed by the sea beforehand.

Two weeks later

Derrick scaled the ladder and hopped onto the upper deck of HMS *Swallow*. He located Captain King on the quarterdeck and set course for his commanding officer. The captain listened to the ship's carpenter with a sullen expression.

"What is our diagnosis?" Derrick asked.

"That gale nearly finished what the French frigate could not." Captain King swore. "Thank you, Mr. Merrell." The carpenter nodded, bringing his hand to the brim of his hat in salute.

"How long will repairs take?" Derrick scanned the rigging, much of it drooping to the deck. It wasn't difficult to tell they'd be sitting in the Deptford dockyard for quite some time.

"Three weeks at least," King grumbled. "The foremast held up well enough, but we'll be replacing much of the main and mizzen. Then there's the pumps and starboard hull. What a disaster."

Derrick winced. An embarrassment for a captain's first mission. "There was nothing we could do about the storm. And the Frenchmen suffered more than we did in the altercation." Then slipped away like a nose-sniting, yellow-bellied coward. Captain King had done as well as any more-experienced captain, given the circumstances. They hadn't lost a single man in battle, only a few wounded. Still, it was difficult to limp back to Deptford after the storm with their heads held high.

"We'll be in for a thrilling few weeks." Captain King wandered to the helm, taking it in hand as though ready to steer the frigate out to sea, hang the repairs.

"Nothing boosts crew morale like sitting in a rolling tub of bilge water going nowhere with a hundred of your closest friends," Derrick said, joining him.

"Or closest enemies," King said wryly. "Dare I grant shore leave with every captain from here to Chatham scrambling for a crew?"

"We're patrolling the Channel. Surely, given the choice, many would prefer to stay closer to home." Whatever home they had.

I don't want a home in Bristol. I want a home with you.

Derrick blinked rapidly. How did she manage to invade every thought? Her voice was both a balm and a torment.

"I will certainly be giving leave to officers, if asked."

The implication in the captain's tone made Derrick squirm. "I won't be needing leave, but I'm sure Christian and Willis would appreciate it." A small part of his heart protested. She was in London. He could at least enquire as to her well-being.

"You are the one I thought could benefit from a few days on land."

"Me?" Derrick tried to laugh. "I have no home, no family. Of all your officers, I am least in need of time ashore."

Captain King tapped the wheel thoughtfully. "You are not the carefree Lieutenant Owens who kept our spirits up the winter of '89. Either something happened in the three years since we served on *Bountiful* or you are not being entirely truthful."

Derrick looked out across the river toward London, tendrils of fog lingering in the April morning air. Somewhere in the bustle, she must be waking up to ready for a day of social calls and parties. Or perhaps she'd decided to smuggle one of her romance novels into bed and was spending the morning hiding under the covers. Was she thinking of him as she read and about all he'd denied her?

"Join me in the main cabin, would you?"

"Yes, sir." Derrick followed him in descending from the quarterdeck and down the hatchway to the captain's quarters. He nodded to the marines on watch outside the doors.

King shut the door behind them, then made his way to his desk. "You've been distracted, Owens. Everyone can see it."

Derrick folded his arms over his hat. "I am doing my best." If only Corah hadn't been such a wonder.

"It's a girl, isn't it?"

He groaned, swiping a hand down his face. "Captain, it is a ridiculous matter that I will sort out. I will do better at ensuring it does not affect my duties." He didn't think it had, but it seemed he'd been wrong.

King clasped his hands on his desk. Barely five years separated them, but King seemed to live a vastly different life. He had a wife and child, a command, the respect of the navy. They'd bring in prizes aplenty patrolling the Channel, picking off as many French merchants and smugglers as they could, which would give him a comfortable fortune. Even if Derrick received an appointment to post-captain, he could not see that cozy life in the cards for him. Not for many years, when Corah was married and gone.

"You won't confide in an old friend?" the captain asked.

Derrick leaned against the bulwark, attempting to look unconcerned. "There is nothing to confide."

"Is she a captain's daughter?" King took out a writing box and set about trimming a pen.

Derrick blew out. The indefatigable weasel. "Midshipman's sister."

His friend did not react to being proven right but kept his focus on shaving off bits of the quill. "Anyone I know?"

"Bradford from *St. George*. I doubt you know him."

King fashioned the tip into a point and held it up to the light coming from the stern windows. "Is she waiting for you?"

"I told her not to. She's in London for the Season trying to find a husband." It was the hard thing to do, but it would work out better for the both of them. He couldn't be so selfish as to make her wait years.

"You daft-headed son of a landlubber." The captain set down his pen and knife. "London is crawling with dandies. She'll be nabbed in no time."

"As I hope she will."

Captain King planted his elbows on the desk. "No, you certainly do not. And that is why you've been in such a terrible gloom."

Derrick chewed the inside of his cheek. He couldn't deny it. His lowest moments came from imagining her in the arms of another man. "You know, your insults could use a splash of originality." Anything to change the subject.

"I'm a captain, not a lovesick lieutenant. I don't have time to practice words, be they poetry or insults." The captain plucked up his pen and began writing. "I'm sending you ashore."

"Captain, no." Panic flared in his chest.

"Does she return your affections?"

Derrick threw up an arm. How was he discussing this with his captain? "I do not know." He hesitated as Corah's tearful face swept across his mind's eye. The feel of her gripping his waistcoat, begging him not to push her away, made his breath catch.

"Then go be certain."

"What good will that do?" Derrick fiddled with the cockade on his hat. Curse his blasted sensibilities. He wanted to find her and take back everything he'd said.

"If she's in agreement, get a house in London and care for her. You aren't destitute. I know a clergyman who can procure you a license."

"'I love you, darling, let's marry, and then I'll leave you for war,'" Derrick grumbled. "That's a very romantic proposal."

"Nothing brings more comfort at war than knowing you are giving everything to protect the one you love," Captain King said, pausing his writing. "Unless it is knowing that she'll be there when you return."

His whole life at sea, he'd watched seamen and officers reuniting with their wives and sweethearts. He hadn't had family waiting for him since Grandmother's death, and even then she hadn't come to the docks. Corah would watch for his ship and be the first to greet him, just as Richard Bradford said she did with him when he returned to Bristol.

"I can spare you the next few days as we're demasting," the captain said. "We'll discuss further leave if needed."

Hope threatened with excruciating exhilaration. He wanted Corah as his wife. He'd known that deep down since not long after their first meeting. "I never took you for a matchmaker, King. Why are you doing this?"

His friend rose, grinning. "I want my first lieutenant back to working form." He extended his hand. "But I also want my friend to not make a mistake he'll regret the rest of his life."

Derrick grudgingly shook King's hand. He was a dunce on a fool's mission, but how could he turn down a chance to make things right, to heal his heart and hers?

"Hurry along, then." Captain King grinned. "I expect a full report."

Derrick nodded and quit the cabin, his feet carrying him faster than he intended. He raced down the ladder to the gunroom. A report. As though he were going out on official navy business. He *was* a lovesick lubber, and as he scrambled about his cabin deciding what to bring, he hadn't space in his mind to care. He pulled a little box out of his sea chest, which had been delivered soon after their return to Deptford. A grin spread across his face as he pocketed the box. He'd see Corah today. Never mind the cost.

Corah twirled an ostrich feather between her fingers as Jemima arranged her hair. The feather's curled barbs swayed at the slightest movement. Watching them flutter made it easier to ignore the dread that had settled into her stomach. Another assembly ball, where she'd act the part of a perfect young lady while inside her, hope died a little more.

At least there were no wagers to worry about.

Aunt Mary sat on the bed like Melinda would before balls in Bristol. "With Easter having passed, we'll have more people to meet. And more potential partners to dance with."

"Thank heavens," Corah said flatly.

"I noticed you searching the papers the last couple of weeks," her aunt said casually. "Did you find news of him?"

Corah blushed, dropping the feather. "I do not even know the name of his ship." But she'd hoped there would be some mention of him so she could discover it. Preferably a mention for an act of bravery, and certainly not because he'd been lost.

"Perhaps if you are trying to forget him, that is not the best method." Aunt Mary said it kindly, but the advice still cut. She was right, of course. The hope of seeing his name in the newspaper kept alive the flame of her devotion. In fact, it made it grow.

"I shouldn't have so hard a time forgetting." Corah swallowed.

"We will find you a wonderful man, love. One who is kind and respected."

She laughed to prevent her eyes from filling. "I so wanted it to be him. I don't know why I did. He has no real ties to Bristol. My whole life I feared being sent away from Kirkby Park like you and your sisters, and the first man I set my cap at was a man who would take me far from it all."

Aunt Mary stood and went to her side. She took Corah's

hand in both of hers. "Seeing the world is not a bad thing. Bristol will always be there to welcome you home."

"Is that how you could bear leaving when you married?" Behind Corah, Jemima produced the box of powder and the cape to protect her clothing.

"Bristol will always be home," Aunt Mary said, helping Jemima smooth the cape over Corah, "but it is not the only place in the world to find comfort and love. I think you will learn, wherever your husband takes you, that you can find home in more than one location."

"We shall see." How she wanted to believe it. Corah bit her lips, gazing into the mirror. She was only half ready. Each time she prepared for a ball, it seemed to take longer.

"Likewise, if the door that was Lieutenant Owens has closed, don't despair that you will never find another. He is not the only good man in England."

Corah nodded. She knew there were other gentlemen with whom she could create a happy life. But she'd chosen *that* gentleman. Did that count for nothing?

Aunt Mary squeezed her shoulders. "Tonight, let's not try to find suitors. Let's try to find good conversation and amiable friends. We'll eat all the food we can find, and when we're full as hogs, your grandfather can roll us back to the carriage like barrels. Does that sound agreeable?"

"Perfectly." Corah smiled, the first truly happy smile she'd had in weeks. No burden to find the right gentleman so as not to waste Grandfather's money. Simply a night to enjoy herself with her dear aunt.

Jemima opened the powder box and set about her work. Corah watched, mind turning. Bristol was only one place. What other lovely things would she find beyond its borders? She didn't fancy the bustle of London much, but London was not the world. Perhaps there was a place waiting to become as dear to her as Bristol. Just as there was a man waiting to become as dear to her as . . .

Well, perhaps she wasn't quite to the point of thinking that yet.

"Very light with the powder tonight, Jemima," Corah said, tilting her head to examine the coiffure. "I want only enough to take off the sheen of the pomatum."

"Yes, miss."

Aunt Mary lifted a brow. "*Au naturel* tonight?"

"Nothing changes one's mood better than doing something different with her look." Good heavens, that sounded like something out of Miss Whiting's mouth. But she needed this. Tonight was for her and Aunt Mary. She would put away the dreams of Lieutenant Owens. The world was bright and large, and she would find her way home, wherever that was.

Eleven

DERRICK PAUSED AT THE ENTRANCE to the ballroom, pulling at the stock about his neck that he must have fastened too tightly. Crystal glittered from the ceilings. Silk shimmered. The brightness hurt his eyes after so many weeks belowdecks on a frigate.

A pair of giggling young ladies jostled past him, not sparing him a glance. How would he find her in here? The rooms were larger than in Bristol's assembly hall and far more crowded.

Mr. Colston's family had been out when Derrick attempted to call at their rented townhouse earlier in the day, but he'd easily convinced the inexperienced footman to relay the family's schedule. There had been little time for him to fetch his dress uniform and change before the assembly. Blast this gargantuan city.

Dancing had stopped and chatter commenced. He couldn't decide if it would be easier to find her in the middle of a set or between dances. The last time he'd found her at the very beginning of a set, after Mrs. Stewart pointed her out to him. He didn't have his friend's assistance this time.

Fifteen minutes of scanning the ballroom left him wondering if the footman had sent him on a fruitless chase. No one matching her features milled in the crush. Perhaps she'd taken sick. He'd make a round about the room, then double back to the townhouse. His palms were sweating inside his gloves. Every moment he couldn't find her rattled his resolve. Captain King had given him a ridiculous mission.

"Why, Mrs. Lee. Miss Bradford!"

Derrick tensed. Where had that voice come from? He swung his head from side to side, searching. At the end of a line of chairs, he spied a gentleman in rich silk.

"I did not know you had made the journey from Bristol. How do you do?"

Haltwhistle. Derrick's lips twitched as he remembered ruffling that peacock's feathers. And standing before the gentleman was a young woman in yellow, her back to Derrick. Brown curls fell over her shoulder.

With a breath to gather his fortitude, Derrick wove through the crowd. The orchestra took up their instruments, signaling the impending resumption of the dancing. He increased his speed, excusing himself as he bumped into others.

"Miss Bradford, would you do me the honor of dancing the next two dances?" Mr. Haltwhistle said, dipping his head in what he must have thought an elegant gesture.

Derrick reached out, catching Corah by the elbow. "Miss Bradford has promised me this dance," he said breathlessly.

Her head whipped around to stare at him. Her eyes widened, the candlelight catching the gold and green in her hazel eyes.

"You!" Haltwhistle turned a brilliant shade of red.

Derrick narrowed his eyes, cocking his head. "Do forgive me, but have we met?"

The man's mouth worked like a fish dropped onto the deck. Any other night, Derrick would have lingered to make sport of the buffoon, but he had things to say that could not wait.

"Perhaps we may dance later, Mr. Haltwhistle," Corah finally said. She seized Derrick's hand, holding it against her arm as though afraid he'd let go. He smoothed his thumb over the back of her arm. He was here and he wasn't leaving her. "I . . . I believe the music is starting. Shall we, Lieutenant?"

He didn't have to offer her his arm before she latched on to it. They hurried toward the other side of the ballroom. Where would he be able to speak to her alone? An assembly was a terrible place to talk about these things. He'd been so consumed with the need to find her, he hadn't thought anything else through.

As they passed a door leading outside, Corah tugged on his arm. He followed her urging, and they slipped out of the hot ballroom into the coolness of the night. His heart thundered in his chest, both at being alone with her after so long and at what he needed to say next.

"Is your grandfather here?" Derrick asked.

"Yes, in the cardroom."

He swallowed. That man would have his head when he learned they'd escaped the assembly. As Corah pulled him across the street to the park on the other side, Derrick found the worry flitting away. He'd worry about the grandfather later. He squeezed her hand. They had happier business ahead. He hoped.

Corah dragged him toward the nearest tree, where a bench rested in its shadows. Brilliant moonlight guided her path, her feet pounding the ground in time with her heart. She didn't take a seat when they'd reached the shelter of the tree. Instead she whipped around to face him.

"Why are you here?" she demanded. How was he standing before her? Lantern light from the streets reflected in the gold buttons and braid that trimmed his dress uniform. Simple ruffles cascading from his throat to his chest rippled in the faint breeze. He raised his arms, adorned in fine sapphire sleeves, ever so slightly, as though longing to wrap her in them. Gracious, Melinda was right. A man in navy blues was a thing to behold. Or was it simply that she couldn't believe this vision of Derrick?

"You seemed to have fallen into the grasp of Mr. Haltwhistle again," he said. "I felt it my duty to step in, as I clearly hadn't scared him off properly."

She huffed, clapping a hand to her forehead. She'd missed his teasing. "If that was all it took, I would have sought the man out weeks ago." Her lungs couldn't draw in enough air. He was here.

"Just so I'd come?"

She turned away. The moon drifted just above the line of trees on the other side of the park. "I don't think you know how much I've missed you." She hugged herself, wishing she hadn't admitted that. What if he weren't here to apologize? This vulnerability only opened her to more hurt.

Strong arms wrapped around her from behind. "I think I have an idea," he whispered in her ear. The words tickled their way through her, sending little thrills across her skin.

"Do you? Your duties to the Crown haven't distracted you?" The scent of his musky cologne, which she'd missed so much in his absence, wafted over her.

"I hoped they would. They didn't."

He'd missed her. She clung to his arms, relishing in their

safety. Was she fooling herself? He belonged to the king, and that meant he had to leave again. She pulled out of his embrace and walked farther into the park. "Where have you been?"

There was a pause, then his footsteps came toward her. "Patrolling the Channel." He sounded disappointed.

She fingered the flowers tied with a ribbon and pinned to her bodice at the neckline. This could end worse than their last conversation. Fate was cruel to give her a glimmer of hope. "And how did the Channel treat you?"

"Very poorly. We barely made it back to Deptford."

"Did you win battles?" They should return to the ballroom. What had she been thinking? She hadn't been, and that was her problem.

He took her hand and pulled her back toward the tree. "Corah, I didn't come to talk about victories. I came to ask your forgiveness. I know, after how I hurt you, I do not deserve to ask for your love."

She tensed, waiting, not daring to believe.

"But here I am, devoid of eloquence and sanity, to tell you not a moment has passed since we parted that I haven't thought of you." His hands encircled her waist and he placed a kiss on her cheek like he had that day in the gorge. The warmth of his breath washed over her skin. "Not a moment has passed that I haven't wished I'd agreed to your pleading. I thought I didn't need anyone in this world, but I was wrong. I desperately need Corah Bradford."

He needed her. The vulnerability of his voice undulated through her, filling every thought, every breath. She slid her arms around him, leaning her head on his chest. Her pulse raced. How many times had she wished to be right here, cradled against his tall, muscled form? "Why would you need Corah Bradford, who sings silly songs in parks at the break of dawn to fulfill ridiculous wagers and searches for diamonds by the river?"

He pressed her tightly against him. "Because she laughs at my teasing, and not many do that. Haltwhistle, for example."

She giggled. "He looked ready to murder you in the ballroom." She traced the buttons on the back of his coat, then ran her fingers along the braid.

"Haltwhistle? Ha! He can't remember which is the handle side of a pistol. There's nothing to fear from him."

Despite his joke, his heart pounded wildly beneath the soft ruffles of his shirt. She closed her eyes, reveling in the sound. He was here. He loved her. He wanted her.

He fished a little box out of his pocket and held it for her to see. "I had this made. I intended to wear it as a cravat pin, but I want you to have it."

She opened the box. Moonlight caught a yellow-tinted crystal encircled by smaller crystals of the same hue. "Are these Bristol diamonds?" she asked, running her finger over the smooth facets.

"I stole a piece that day in the gorge. I wanted something to carry with me. Something that reminded me of you."

She leaned into him and pulled the pin from the box. "Do you not wish to keep it?" She fastened it to the ribbon on the flowers at her neckline.

"I want you to have it so that no matter where you venture, you'll have a little piece of home."

"And a little piece of that magical day I spent with you." She stayed still, at once loving the feel of his steadiness and fearing his speech meant he'd soon be gone.

"I love you, Corah. Can you bring yourself to marry such a blasted fool?"

Marry. She raised her head, which brought her lips dangerously close to his. The sincerity in his eyes drew tears to hers. Had it only been hours ago that she sat at her dressing table wondering how to forget him? She'd thought him lost, if not to the sea, then to duty and benevolence. He hadn't seen the diamonds through life's rough exterior. "Do you not mean 'blithering, addlepated son of a blunderbuss'?"

Derrick chuckled and lifted her from the ground in a crushing hug. Corah laughed with him, not caring what attention it would draw. Then he released her and pressed his lips to hers. Her mind went fuzzy at the warmth of his kiss. A tear ran down her cheek. Hours ago she would have wagered she'd never see him again, that she'd be haunted by what might have been for the rest of her existence. Now here he was, offering his heart and all he had as though he thought it a pitiful payment for her love. He didn't understand it meant more than anything the world had to give.

She pulled back, then went up on her toes to whisper in his ear, "Yes. I cannot think of anything I'd rather be than the wife of the best man in all His Majesty's navy."

He brought his forehead to hers. "It will not be easy."

"Life never is." She slid her hands up his coat to grasp his white lapels. He shivered and she grinned. "But I am ready for this adventure."

Epilogue

2 July 1795
Two years later

CORAH LED DERRICK BY THE hand from the hackney through the doors of their little townhouse in Deptford. Fatigue slowed his pace, but his blue eyes shone brighter than the trim of his full-dress coat. Heavens, that suited him well. She hurried to close the door, leaving them alone in the darkened house.

Not sparing another moment, she threw her arms around his neck. "Post-captain, Derrick? I can hardly believe it."

"You didn't think I'd stay a lieutenant forever, did you?" He embraced her, nuzzling her neck the way he always did when he returned.

"Captain King will be sorry to lose you, but you deserve the recognition." His bravery in action off the coast of Brittany had been too valuable for the Admiralty to ignore. She released him to examine his face. What new scars had he acquired this time? She ran her fingers over the nicks on the sides of his face, then turned to his hands to look for evidence of gashes. He'd returned whole, and she would offer the sincerest prayers of gratitude for that.

He grinned. "You are happier about the time I'll have at home waiting for a command than you are about the commission."

She reached up and pulled the hat from his head. "Of course I am." The first two years of their marriage hadn't been easy, but she'd settled into the life of a navy wife. She was luckier than many wives, as he returned to England with messages and prisoners more often than most officers. She saw him every moment he could spare. It was never enough, but someday France would relent. She'd learned not to give up hope.

Now hope had given her a little prize of her own. It could be months before the navy had a ship for him. With pockets padded from prize money, she didn't even mind the cut in his pay. He was home.

Corah pulled off her hat, the Bristol diamond pin twinkling from its band, and set both on the sofa in the tiny sitting room for the housekeeper to care for later.

"Where is Mrs. Thomas?" Derrick asked.

"She and Matilda are at the grocer's." Corah had sent the housekeeper and maid-of-all-work off to purchase things for dinner before she left for the docks. She and Derrick had been invited to dine at Grandfather's townhouse across the river, but she wanted Derrick for herself tonight. A navy wife could be selfish about this sort of thing. That's what Mrs. King had told her.

"We're alone, then?"

She cocked her head coyly. "If Mrs. Thomas and Matilda are not here, what do you think?"

"Do not play with me." His arms shot around her with a swiftness she wouldn't have expected, given how tired he seemed in the coach. "Do you know how long I've been dying to hold you?"

Corah took his face in her hands. "Remind me."

He kissed her fiercely, as though trying to make up for all the time away. She let him try for as long as he wanted. Every night he was away, she dreamed of this moment. She ran her fingers through his hair, quickening his breath until eventually, she tugged out the black silk ribbon that held his hair back.

"You're certain they won't be back soon?" he asked.

Corah lifted a shoulder. "They don't usually return before noon."

Derrick scooped her into his arms, earning him a laugh. He made for the stairs and proceeded up them with determined vigor. She clung tightly to him, the brightness inside warming her from her head to her toes. How she'd missed him. All the waiting was worth it if it meant being his wife. Never mind that fate had given them a life neither one had planned. They'd both found home—not in Bristol or on the decks of a ship, but in each other.

Acknowledgments

First and foremost, I wish to thank my parents' kitchen table for providing me a place to write while waiting for our house (and therefore my office) to be finished. And thank you to my parents for lending it, as well as my siblings, children, niece, and nephews for (sort of) allowing me to write without distraction. Love you all!

Much appreciation to Commander C. A. Sorensen and the Chathams for welcoming me into their numbers and allowing me to ask my hard-to-research Royal Navy questions. Thank you for providing entertaining and enlightening conversation about a topic few in my life understand. Despite researching for years, I still have so much to be taught by you learned coves.

Thank you to my critique partners, Jo, Heidi, Meg, and Deborah, for cheering me on during this quick turnaround in an impossibly busy summer. My writing would not be what it is without each of your insights and encouragement.

My amazing beta readers were such a huge help. Thank you, Jo, Heidi, Deborah, Ashlee, Tasha, Ruth, and Sharleen! Your comments helped me make this novella shine.

Thanks to Timeless for giving me this opportunity to go beyond my usual time periods. It was so fun to get to do a novella again after a two-year break.

Of course, much thanks and love to Jeffrey for protecting my writing time and my space to develop my talents. I could not do this without you. Thanks for being my greatest fan.

And thank you to my Heavenly Father for giving me these passions and interests and a way to use them for good.

ARLEM HAWKS began making up stories before she could write. Living all over the Western United States and traveling around the world gave her a love of cultures and people, and the stories they have to tell. She graduated from Brigham Young University with a degree in communications and emphasis in print journalism, and now lives in Arizona with her husband and two children.

Visit her website here: ArlemHawks.com

Women of a Certain Age

Josi S. Kilpack

One

COLLETTA MARKSHIRE HAD BEEN INVITED to the first Queen Charlotte's Ball in 1780, never imagining that eight years later, an entire social season would have sprung up around the event. As a year-round resident of London and former attendant to the queen, Etta had positioned herself to be an excellent player in this new opportunity becoming known as "the Season." Tonight, therefore, she surveyed the room with the confidence of an expert perfectly comfortable in this arena.

That the prey was not for herself made the hunt even more satisfying.

The twelve debutantes who Etta nominated in previous years had made their matches and were as secure and happy as anyone could expect a married woman to be. Rachel—Etta's lucky number thirteen charge—was on her way to finding an equally good situation. Rachel had been presented to the queen weeks ago at the Queen Charlotte's Ball of 1788, thereby gaining entry to the most exclusive entertainments in London, such as this ball tonight at the London home of the Duke of Brenton.

As part of her duties to help Rachel find her place in the world, Etta had been tracking her top husband choices amid the glamorous crowd in the ballroom and gauging their interest in the other young women as well as their attention to Rachel.

Wilfred Carrington? He would be a viscount one day, so long as his uncle did not marry again and produce his own heir. The Carrington's primary estate was within a day's journey of London, and though he was rather short, he had a similar demeanor to Rachel—quiet, introspective, a bit boring. Rachel could be happy with him.

Edward Longshore was a viable candidate, thanks to his merchant fortune and current clerkship for a member of Parliament, but he was thirty-four years old—exactly twice Rachel's age. An older husband was, of course, optimal for matters of security, but Rachel had a sizable dowry and did not need to marry for money alone. He was ambitious, paid Rachel a great deal of attention, and she did not seem put off by his age or expanding waistline. He was a bit of a flirt, but that did not seem to bother Rachel either.

Jonathan Rigby III was Etta's favorite, however. He had no title coming his way but was connected to several of the most influential families in England. His father was a heralded general currently watching France closely, and Mr. Rigby's grandfather on his mother's side was a marquess. The young man made a point of engaging Etta in conversation at each event where they crossed paths, and while she knew his attention was to earn her good favor, Mr. Rigby's understanding of the game impressed her. He was also the right height, had good teeth, and had just purchased a fine piece of horseflesh at Tattersalls. Rachel adored horses.

Yes, Jonathan Rigby III was top of Etta's list so far, yet it was not quite June. There could very well be more players joining the Season before a winner was declared. Unlike the debutantes who were expected to attend the whole of the Season or until an engagement was imminent, eligible young men came and went.

It was a boon to have all three possibilities in attendance tonight. In fact, the evening had been nearly perfect . . . save for Etta's wig.

Tonight's headpiece was new: a delightfully large powdered confection of rolled and stacked curls that fairly sparkled in the light, as it was shot with tiny crystals meant to engage that exact effect. The elaborate wigs and cosmetics, inspired by the ostentatious French, were beginning to fall out of fashion in London as political tension across the Channel increased, but Etta loved the excessive costuming for formal balls such as this one. As a Woman of a Certain Age, she could do as she pleased in regard to fashion, so long as it was well executed.

However, the pins that secured the wig to the tight linen head wrap covering her actual hair had been gouging her scalp all night. During a visit to the refreshment room half an hour ago, she'd pulled out the three worst offenders, thinking that they would not be missed amid the dozens of other pins holding the wig in place. She'd dropped the pins into a bowl on some side table somewhere and expected not to worry about it any longer. The wig was not sitting quite so steady on her head, however, making her wonder if perhaps she'd overreacted. What was a little scalp impalement compared to losing one's hair in public?

A voice just behind Etta's shoulder almost made her jump, which her wig could not afford her to do just now. A lifetime of practice kept her from reacting at all, thank goodness.

"Where is she?"

Etta turned her head to carefully look down at Elizabeth Pettengill, one of her closest friends despite the fact that Elizabeth took great pleasure in discomfiting Etta whenever she could manage it. Etta gave as well as she received, however.

"Oh, it's you," Etta said with exaggerated dryness as she faced forward again. "How nice of you to join us."

"Isn't it though?" Elizabeth said, rouge amplifying the rounding of her cheeks as she smiled. She never did herself up as elaborately as Etta did, but she always hit the mark. "Where is your charge?"

"Good to see you as well, Elizabeth," Etta said dryly.

"Of course I'm glad to see you. Which one is she?" Elizabeth was wearing gold satin tonight, a bit more flamboyant than her usual choices but appropriate for her first elite event since her return to Town. All her friends and acquaintances would notice her, to be sure.

Etta pointed her fan toward Rachel gathered with some other young people as they waited for the next set of dancing to begin. "Far corner, near the south veranda. Light blue silk."

Elizabeth lifted her quizzing glass—another eccentricity Women of a Certain Age could get away with—and pursed her rouged lips.

"Do you mean the blonde with the square neckline?" Elizabeth asked.

"Yes, that is my Rachel," Etta said, choosing not to nod.

"She's fat."

Etta narrowed her eyes as she scowled at her friend, careful not to incline her head too sharply toward the shorter woman. "She is pleasingly plump."

"Fat," Elizabeth repeated, lowering her glass, which was secured to the bodice of her golden silk ball gown. "I certainly do not mean it as anything other than an objective observation, of course. Frankly, we need more of us stout women to offset the balance of you gangly things." She turned her glass on Etta. "Case in point, you look like a powdered stalk of asparagus."

Etta bit back a laugh. When alone, she and Elizabeth could roast one another and laugh until their stomachs hurt, but in a forum such as this, Etta needed to maintain her dignity.

"If I am asparagus, you, my dear, are a golden pumpkin," Etta said once she could trust herself to speak.

Elizabeth let out a single snort of laughter, and they both looked over the crowd once more.

Do I really look like asparagus? Etta wondered, smoothing the bodice of her gown—green muslin with a silver underdress to match the sparkle in her wig. She wore her widest hoops tonight and her tightest corset, which meant she had to take small breaths and had only dared eat two bites of dinner. Fashion was not without its sacrifice.

She probably did look like asparagus though. Pity, that.

"Rachel is a delightful girl, thank you very much," Etta said. "She speaks nearly fluent French, is an excellent rider, and exhibits great poise. The queen was quite taken with her."

"Oh, I'm certain she is all those things . . . and fat. She is Nathan's youngest, yes?"

"Yes," Etta confirmed. "Her mother came to London for the first two weeks but returned to Northampton once Rachel was settled in."

"Which you did not mind one bit, I'd wager," Elizabeth said with a knowing grin.

By way of response, Etta fluttered both her fan and her eyelashes in Elizabeth's direction, making Elizabeth laugh again. Without children of her own, Etta took full advantage of the opportunity to spoil and primp the girls she hosted. It was much easier to do this when the mothers did not interfere.

"Who was Rachel's older sister again?" Elizabeth asked.

Etta paused a moment before she answered, preparing herself for a predictable reaction. "Beatrice."

"Ah, Beatrice, number ten. A great beauty." Elizabeth frowned. "That will be a difficult act for Rachel to follow."

"Rachel is lovely," Etta defended.

"But she is no Beatrice."

"Oh stop," Etta said, tapping her friend's shoulder with her fan. She really did want Elizabeth to stop. There had already been an uncomfortable number of comparisons between Rachel and Beatrice—many of them made by Rachel herself. "Rachel will make a fine match."

"Of course she will," Elizabeth said, her small tightly curled wig very securely fastened to her own head. Etta was coveting that wig. "Your nominations always do. And Rachel is your lucky thirteen, is she not?"

It was a wonderful thing to be known so well by one's friends. "Indeed," Etta said, snapping open her fan and using it to conceal her self-satisfied smile—no need for the rest of the guests to suspect how impressed she was with herself.

One of the papers had called Etta a matchmaker after the engagement of her seventh debutante a few years ago, but the title sounded rather . . . occupational, and a woman of breeding could never have an occupation. No, she was simply a designer of partnerships that, thus far, had been satisfyingly successful for everyone involved—including herself.

Women of a Certain Age needed to have passions and pleasures after all, and there were worse vices than helping young women make good decisions when choosing who to bind themselves to for life. A bad match could be ruinous for a woman. Etta had learned that the hard way . . . twice. This gave her important objectivity.

"Did you see that Wynn Firth is in actual attendance at an actual ball?" Elizabeth asked. "I nearly fainted when I saw him."

Etta moved her head too fast, and the wig definitely shifted. She covertly raised a hand and pushed it ever so gently back to center. Blast herself for removing those pins!

"What on earth would bring him to Town?" Etta asked.

Wynn Firth had never cared for noble connections, though he was the second son of an earl with a significant estate up north. An estate that primarily raised pigs, it should be noted. The late Mrs. Firth was the cousin of one of Elizabeth's childhood friends, so Etta knew a bit about the family. She'd have never expected him to partake of this new social season.

"He's attending the ball with his son tonight," Elizabeth said.

"His son?" Etta asked, annoyed that she was hearing this information only now. She made a point of staying on top of such important gossip amid the *ton*—especially when there was an eligible young man involved.

Elizabeth nodded. "The eldest daughter, Lydia, has come to Town as well, though she was not feeling well tonight. Ethyl Marble is hosting the girl. I met up with Mrs. Marble in the foyer and she is quite pleased to have brought the Firths out of obscurity, that is how she said it."

Etta snorted—in a very ladylike way, she quickly covered with her fan, careful not to move her head. Mrs. Ethyl Marble was known to take payment for making introductions for girls who lacked London connections of their own. Though Wynn Firth was only one degree removed from a title, none of his family had done the noble thing of making a place for themselves here in London. His brother, the current earl, did not even bring his family to London when he had to come for Parliament and refused every invitation that did not feature a hand of cards. In Etta's opinion, if a girl did not have relatives of her own to offer introductions, she ought not attend the

London Season at all. "She was not presented to the queen," Etta said, pointing out yet another mark against the Firths.

"No, she's only just come to London."

Etta nearly snorted again. After the first Queen Charlotte's Ball, a nomination system had been created where a woman with royal ties could nominate unmarried young women to be presented to the queen. If the girl's family and status was approved by the lord chamberlain, she could attend the ball and be presented, earning her a royal stamp of approval that she could carry with her as she danced and flirted her way into a successful match with a man of her same station. Etta had been an attendant to Queen Charlotte for over a year in between marriage one and marriage two, when the royal family had lived in Buckingham House. That connection allowed Etta to make nominations, which she had done thirteen times now, with thirteen approvals, thirteen presentations, and twelve marriages thus far. As the granddaughter of an earl, Lydia Firth's nomination likely would have been approved, which meant no one had bothered to nominate her. Poor thing.

Etta had been scanning the ballroom for Wynn Firth while Elizabeth filled in the details Etta should already have known, and she finally found him. They had met a few times these last decades—though Etta could not remember exactly where or why—and he was as handsome as he had ever been; he was tall and broad, with thick dark hair tied back at the base of his neck. She remembered from their encounters that in addition to his good looks, he had a loud laugh and a casual demeanor. Country manners, to be sure.

"I am flatly shocked," Etta said, rather annoyed that the Firths felt they could step away from the Polite World and then step back in when it suited them. She, on the other hand, had made navigating this world her sole pursuit. It occupied every minute of her life. She was also annoyed that he was still handsome, though she noted that his evening dress was outdated and he had no buckle on his shoe.

"I hope you will be kind to him when your paths cross," Elizabeth said.

Etta looked oddly at her friend, still mindful of the unstable wig. "Of course I will be kind. I am kindness to the core, thank you very much. Why would I not be kind?"

Elizabeth nodded in the direction of Rachel. "Because Reed Firth seems to have captured the attention of your lucky number thirteen."

Etta turned her head too fast and had to reach up to hold her wig in place. Rachel was where she'd been a few minutes earlier by the south veranda. A tall young man—too tall for her stout frame—with thick dark hair in need of a trim and barely a polish on his boots, stood closer than he should. Rachel, bless her pleasantly plump heart, was looking at him with complete adoration.

Rachel had not looked at Mr. Rigby like that. Not once. She had not looked at any of the men she'd met here in London with anything near the sheer joy reflecting off her face like the very sun.

"Oh dear," Etta said, keeping her head steady as she began to make her way through the crowd.

This would never do.

Two

"Good evening," Etta said, sliding into the too-small distance between the young people.

Young Mr. Firth took a polite step backward—he was very young—and Etta kept her eyes fixed on him. She extended her hand, palm down. "Mrs. Colletta Markshire," she said as he took her hand in the country style and gave a slight bow. She could not nod her acceptance of his courtesy due to the wig, but it was just as well that she keep the intimidation levels high.

"Pleased to meet you, Mrs. Markshire," he said nervously without meeting her eyes. "Mr. Reed Firth."

"Pleased to meet you, Mr. Firth," Etta said with decided coolness. She let the silence hang between the three of them as he released her hand and immediately began to fumble with the button of his coat.

"Mr. Firth is from Shrewsbury," Rachel said in rushed tones. "Mrs. Markshire is my aunt, Mr. Firth. She is hosting me here in London for all the social events."

"Ah," Etta said, still staring at him. "Who introduced the two of you?" Introductions were rather formal affairs here in

London made through a shared acquaintance—Etta would have known if someone had introduced them.

"The Firths live near my grandfather's estate, we have known one another for years."

"Is that so?"

Another awkward silence descended. Etta did nothing to appease it. She knew that Rachel's maternal grandparents lived in the far north but did not realize it was Shrewsbury. She did not like being ignorant of such things.

"He is here in London with his sister, Lydia," Rachel offered. "Though she is not here tonight."

"And they've only arrived now? In late May?" Etta asked, even though Elizabeth had already informed her of these details.

"Well, they spent some time in Manchester—there are some social events there this time of year as well—but now they are in London for the duration."

"Hmmm."

Mr. Firth took another step back and ran a nervous hand through his overgrown hair, still looking at everything except her, which only emphasized how out of place he was. No refinement at all. "Well, I should, um, go. It was wonderful to see you again, Miss Johnson."

"As it was to see you, Mr. Firth. Please give my regards to Lydia, I hope her health improves."

He nodded again, then turned without saying good night to Etta. Country manners were not very charming, in her opinion. As he walked away, she could see the similarities between him and his father—handsome, thick-haired, and so very country.

Etta smoothly put Rachel's arm through hers and turned toward the back of the room where they could walk together. For the moment the wig was holding its place well enough so that she could divide her attention between both troublesome issues of the evening.

"Tell me about your acquaintance with that young man," Etta said, smiling at a friend who caught her eye but not slowing her steps or nodding a hello.

"As I said, he lives near my grandfather's estate. The families dine together and, well, we would go walking sometimes."

"Walking?"

"Through the woods there. To the village."

"And when you say we, do you mean Lydia and yourself?"

"A-And Reed. Sometimes."

"Reed? You are so familiar as to use his Christian name?"

She glanced sideways enough to see Rachel's cheeks redden—she was too young for face powder, but then most of the young people were forgoing such things. "I mean Mr. Firth, of course. Manners are different in the country."

"Not so different as they should be when it comes to propriety, my dear. Did you ever have time with just Mr. Firth?"

Rachel did not answer, and Etta took a breath before stopping and turning to face her niece—far enough from the other attendants that she could even dare have this conversation. She gave Rachel a look almost as hard and strong as the look she'd given young Mr. Firth a few moments earlier. "Rachel, is there an agreement between the two of you?" So help her, if Rachel said yes, the girl would be on the next carriage home. Etta was clear with all her charges that if they had an attachment to any man, there was no reason for her to invest the time it took to host them here in London.

Rachel shook her head quickly and her eyes widened enough that Etta believed her.

Etta allowed herself to relax. A bit. "Do you trust me, Rachel?"

"O-Of course I trust you, Auntie."

"Good, then I will ask you to give Mr. Firth his distance." Rachel started.

"Whatever feelings of affection you might have had toward him are part of your childhood and have nothing to do with your future. A solid representation of men who can give you everything you need for a happy and successful life have expressed their interest in you, and if you allow Mr. Firth to capture your attention, you will lose theirs. Do you understand?"

Rachel was silent a few moments. "He is my friend." The tone was cautious rather than argumentative. Good.

"Not here. In London, unmarried men and young women interact for one reason: to make a match. Mr. Firth is not a good candidate. He is too young to offer security and his holdings are not sufficient to assure us that he would not be after your fortune."

Rachel swallowed, then dropped her eyes and nodded.

Etta allowed the words to sink in for a few moments, then patted Rachel's arm. The truth was painful at times, to be sure, but it was still the truth, and Etta would be no host at all if she were not confident enough of the process to keep Rachel on course. "And it is time for us to return home for the night."

Rachel's eyes snapped back up, her expression showing that she thought it was her association with Mr. Firth causing the early departure. Etta did not mind that she'd made this assumption, as it could only help impress the importance of the topic. But it was time to make some amends as well and shore up her own connection to her darling niece. They were in this together after all. Rachel's success would be Etta's triumph.

Etta leaned in conspiratorially—and very carefully—opening her fan to give further privacy. "I took some pins out of this monstrous wig because they were impaling me, and it is beginning to slip. If we do not leave soon, I am afraid it shall unseat itself entirely." She quirked a smile and Rachel responded instantly with a smile of her own, good graces restored.

"Do you mean your hair is going to fall off?" Rachel whispered as Etta straightened.

"It just might," Etta said, moving her head just quick enough to make it slip. Rachel's hand flew to her mouth, but her eyes were dancing as she tried to hide a smile. "I shall call for the carriage," Etta said, closing her fan with a snap and delicately pushing her hair back to center. "You may say goodbye to your friends with the excuse that we have an early morning tomorrow, then meet me in the foyer in ten minutes."

"Yes, ma'am."

Etta squared her shoulders in an exaggerated manner and added crisp elocution to her words. "Very good. According to the ton, I am a dignified woman, and having my wig flayed out upon this ballroom will not support that position."

"No indeed," Rachel said with a giggle, then her expression changed to concern. "You will be all right without me?"

"For ten minutes I shall. At minute eleven, I shall begin reducing your pocket money by the minute."

A smiling Rachel hurried off in the direction of the crowds where her friends were waiting for the next round of dancing to begin. She really was a dear girl.

Etta turned toward the foyer but stopped short due to a man standing directly in her path—Mr. Wynn Firth, in fact. She had to reach up for her wig with both hands to keep it in place but dropped her hands immediately, though the wig felt barely balanced. She schooled her expression so as not to give any hint of her predicament.

"Mr. Firth," she said in an even tone. "What a pleasure it is to see you in London."

He inclined his head politely. "Thank you, Mrs. Markshire, I'm glad you have so much pleasure in seeing me."

She narrowed her eyes slightly, sure she'd missed something in his meaning but unsure what it was. Every other man of his age had been covering their thinning pates with wigs for more than a decade, yet his hair was still thick and full. She was close enough to see the silver flecks weaved throughout the dark brown, and though his skin reflected too much time in the sun, the browner tones set his blue eyes off to an even greater contrast.

"You look absolutely stunning tonight," Mr. Firth continued, giving her a warm smile that only made her more suspicious.

"Thank you, sir. Unfortunately, my niece and I are leaving early, so if you will excuse me, I need to call for my carriage."

Mr. Firth nodded but did not step out of her way, demonstrating the same mushy manners as his son. Men in general were incredibly irritating sometimes. Well, most of the time, if she were truly honest. She had very little use for them at all and no use for a country gentleman farmer with no real place in noble circles.

"Your niece, Miss Johnson. She is previously acquainted with my son, Reed."

"So it seems." She looked past him toward the door that would take her to the foyer.

"Because of that previous acquaintance," Mr. Firth continued, "he was not being presumptuous to have spoken with her."

Etta looked back to meet Mr. Firth's eyes, keeping her head perfectly still. "I have no qualm about their speaking," she lied.

He held her look . . . much as she'd stared down his son a few minutes earlier, and his smile tightened, which caused her spine to tighten as well. What was this man about?

"I am glad to hear it. Our connections here in London are limited, thus it is important that we foster a good opinion. I only want to ensure that possibility for my children."

He still did not move, and she clenched her teeth together for a moment while she waited, then finally said, "Indeed. I wish you a good evening, Mr. Firth." She stepped around him and did not look back—both out of pride and the preservation of her blasted headpiece.

A footman posted near the door of the ballroom opened it for her, and she breathed a sigh of relief to be free of the room and all the eyes within it. She immediately lifted one hand to her hair now that no one would see—a stiff wind or a too-fast turn would be her downfall. The wig seemed to be losing balance a bit more with every step she took.

"You there," she called out when she reached the foyer, getting the attention of one of three men in livery standing by the main entrance. The tallest of the three hurried forward. "Please call round the carriage for Mrs. Markshire. My driver is Robert Kent."

"Yes, ma'am," he said, bowing before heading down the opposite hallway. She watched him go and willed that he would hurry. The foyer was blessedly empty just now, but anyone could enter at any time and wonder why she was holding her hair up.

She heard the sound of a footfall and turned enough to find that Mr. Firth had followed her. She attempted to lower her hand, but the wig shifted a quarter inch to the right when she did so, necessitating that she quickly put her hand back. She must look idiotic, but to her preservation, he was a man, and men in general were usually inattentive to details.

"What can I help you with, Mr. Firth?"

"I do not feel that we finished our conversation."

"I believe that we did," Etta said, looking past him toward the hallway where the footman had disappeared. A full minute had not yet passed, but her impatience was rising quickly.

"Do you object to my son's attention toward your niece?"

Her focus moved back to his face. *Of course I object!* she thought. "Of course I do not have an objection," she said out loud, because truly, what else could she say?

"Then why did you interrupt them?"

"Did I interrupt them?"

"Yes," he said with a nod. "You stepped between them, and from what I could see from my side of the room, you were rather severe. I am sorry to press this point, but as I said, we have few connections here in London, therefore each association we do have is precious. I want to resolve whatever concerns you might have so as to shore up this one."

Etta did not like that her interference had been noticed, and yet she was fulfilling her responsibility to Rachel and Rachel's family by looking out for the young woman's interests. Etta lifted her chin to show her confidence, only to feel her wig shift to the left this time. She quickly caught it with her left hand so that she was now standing before this virtual stranger, holding her wig like a basket on her head. Thank goodness for face powder to conceal the heat rising in her cheeks. As a rule, Etta tried not to be rude—there were almost always better ways of making your point that kept everyone's pride intact. Mr. Firth, however, was proving himself rather thickheaded.

"Mr. Firth," she said tightly. "I am Miss Johnson's sponsor here in London as neither of her parents are on hand. It is my responsibility to see that she behaves appropriately and is treated equally so. I saw a man she had not been introduced to dominating her attention, and I did what any good sponsor would do: made his acquaintance and reminded him that there are protocols."

Mr. Firth's expression, which had been relatively open before, hardened slightly. "He had not broken any protocol; they have known one another for years and did not need additional introduction."

"They had been friends as children, Mr. Firth."

"As people, Mrs. Markshire. Surely the trappings and fripperies of this city do not overpower the humanity of previously acquainted young people."

She narrowed her eyes, yet she was still holding this blasted wig on her head, which seriously undermined the position of authority she was trying to present. "As children," she repeated. "Rachel is here to make her match, and I am here to ensure that she makes a good one."

"Are you saying my son is not a good match?"

Oh, but he was bold. Lucky for her—and Rachel—so was she. No one survived London if they were not bold enough to defend their position and tradition. "Your son cannot be more than twenty years old."

"Twenty-two."

She gave a sardonic laugh but could not move her head to show a full reaction. "As though that is a better credit? He is not ready to support a family."

"Things do not always have to be done one way. He's a grown man helping run the estate he will inherit one day, and he did not dominate your niece's attention, he simply said hello. I would not want any of that misinterpreted, which is why—" His eyes traveled from her face, where his attention had been focused, to her hair. "Are you all right?"

"Of course I am all right." She looked down the hallway again. Where was the footman?

"Is there something wrong with your, um, hair?"

"Mr. Firth, you are being indecent."

He looked back at her eyes and suddenly smiled—a flat-out grin on his country face. "If I am being indecent, perhaps you should slap me."

She was sorely tempted, but the fact that she was holding her hair in place with both hands made it impossible, and well he knew it. Never mind that she would never do something so undignified at a ball. This was so humiliating.

The footman who had called the carriage came out of the hallway with two velvet cloaks over his arm. Blast—she'd forgotten that she and Rachel had worn wraps tonight. How would she manage to put her arms through while holding her hair?

As though reading her thoughts, Mr. Firth stepped forward and reached up to put his hands beside her own on either side of her wig. She felt the pressure on her scalp and closed her eyes as the humiliation became more than she could bear for a moment. "You can let go," he said.

She opened her eyes—his face was very close to hers. Closer than any man had been in a very long time. The scent of his cologne caused a tickle in her belly that she refused to think on.

"Let go and put on your wrap," he said again, and she lowered her hands, having to look away from him as the footman helped her put her arms through the sleeves and fasten the clasp at the neck. Women of a Certain Age should never be diminished in this way.

"Your carriage will be out front shortly, Mrs. Markshire," the footman said, stepping away.

Mr. Firth did not let go of her hair, keeping himself close. "Your niece gives my children the opportunity to find their ground in unfamiliar territory. Please take the time to get to know Lydia and give my boy a chance. You can let go of your fears for your niece," Mr. Firth said in a low voice.

The impertinence of his words turned the heat in her chest from embarrassment to anger. Whatever masked intimacy their proximity offered only emboldened her determination to put him and his son in their place. "Your boy, Mr. Firth, is not even a contender. It is in everyone's best interest if he focuses his attention elsewhere."

Mr. Firth narrowed his eyes as he held her gaze a few seconds. He abruptly pulled his hands away from her wig as he stepped back.

Etta would never know if he intentionally unbalanced the wig when he removed his hands or if it was just the law of gravity that came into play, but either way, Etta's attempts to catch the massive headpiece were to no avail, and the lovely, glittering confection landed on the floor between them with a thump. The sound was deafening, at least to her ears, and her hands immediately flew to her head, which was supposed to have a tight linen wrap . . . but didn't. She belatedly saw the fabric still attached to the interior of the wig itself. Her real hair was coiled tightly against her head, pinned close to her scalp in a utilitarian way that was unattractive and never intended for anyone's view but that of herself and her lady's maid. Etta looked from the wig—which looked like a pathetically powdered and glittering fir tree—to Mr. Firth. He smiled back at her, then bowed deeply at the waist. "Good evening, Mrs. Markshire."

Three

ETTA WAS IN THE CARRIAGE with the hood of her cloak over her head by the time Rachel reached her. The hairpiece lay beside her on the bench and her chest continued to vibrate with humiliation and amplified annoyance.

"Auntie?" Rachel said as the door closed behind her. "What happened?"

"Nothing," Etta said, forcing a smile. "I took it off once I was in the carriage." She then pointedly looked out the window to show she did not want to discuss it further. Rachel did not press.

Throughout the travel home, Etta's mind played through the final event of the evening and then spun off into other possible things that could have happened—someone could have come into the foyer before she'd made her escape. The hairpiece could have fallen off in the ballroom. She tried to stop the circling thoughts but found it difficult. Her anxiety rose with every repetition and false scenario.

Once home, Etta carried her wig beneath her cloak to her room, though it was impossible to keep the monstrous thing inconspicuous. In her bedchamber, Lowry had laid out her nightgown and was waiting to help her ready for bed. Etta revealed the headpiece from inside the fold of her cape and Lowry gasped, putting her hand to her mouth.

"What happened, Mrs. Markshire?"

Etta told her the story, then said she did not want to talk about it further. Lowry nodded her understanding and took the wig from Etta before taking it into the changing room with the other thirteen wigs that Etta owned. Etta doubted she would ever wear it again, not after tonight. She doubted she would ever see that wig without also seeing the scene of it landing on the floor at her feet, Mr. Firth staring at the thing like it was a dead animal.

Mr. Firth's words repeated in the background of her thoughts—*surely the trappings and fripperies of this city do not overpower the humanity.* Etta walked to the full-length mirror and looked over her costume and face makeup before taking down the hood of her cape and looking at the whole of herself; the caricature of the woman she presented to the world. It all struck her as utterly ridiculous in light of this evening—Mr. Firth's lack of manners, her own rudeness, the trappings and fripperies, and . . . hair. It was what she knew—the way life worked here in London—but tonight it felt heavy and false. What Mr. Firth must think of her . . . dressed up as she was, exhibiting her own lack of manners. Her tired mind was fertile ground for discontent, and no matter how she tried to push away the thoughts, they would not obey.

Lowry returned, and Etta put her arms out so that Lowry could undo the hidden ties and clasps that held together the three-piece dress—bodice, skirt, and back. The lady's maid set each piece on the footstool, then removed the outer petticoat and untied the hoop that accentuated Etta's hips to dramatic proportions. Lowry lowered the hoop to the floor, where Etta stepped out of what suddenly looked like an elaborate birdcage. Lowry took the hoop to the changing room, allowing Etta to look at herself again—hair bound close to her head, face in full makeup, body bound into her corset that forced a shape that was not her own. How many hours had it taken for her to get ready tonight? Two? Four? All to have her hair fall to the floor at her feet.

Lowry returned to unlace the whalebone corset and layers of petticoats and underskirts required for tonight's presentation. Etta's body ached and tingled as it settled into its actual shape after hours of confinement. She removed the shift herself, wincing at a twinge in her shoulder that had been there for years, then rubbed the chaffed area below each arm where the skin was pink and tender from the corset. She undid the garters to her pantaloons and then slid her arms into the sleeves of her dressing gown, which felt smooth and cool against her bare skin. Then it was the stockings that Lowry unrolled one leg at a time after Etta sat down, her skin flushing warm as the blood flowed and her muscles relaxed. She turned to face the mirror while Lowry fetched the washbasin, soap, and towel needed to remove the white face powder, bright rouge, and black eye charcoal from her face. Yet another part of this persona she'd become—Colletta Markshire, London socialite, hostess extraordinaire.

Trappings and fripperies replacing humanity. Blast Mr. Firth for putting such thoughts into her head. Making her question the only life she knew. Society needed structure and rules—there had to be proper ways to go about things.

"I would like my hair taken down tonight, Lowry."

Lowry met her eyes in the mirror, and Etta nodded confirmation of the detour from their usual arrangement. She wore wigs every day and therefore kept her hair pinned for days at a time between washings. She'd washed her hair just yesterday. The maid did not hesitate long and began to unpin the coiled loops of hair. When she finished, Etta's own hair hung nearly to the middle of her back in kinked and frizzy waves. Etta's scalp throbbed almost to the point of being painful. It was a familiar sensation—it always felt this way when Etta took her hair down—and the feeling matched the similar sensation she felt in much of her body right now, undone as she was.

"Shall I put it in a sleeping braid?" Lowry asked.

"No, thank you. I shall manage. Good night, Lowry."

After Lowry took the linens and left the room, Etta went to the basin and flipped her hair over to pour water from the pitcher over her head. She dried her hair with a towel, then brushed it out, long and smooth. She sat in front of her mirror and looked at her skin free of cosmetics, her hair free of pins, and her body free of the contraptions that kept her in fashion.

She noted the fine lines around her eyes and the texture of her skin that had once been smooth. Her sandy-blonde hair was streaked with grey, her small breasts soft beneath her dressing gown, and her waistline no longer held the contour it once did. Yet this was her body, her true self. The trappings were just that, trappings, decoration . . . distraction?

She stared for a long time, thinking over her interaction with Mr. Firth and not sure why it felt like so . . . much. Why did it feel important enough to think of at all?

Because she hadn't liked who she'd been.

She'd structured the interaction to give an impression and make a point, all of it based on pretense and expectation. None of it based on the fact that she'd talked to a man new to Town who'd been trying to look out for his children and asking for her help in doing that. She had chosen the trappings over the humanity, and it did not sit well with her. Yet what else could she do?

She finally turned away from the mirror with a sigh,

hating how unsettled she felt, but hopeful that morning would bring a better mood and less depth to her thoughts. They did not serve her and the life she'd made. They only made it harder to live it.

 Four

IT WAS A WEEK BEFORE Etta had to face Mr. Firth again. She saw him across the lawn at a garden party before he saw her, and she managed to keep a distance for some time. The uncomfortable thoughts had eased by morning but had not disappeared completely. She did not like that seeing him again reminded her of those thoughts all over again.

Eventually, the inevitable happened, and they stood across from one another amid a circle of other attendees, including his son and daughter. Etta looked Mr. Firth squarely in the eye to show him that she was not going to let their last meeting set the tone for their interactions going forward. She had been at a disadvantage, and he had not behaved as a gentleman—that was the point she would focus upon. He held her gaze a moment, then introduced himself to the other women in the circle, which she took as an acknowledgement of his understanding. Rachel, luckily, was taking a turn around the pond with Mr. Rigby. With a bit more luck, that walk would last longer than this exchange.

"Mrs. Markshire," Mr. Firth said after having greeted every other person in the circle. "I would like to introduce you to my daughter, Lydia."

The wisp of a girl Etta had also seen from a distance much earlier in the day could not be more than eighteen years old and looked absolutely terrified. Etta could not help but feel compassion for the only Firth who seemed to know how out of place they were in Town—proof that her humanity was not entirely depleted after so many years in London.

"How do you do," the girl said, dropping into too deep a curtsy for a casual afternoon event.

Etta appreciated the girl's effort and let her heart remain soft toward her. "I am well, Miss Firth, thank you. Your dress is lovely, that shade of green is perfect for your coloring."

The girl met her eyes with desperate gratitude. "Do you really think so?"

Etta did not show her surprise at the girl's response, though Lady Wilkins, standing to Etta's left, made a soft snort. "I do," Etta said, glad that her compliment had been genuine. It was a lovely dress, and it set the girl off to as much advantage as a dress could. "It can be a challenge to choose amid current fashion and still find the designs that set us off to our best representation. Your dress is an example of success in that field."

"Oh, thank you, Mrs. Markshire."

Mr. Firth shifted awkwardly, which told Etta that he knew his daughter was not ready for London. Reed Firth stayed a step back from the group, looking as awkward and out of place here as he had at last week's ball.

"You are welcome, Miss Firth."

There was a bit more small talk amid the group and then the Firths moved on, and Etta hid her relief.

Lady Wilkins snorted more loudly once they were gone. "Gracious, is this what London has come to? Every country bumpkin can crash on through?"

"It is not her fault," Etta said, opening her fan. The day

was warm, and though she'd chosen a much more subdued wig today and a lovely wide-brimmed hat, she was feeling the prickling sensation of sweat beneath her layers. "She seems very sweet-tempered." Again, Etta was glad to be able to speak the truth. The girl was not ridiculous, just unpolished.

Lady Wilkins snorted again. "She'll not make a match here."

Etta did not want to prolong the topic, but she silently agreed.

Mr. Holladay and his sister joined the party and the topic of conversation blessedly changed, but Etta found herself continuing to track the Firths as the afternoon continued. Mr. Firth did not leave his daughter's side, which was sweet but silly if he wanted her to make acquaintances her own age. Eventually, Mr. Rigby returned Rachel, and for the rest of the party Etta made it a priority to move her in circles opposite those the Firths were making. She was both smug and satisfied when she and Rachel were finally handed into the carriage without having another encounter.

"How was your afternoon?" Etta asked once the carriage was moving. "Did you enjoy yourself?"

"I did enjoy myself, it was a lovely time," Rachel said, sitting perfectly straight in her seat and looking as contented as her words implied.

"You had some time with Mr. Rigby," Etta said, lifting one eyebrow. "He is very attentive to you."

Rachel lowered her chin and Etta was unable to read her expression. "He is," Rachel said, then lifted her head, her cheeks pink.

Etta smiled, then took a satisfying breath and looked out the carriage window, already thinking ahead to the Cronshaw's dinner party tonight. It would not be a large affair, twenty people or so, but Mrs. Cronshaw was Mr. Rigby's aunt and he was sure to be there. Two opportunities in a single day for the two young people to further their connection. That was excellent.

"I did not get to talk to Lydia or Re—Mr. Firth."

Etta turned back to Rachel and raised her darkly penciled eyebrows. She did not wear powders during the day but still accentuated her brows, eyes, and lips. "Oh?"

"I saw you speaking to them when I was walking with Mr. Rigby and had hoped I would have another chance. I have barely seen Lydia at all since she's come to Town. When we did speak last, she was finding it all a bit overwhelming."

"Yes, I am sure it is overwhelming. The farther from Town one lives, the more difficult it is to feel comfortable here. I am surprised they did not stay in Manchester and simply find satisfaction with the events there. I think it would have been more comfortable for all of them." Manchester was nothing like London, of course, but a much better place for someone ill-prepared for the expectations of the city.

"As does Lydia," Rachel said. "She had quite liked it there, but her father insisted they come to London for some reason. I just hope she is all right. It was a difficult adjustment when I came to London as well."

"But you have many ties here," Etta reminded her, not wanting her to empathize too much with Lydia. "And you have visited many times, so you were much better prepared."

"Exactly," Rachel said. "It is far easier for me to find my comfort here than it is for Lydia, to be sure. Would it be all right if, perhaps, I invited Lydia to attend with us from time to time? It is always so much easier to feel comfortable when you have a particular friend beside you."

"I suppose," Etta said, not liking this suggestion at all. "Though at some point, each debutante must find their own way."

"Of course," Rachel said, nodding. "I am certainly not in any position to manage her experience; I would just like to help her find her feet."

Etta rolled that idea around and then decided to be direct in her concern. "Would having additional time with Lydia be at all connected to the desire to have additional time with Mr. Firth?"

Rachel looked to the side and did not answer as quickly as Etta would have liked. "I know he is too young, Auntie Etta, and a bad match."

Etta felt a weight lift off her shoulders at Rachel's admission.

"But they are my friends," Rachel said before Etta could speak. She looked at Etta again. "I have so many opportunities that they do not, and their mother's death was particularly hard on Lydia. I only want to help her have as good an experience as possible—nothing more." She smiled a bit shyly. "That sounds terribly pretentious, doesn't it?"

"Not at all," Etta said, moved by this girl's compassion and yet uncomfortable with the possibility of how that compassion could play out. "Of course you should help Lydia feel more comfortable, it is only . . . I only want to ensure that it does not detract from your own experience too much. The Firth family is not, what one would say, quite the thing, if you get my meaning, and there may be a fine line between how much benefit your association can offer without them interfering with your own objectives."

Trappings, fripperies, humanity.

"You think time with them could hurt my own prospects?"

Etta considered what to say, but now was not the time to resolve the ethics of what life was. It was not as if she had set the rules. "Too much time, yes, especially with Mr. Reed

Firth," Etta said. "If other men feel that you have interest in Mr. Firth, they may keep more distance. It has been at great expense and attention that you are here, Rachel, and those of us who have facilitated this opportunity are counting on you using it to your highest advantage, not sacrificing your potential on behalf of those who have not put the time and attention into preparing for their experience."

Rachel pulled her eyebrows together in a thoughtful expression. Etta let her process for several seconds before extending an olive branch.

"Why don't you invite Lydia and a few of your other friends to tea tomorrow? Something small and intimate. That would strengthen her association with other girls as well as show your interest in those connections."

Rachel brightened. "That is an excellent idea," she said. "I can think of a few girls who would be inviting to her, especially in a setting like that. Thank you, Auntie."

"Of course," Etta said, waving away the thanks. "A young ladies' tea is just the thing." The best part was that young Mr. Firth did not fit the party regime at all.

Five

THE TEA WAS A SUCCESS, and three nights later, Rachel invited Lydia as her particular friend to a dinner party at the Whitcombs'—an event that the Firths had not been invited to. The association between the girls naturally created increased connection to both Mr. Firths as the first week stretched to two and then three. Etta watched carefully and felt secure enough in the public distance that young Mr. Firth kept that she did not feel the risk was too great. Mr. Wynn Firth seemed to always be on hand at these events, but she was careful to keep him at a distance emotionally, if not physically, because she could not risk losing her vigilance regarding his son or allowing his censorious thoughts to impede her work.

To her surprise, however, the rest of London warmed up to all three of the Firths far quicker than she would have expected. Wynn Firth had better social graces than Etta would have guessed and conversed easily with both men and women. The older women were particularly attentive to him, and he was never without female company at the events they attended. An odd jealousy began to attach itself to the annoyance Etta felt toward him. She had lived in London most of her life and worked hard to build up the friendships and connections necessary to be successful here. That Wynn Firth could do the same in mere weeks made her question the value of those relationships as a whole. These were uncomfortable thoughts that took a great deal of effort to keep at bay, and too often Etta found herself watching him from across a room as she tried to make sense of it all. Make sense of him.

"Miss Firth has certainly blossomed beneath the London skies," Elizabeth Pettengill remarked one day as she and Etta sat in the shade of a tree at a garden party on an excruciatingly hot day. They both waved their fans and dabbed at their sweaty foreheads and necks as decorously as possible. Women of a Certain Age really should avoid such undignified situations. If not for Rachel, Etta would have left an hour ago.

She looked to where Rachel and Lydia played lawn games with a dozen or so other young people, Mr. Rigby among them and Mr. Reed Firth blessedly absent. Etta was still hopeful that Mr. Rigby's attentions would lead to a match, though he was certainly taking his time about it. There were only a few more weeks of concentrated social events left before Parliament would end and the majority of nobles would return to their country estates. "Yes," Etta confirmed, returning to Elizabeth's comment about Lydia Firth. "Lydia has done quite well. I would be hard-pressed to recognize her as the girl I first met."

"And Rachel has quite taken to her role as mentor," Elizabeth remarked.

"Indeed, she has," Etta said, focusing her attention on Rachel as she laughed at something Lydia had said. Etta smiled, proud of Rachel's compassion toward Lydia but . . . "Not all the changes in Rachel have been good ones," she confided to her friend. "Though I am gratified by Rachel's confidence, it has brought with it some concerning . . . arrogance. She refused Lady Medford's Sunday tea last week. She called it pretentious."

"Well, that tea is rather pretentious," Elizabeth said, still fanning herself. "Making everyone wear pink and then having to wear one of her gaudy hats."

"Be that as it may, it was an honor to be invited—even Beatrice did not merit an invitation while she was here in London. It concerns me that Rachel is not appreciating the opportunities, and it was terribly embarrassing to send regrets. I am dreading my next encounter with Lady Medford, as I'm sure she will mention it."

"Oh, she most certainly will," Elizabeth said, pausing her fan to take a sip of her warm lemonade. She scowled and put the cup as far away from herself as possible. "I'm surprised you let Rachel bow out; in the past you were the one who decided which events you attended and which you did not."

Etta considered that and felt her shoulders slump with the realization that Elizabeth was exactly right. "I suppose I am getting soft, aren't I? She's become rather distracted with her friends, and I do not feel that we are as . . . close as we were in the beginning. Twice last week she agreed to invitations without discussing it with me and then she refused Lady Medford's tea."

"Then you must rein in that independence," Elizabeth said, looking at Etta over her fluttering fan. "Remember Sarah Lynn when she became determined to only interact with titled gentlemen? You cut off all events until she promised to behave with grace at any event, and it reminded her who was truly in charge."

"I had forgotten that," Etta said. Goodness, Sarah Lynn had only been her third charge. Had Etta truly had that much fortitude? Of course, that was six years ago. Etta straightened a bit in her chair. "You are right, Elizabeth. I need to remember who is in charge. Rachel came to me because I could help her navigate those things she cannot navigate on her own." She felt the infusion of credibility. "I must not be so flexible with her that she chooses her uneducated and immature judgement over my own."

"Precisely," Elizabeth said.

Etta sat back in her chair, revived and freshly committed to her course. She was the sponsor; Rachel was a child. Etta would not forget again.

Just then, the older Mr. Firth, who had not been in attendance at the party so far—it was primarily for women and a few of the bucks closely connected to the hosts—appeared on the lawn near a group of women. Etta's awareness, always too easily tuned in to Mr. Firth, was heightened, and she began fanning a bit faster. He laughed at something with Mrs. Gordon—a widow of means with wide hips and a pug nose.

"And then there is Mr. Firth," Elizabeth said as if she were a narrative voice in Etta's head.

"What about him?" Etta said with conscious coolness.

"He is country and lacks the polish of Society, but there is something rather . . . intriguing about him."

"I'm sure I don't know what you mean," Etta said amid the flutters of her fan. "I find him very much as I did when he arrived."

"If that is true, you are the only one. The matrons and widows of London are all quite taken with him."

"He is handsome," Etta said dismissively. "It would not be the first time a handsome man distracted the ladies of this town."

"He took Mrs. Winters to the opera last week."

"I know," Etta said, even though she hadn't known.

"And Lady Carmichael invited him to her box at the opera."

"That is excellent," Etta said, realizing she'd been tapping her foot. She forced herself to stop. "Perhaps if he makes connections of his own, Rachel shall not feel so responsible to make them for Lydia."

"He seems to pay you a great deal of attention."

Etta stopped her fan and looked sharply at her friend. "He does not."

"Yes, he does," Elizabeth countered. "At any event you both attend, he always seeks you out."

Did he? Etta wondered. She shook her head. "Because of Rachel and Lydia's friendship, that is all. He confirms which events they are attending together, arranges who shall provide transport, that sort of thing."

"The sort of things the girls could easily manage without him."

"He is an over-involved parent," Etta said with a shrug, going back to her fan and stopping her tapping foot again.

"Or he is looking for excuses to interact with you."

"Stop it, Elizabeth," Etta said, looking away from Mr. Firth to watch the young people's game. Not looking at Elizabeth.

"Stop what?"

"Teasing me."

"I am not teasing you," Elizabeth said in a non-teasing voice. "Only pointing out that his attention to you is curious. I think he has some intentions."

"His intentions are surely no interest of mine," Etta said, and she meant it, except that the heat she felt in her chest was not consistent to her position. Was there more in his attention than she had seen? And if there were, did she truly have no interest? "Any number of men have had intentions toward me, as well you know."

"Yes," Elizabeth agreed. Etta could see her head nod from the corner of her eye. "But none that you watch quite so closely as you watch Mr. Firth."

Etta clenched her teeth together, a quick shot of defensiveness testifying that Elizabeth spoke the truth. She took a breath and forced the defensiveness down with a reminder that Elizabeth was her closest friend—one of very few people Etta could truly trust. "I do not understand it," she said so soft, she thought—partly hoped—that Elizabeth would not hear it.

But Elizabeth did hear it. Etta could feel the softening of her friend beside her. "I have no want of such notice, Elizabeth. None at all."

"Which is understandable, Etta, and beyond any right anyone has to judge and determine. However, that you do pay such particular notice might mean something."

"What?" Etta said, turning to look at her friend directly. "What might it mean?"

Elizabeth smiled kindly, cocking her head to the side and slowing her fan a bit. "Sometimes an uncomfortable feeling can be easier to tolerate if we give it a different meaning. For example, we might be afraid of something, but it feels like anger. Or anxious about something else and it feels like excitement. Or, perhaps, what feels like irritation is actually . . . attraction, curiosity, interest."

"Interest," Etta repeated. Was she interested in Mr. Firth? Surely not, she was not interested in any man. She was interested in an independent life where she did what she wanted, when she wanted, without anyone's disapproval or prevention. That was what she was interested in.

And yet . . .

There was a thinness to her life that hung just outside the window of her mind. A sense that she had not quite accomplished all that she wanted to accomplish. Yet she had accomplished so much that she was proud of. She had wonderful friends, respect of her peers, opportunities, travel . . .

and a perpetual question as to whether she had ever been truly loved.

Trappings and fripperies were not silencing those things as they once did. She blamed Mr. Firth. Ever since that night all those weeks ago, the discomfort with her life had felt closer, brighter, harder to ignore.

She shook her head, irritated at the thoughts while at the same time remembering Elizabeth's theory that one feeling might mask another. Was her irritation actually the fear of admitting such things? Of looking too closely into the void of what she'd never found? Fulfillment with a man. A trusting relationship where she was wanted and loved. Could that be more important than the other things she had accomplished?

Sometimes she looked at married couples who had grown into such comfort with one another and wondered what that might be like. Facing such thoughts raised her fears and hesitations, however, and reminded her of all the reasons she was determined to remain independent. No matter the handsome man and fluttering feelings and the inability to ignore where he was in any space at any given time.

"Oh, Elizabeth," she said softly, resting her open fan on her lap and looking at the oriental flowers painted across the paper. "Sometimes the thoughts in my head are exhausting."

Elizabeth's quick clearing of her throat drew Etta's attention, giving her precious seconds to set herself to rights before the very subject of her thoughts was upon them.

"Good afternoon, Mrs. Pettengill, Mrs. Markshire."

"Good afternoon, Mr. Firth," Elizabeth said for them both. "How nice to see you."

"Thank you, Mrs. Pettengill." He looked at Etta, but she felt rather overwhelmed by all the thoughts she'd let in during the minutes before his approach. She nodded politely and looked away, pretending to be absorbed in the young people's games.

"How are you liking London?" Elizabeth asked him.

Etta already knew the answer because she and Mr. Firth had discussed this topic last week at the Forsham dinner when he was suddenly at her side for no particular reason. She remembered that when he'd excused himself after a few minutes, his shoulder had brushed hers accidentally and she'd felt it shiver through her. She only listened to his answer now with half an ear, looking pointedly away as the small talk continued while the confusing feelings in her chest morphed into one that was easily identified and perfectly comfortable for her to act upon—annoyance. She'd gone soft and allowed Rachel to take more control than she should have—that must stop. She'd also gone soft in her determination to want anything more than she had—that must stop too.

"Well," she said suddenly, standing quickly enough that both Elizabeth and Mr. Firth started. "I do believe it is time for us to go, good day." She marched away from them and called for Rachel. Several young people looked her direction, then at Rachel as she obediently broke away from the group.

"Yes, Auntie Etta? What is it?"

"It is time to go," Etta said.

"Our game is not yet finished," Rachel protested. "Perhaps in a quarter of an hour."

"Rachel," Etta said, fixing her with a look that Women of a Certain Age had mastered. She spoke slowly, enunciating each word. "It is time to go. I expect you at the carriage in five minutes."

She turned on her heel to avoid another protest and moved toward the drive, aware with every step exactly where Mr. Firth's placement was to her and knowing without a doubt that he was watching her just as she so often watched him.

Six

"Mr. Winfred has asked Abigail Horsley to marry him!"

Etta looked up from her morning paper, as surprised by Rachel bursting into her room unannounced as she was by the news Rachel had just trumpeted.

"Abigail Horsley?" Etta said as Rachel threw herself backward across the foot of Etta's bed. It was a Friday morning, and they did not have an event until three, so Etta was taking the morning to herself. Or such had been her plan. "She has been here in London less than a month, and she is so... pale," Etta said. The girl blended so well with the pastels afforded to debutantes that she often looked like a ghost amid the other girls.

"I know!" Rachel wailed, throwing a hand over her eyes. Truly, Etta had never seen Rachel so animated. "He had been so attentive to me before she arrived, and I thought that once he realized how insipid and dull she was, he would see me in an even better light."

"You need not be critical of other girls to feel good about yourself," Etta chided softly, surprised again as she had not seen such judgement from Rachel before. Never mind that

Etta had thought the same thing. It was one thing to think a thing, however, quite another to say it out loud where people could flog you with it.

Rachel stayed in Etta's room for a full half hour talking through her disappointment, and when she left, Etta felt a new sense of satisfaction. To be the receiver of Rachel's sorrows helped center her concerns over Rachel's increasing independence. And hopefully, this loss of Mr. Winfred's attention would help Rachel understand the stakes. Parliament would end soon. More and more engagements were being announced. It would not be the worst thing in the world for Rachel not to make a match—two of Etta's sponsors made their matches on their second Season—but she would like the girl to find success this time around if possible.

Two days after Rachel burst into Etta's room, Mr. Rigby left Town for his grandmother's birthday celebration in Sussex. Rachel became very quiet, and the following evening claimed she was too tired to go to the ball they had been planning to attend. She spent the night alone in her room while Etta caught up on correspondence. Mr. Reed Firth sent her flowers the next day, and Etta would have read the note that accompanied the arrangement if her staff had done their job and alerted her before taking it to Rachel. Etta sent Lowry to find the note when they were out that evening, but upon her return, Lowry claimed the note was nowhere to be found.

Despite the rousing of their connection that Etta had felt the week before when Rachel had shared her disappointment over Mr. Winfred's engagement, tension began to set in between them again. Rachel only wanted to go to the events Lydia attended, most of which had Reed Firth on hand as well—and Mr. Firth too. When Etta forced Rachel to go to events without her friend, Rachel kept herself apart from the main crowds, not putting herself forward to dance and sometimes disappearing into a library or garden or someplace she could be alone. Etta counted the days for Mr. Rigby's return, as she was sure the young man's renewed attention would be just what Rachel needed. She talked at length with Elizabeth about how to best strategize a restoration of spirits in her young charge. And how to keep Mr. Reed Firth as far away as possible while Rachel was so out of sorts. She would be even more vulnerable in her melancholy.

All these things were on Etta's mind when they attended a musical performance at the Royal Opera House. Rachel was not terribly keen about music, and Etta had to keep tapping her with her fan to remind Rachel to sit up straight and at least look attentive to the evening. At intermission, Rachel darted out of their box before Etta could contain her. With a heavy breath, Etta stood and followed at a more decorous pace. There were refreshments in the gallery, and Etta narrowed her eyes when she saw Rachel deep in conversation with Reed Firth. She was waylaid on her way to interrupt them by Mr. and Mrs. Willington, and by the time she was able to end that conversation, Rachel was talking with a group of young women, and Reed Firth was on the other side of the room. Etta looked between them, trying to sort what was happening and feeling very—very—tired. It was good to see Rachel socializing with her friends, but Etta could not help but feel unsettled.

"Confounding, isn't it?"

Etta knew the voice of Wynn Firth by now and took instant offense at the tone, though she did not show it as she turned to face him and gave as polite a smile as she could gather.

"Good evening, Mr. Firth."

He inclined his head slightly, then took a sip of his wine, watching her above the rim of his glass. "Do you agree?" he asked when he lowered his glass. "That these young people are completely confounding."

She was not in the mood for his teasing, so she looked past him in search of any reason to excuse herself. And yet part of her wanted to stay. Confounding indeed.

"You do not need to worry yourself so much."

She looked back at him, keeping her expression bored. "Worry?" she repeated.

"About your niece. Things have a way of working themselves out, and she is a well-behaved and thoughtful girl."

"She is a young woman, not a girl," Etta corrected, solely for the purpose of correcting him. "And I have no doubt that her best future will absolutely work out." She said the last words with flat articulation to reference his own casual mention.

"Then why do you take on so much concern for such things as who she is talking to and for how long?"

Ah, they were back to her not approving of Reed Firth's attention to Rachel. The same conversation that had begun their connection all those weeks ago. She let out an audible sigh. "Have a good evening, Mr. Firth. Your impertinence is what I truly find confounding." He laughed as she turned and clenched her teeth—oh, why could the Firths not return to where they came from? In this exact moment they seemed to be the cause of all the tension she was feeling.

She suffered through the second half of the performance—chiding Rachel the whole time on how to sit and how to smile—and they rode home in complete silence. Perhaps Etta could arrange for Rachel to go riding; she had done very little since coming to the city. Some time on horseback, arranged by her dear auntie, might remedy the melancholy, or at least lead her to discuss her feelings with Etta.

She let the silence continue while she put together a plan that she would start on first thing tomorrow, but she also questioned if she wanted to do this anymore. She did not feel the same about her hosting responsibilities as she once did. What had once been fun now made her tired.

It was something to think about . . . later.

Seven

ETTA WAS LINGERING OVER HER breakfast the next morning as she planned out an opportunity for Rachel—Elizabeth kept horses for riding outside of Town—when there was a quick knock at the door. It opened before Etta had swallowed her bite of toast enough to respond. The housekeeper, Mrs. Thomas, was in a state as she charged into the room.

"I am sorry to interrupt your breakfast, ma'am," Mrs. Thomas said, her voice high and her apple-cheeks bright. "But we are unable to find Miss Johnson this morning."

Etta straightened where she sat in her bed with the breakfast tray over her knees. "What do you mean you are unable to find her?" She immediately thought of last night when she'd entered the gallery to see Rachel and Mr. Reed Firth deep in conversation.

"She was not in her room when her maid went to wake her half an hour ago. We have looked throughout the house and cannot find her anywhere."

Etta was already moving the breakfast tray from her lap. "When was she last seen?"

"Last night, after your return from the performance."

"Was her maid the last to see her?"

"Yes, ma'am."

Etta threw back the covers and stood, crossing to where her dressing gown was hung before throwing it over her shoulders.

"Have you talked to all the staff?" Etta asked, tying the sash around her waist and feeling the fury rise in her chest. She knew from the first time she'd set eyes on the young Mr. Firth that he was trouble.

"Yes, ma'am, no one saw her after Gretchen helped her ready for bed. She did ask Gretchen to let her sleep late, as she said she was very tired, which is why we have only just realized she's missing."

Etta was hurrying toward the door when she realized there was nothing she could do from her home in her dressing gown. She pulled the sash to undo the knot she'd just tied and turned back to the wardrobe. "Order my carriage and send Lowry up to help me get ready. Send the footmen through the nearby parks just in case, and make sure you speak to every staff member personally and press upon them the need for absolute discretion—there is no space for anyone here in Town to know what is happening in our household. I want to interview her maid myself before I go."

"Where are you going?"

"The London home of Mr. Wynn Firth—the man to blame for my niece's disappearance, I have no doubt."

When they arrived at the Firths' town house—a rented town house, mind you—the footman went ahead of Etta and banged on the front door. Etta reached the door just after it had been opened and therefore stepped over the threshold without pausing, then turned to look at a rather surprised butler standing to the side of the door he'd just opened. "Where is Mr. Firth?"

"I am here."

She spun around and looked to the top of the stairs where Mr. Firth stood in his shirtsleeves, looking down at her with a sheaf of papers in his hand. She opened her mouth to speak, but then closed it, mindful of the delicate nature of this conversation and the curious eyes of the servants in their vicinity. "Where is your study?"

He furrowed his eyebrows. "Where is my study?" he repeated.

It would be upstairs, so she lifted the skirts of her day dress and started up. "You shall direct me, or I shall find it myself."

"My word, Mrs. Markshire, what are you about?"

She glared at him as the distance between them shortened but said nothing. Amid her high energy and the fury still building in her chest, she noted that his hair was unbound today, the ends trailing over his shoulders, silky smooth and reflecting the morning light that came in through the foyer windows. The notice annoyed her even more, and she looked away from his face as she marched past him on the stairs. He turned and followed but did not offer direction. She tried the first door in the hallway—a linen cupboard. The second was a bedroom with blues and greens and a decidedly empty feel. The third was another bedroom that smelled just like him. She paused long enough in the doorway to notice the coat casually slung over the back of a chair and the rumpled bedcovers that brought a shot of embarrassing warmth to her chest. She pulled the door shut with a snap.

Her hand was on the fourth door in sequence when he finally spoke.

"Lydia is still abed in that one and will likely squeal if we barge in on her."

"Then where is your study so that we might have a

private conversation?" she said between her teeth as she spun to face him.

He inclined his head and moved past her. It was the fifth door—fifth of six, she noted—and he opened it before giving a flourished wave to show her in. She moved past him with her chin high, then turned to face him. He closed the door without urgency and then clasped his hands behind his back. "To what do I owe the pleasure of your morning visit, Mrs. Markshire?"

"Rachel is missing—where is your son?"

A momentary expression of surprise crossed his face. "My son is in Luton."

"Oh dear heavens," Etta said at the confirmation that young Mr. Firth was not here. She turned toward the window and put a hand to her chest. "When did they leave?"

"They did not leave; Reed left. He was invited to a house party of a friend from school. He left last night as soon as we returned from the performance—in fact, we did not stay for the second half due to his journey."

"Rachel is with him," Etta said, facing him again, her whole body tight.

"She is not," Mr. Firth said, shaking his head, his eyebrows drawn together. "I saw him off myself—he was very much alone, save for his valet and the driver."

"They must have met her somewhere along the way."

Mr. Firth shook his head again and set his papers down on the desk. He crossed his arms over his chest. "My staff is fiercely loyal to me, Mrs. Markshire, they would never execute such a plan behind my back."

Etta cocked her head to the side and folded her arms to mirror his stance. "How interesting that you will defend your staff's honor, but not your son's."

He pulled himself up a bit taller and his blue eyes flashed.

He took a deep breath before he spoke, and therefore his tone continued in that calm tone. "Because there is nothing to defend. Reed would never disgrace a young woman or his family through such an action that you are suggesting."

"And yet Rachel is gone. We have searched our home, interrogated our staff, and no one knows where she's gone. Since crossing paths with your son, her behavior has become subversive, and now they are both gone from London on the same night—can you truly stand before me and say that is sheerly coincidental, Mr. Firth?"

She could see it in the tightening of his jaw that he could not. "I shall go to Luton straightaway."

Etta was already shaking her head. "They did not go to a house party in Luton, Mr. Firth! Your son lied to you and has escaped the city with my charge." She placed a hand to her chest, feeling the weight of her own words. She was responsible for Rachel's care and safety. She had failed everyone. "They must be going to Scotland," she said, the weight of reality heavy in every word. Since the Marriage Act of 1753, marriages in England required a minister, a church, and parental consent. Scotland, however, could legally marry without any of those elements. Unless . . . they weren't going to Scotland at all and were instead making an even worse decision. Surely Rachel would not be that stupid . . . and yet Etta was beginning to think she did not know Rachel all that well.

Mr. Firth turned from her and began to pace. She watched him for six turns before she spoke.

"Well?" she said, putting out her arms. "Have you nothing more to say?"

He glared at her a moment, but then his expression softened. "Let me speak with Lydia."

Etta followed him into Lydia's room, where she did, in

fact, squeal with surprise when they entered, even though she was readied for the day and reading a book in her window seat. The book fell to the floor when she jumped to her feet. When Mr. Firth explained what had happened, she got tears in her eyes and swore that Reed had nothing to do with Rachel's disappearance.

"Then who does?" Etta demanded, sure this girl was lying. "You and she have been thick as thieves these last weeks—if not Reed, then who?"

Lydia began to cry and shook her head. "I do not know, Mrs. Markshire. I swear I don't. I wish that I did. Oh, poor Rachel!"

Mr. Firth turned suddenly and left the room, leaving Etta to blink after him. A few moments later she followed. He was halfway down the stairs before she caught sight of him, and by the time she reached the bottom of the stairs, she could only hear his footsteps as he had disappeared around a corner. She lifted her skirts and hurried after, catching sight of him again just a moment before he disappeared through an unadorned door that must lead to the servants' quarters. Mentally, she hesitated to follow him, but physically, she increased her pace. She pushed through the door and could already hear him calling for all his staff—bellowing, really.

When she came around the corner of the narrow hall, he was stopped in the middle of the kitchens that smelled of pork and hot bread. She stopped a few feet behind him as he barked out names and sent staff members scurrying to find those servants not already below stairs. It took a few minutes before nine servants were standing shoulder to shoulder before him. Nine? She would not have expected him to have so large a staff in his employ. Country gentlemen were notorious for running understaffed when they came to the city.

"This is Mrs. Markshire," Mr. Firth said, waving toward

her. "Her niece is missing, and she believes that she absconded with Mr. Reed. Do any of you know anything about that?"

The staff blinked back at him, shifted their weight, then gave answers to the negative—"No, sir." "Not a thing." "That does not sound like young Mr. Reed at all."

"I understand your loyalty to my children, but this is beyond that. I've a shilling for anyone who knows anything at all." The members of his staff still shook their heads. "And a firm termination for anyone I learn has withheld information." The headshaking became more adamant.

He turned to look at Etta. "I stand by my determination that Reed has had nothing to do with your niece's disappearance, but I will send my grooms to begin checking the posting inns along the road to Scotland. Meanwhile, I shall order my traveling carriage for Luton so that I might confirm that he did not lie to me and that you are a prejudicial woman who puts blame on innocent young men simply because they don't measure up to your pretentious standards."

He strode past her, leaving her staring at his staff as his words looped and twisted around the lot of them. She swallowed her embarrassment, then turned and hurried after him.

"That was uncalled for," she said once she'd pushed through the door into the hallway. He didn't even turn back to her, just kept his long-legged stride moving toward the stairs. She was fairly running to catch up.

"Mr. Firth!" she yelled when she reached the bottom of the stairs and he had not showed the least sign of slowing.

He stopped at nearly the same place on the stairs where he'd been standing when she'd arrived and turned to face her. He said nothing, just lifted his eyebrows and looked at her expectantly, his jaw tight and his patience thin—she could feel it. She missed what she usually felt from him—curiosity and gentle teasing.

She opened her mouth to speak. Closed it. Opened it again and then felt her shoulders fall and her fury turn to fear and indecision. "What am I to do?"

Her words were the softest either of them had said since she'd arrived, and she began blinking back tears, which were the last thing she wanted. She looked away in an attempt to disguise her reaction, feeling ridiculous and yet paralyzed.

"Go home," he said.

She felt her heart sink as even more humiliation rose inside her. He was not going to help her. What was she to do?

"Gather your things," Mr. Firth continued. "I shall be at your door in an hour's time after we have both made our arrangements and instructed our staff on not sharing these details—even the gossip could be ruinous for all of us."

She looked up, grateful but slightly confused at what he was offering exactly.

Mr. Firth continued. "Luton is not so far off the route to Gretna Green. If you engage a few of your men to add to my two, they can cover a great many stops before nightfall. We will go to Northampton and then, depending on the outcome, we can plan the next steps."

If he was so sure Rachel and Reed were not together, why take Etta with him? Had he not just insulted her in front of his staff? And yet what was she to do otherwise? She was certain that Rachel was with Mr. Firth's son, yet she did not know how to organize a search without alerting all of London to the circumstance. Mr. Firth was helping her, and she made the instantaneous decision to trust him.

Eight

MR. FIRTH WAS FIFTEEN MINUTES late, but Etta had needed every second. Lowry was staying behind to manage event regrets and correspondence, which meant Etta had to be satisfied with traveling clothes that did not require the assistance of another person for her to dress. It had been years since she'd been in public without a costume of one kind or another, but Lowry helped her choose a simple wig that Etta could style herself and a set of clothes she could manage, complete with a small corset rather than the full set Etta usually wore. Etta brought a pot of rouge but none of her other cosmetics or finery—there was no use for them in the places they were going. She felt strangely naked without the hoops and corsets but far more comfortable as she came out of the front door of her home, a simple hat with a single pheasant feather pinned to her hairpiece.

The footman loaded her smallest traveling trunk beneath Mr. Firth's carriage—a lightweight configuration that looked to be impeccably kept—and handed her inside, where Mr. Firth was already seated. He was wearing the suit coat she'd seen on the chair in his bedchamber, and his hair was tied back.

She settled onto her seat across from him and straightened her skirts about herself. As soon as she finished, Mr. Firth knocked on the ceiling of the carriage and it jolted forward. Etta grabbed hold of the fabric cord hung from the ceiling for such a purpose and then relaxed when the cadence became smoother.

"My grooms arrived on time?" Etta asked after a few turns of the road.

"Yes, my head groom—George—had already organized their course. We'll all be meeting at the Straw Hen Inn tonight, just before the turnpike."

"They'll be stopping at each posting inn along the way?"

Mr. Firth nodded. "If Rachel is found, they will bring her with them. It is not a perfect system but the best we could do on short notice. Is someone standing by at your home should she return?"

"Of course," Etta said without the defensiveness that had become her base communication with him. She'd penned a quick note to Elizabeth—the only person she dared tell the truth—so that she would help cover for her at the day's events with word that both Etta and Rachel were not feeling well.

"Very good," Mr. Firth said.

They both fell silent, staring out opposite windows as the streets of London passed by at a steady pace. The buildings began to thin and the smells of the countryside began to replace the mustiness of the city, which Etta never noticed when she was actually in the city, only when she departed.

"Miss Johnson is the daughter of Nathan Johnson, yes? He is your brother?"

Etta turned away from the window to look at him. "Yes, do you know him?"

"To a point; he would sometimes come to Shrewsbury with his family. He purchased a pup from me when my terrier had a litter some years ago."

"Oh," Etta said, knowing nothing about a dog, but then why would she? Nathan did not keep her updated on his chattel. They lapsed back into silence, but that only seemed to heighten her nerves. Etta decided to continue to make conversation in hopes it would distract her from her anxieties. "How many children do you have, Mr. Firth?"

"Four. Simone and Rachel are both married."

"You have a daughter named Rachel?" Etta asked.

He nodded. "She lives in Shropshire, where her husband practices as an attorney."

The judgement of the granddaughter of an earl marrying an attorney was quick and spry in Etta's mind, but she managed to hide it. "And your other daughter is a countess, I believe."

"Will be one day," Mr. Firth corrected. "She married Lord Dewmont, whose father is Lord Burbury, Earl of Lonstead."

"Yes, that's right. I do remember that."

They lapsed into a fresh silence broken only by the creaks and bumps of the carriage, which were really quite loud when no one was conversing. She wasn't sure what else to talk about.

"You live in London year-round?" Mr. Firth asked.

"My second husband provided well for me, including the town house in London where I live. I quite like the city."

"Really?" he said, wrinkling his nose. "You do not long for the open spaces of the country?"

"What good would longing for anything do?" she countered, pushing away the dissatisfaction she had felt these last months . . . in part because of this man himself. Trappings and fripperies.

He was thoughtful as he looked at her across the space of the carriage. "You have been married twice."

She felt herself stiffening up but did not shut down the thread—his curiosity was . . . curious. "Yes, sir."

"But you are not married now."

"No, sir."

"And you help young girls make their match when they come to London for a Season?"

"When they need a sponsor for different events, yes, but primarily, I offer nomination to be presented to the queen, which gets them started. Often their mothers will do the job of hosting their time here, but not every mother is much good, if I'm honest. Few people know the city and its players the way I do."

"And do your nominees always make a good match?"

"Yes," she said without the confidence she might have otherwise relayed. Her lucky number thirteen was not on track to do the same, and she felt a stabbing pain in her stomach to think of what was happening. However, she finished the answer because Mr. Firth was still looking at her. "Every one of my charges have made an excellent match."

"What is the definition of an excellent match?"

"Security," Etta said. "Securing one's care and confidence about the future is the very purpose of marriage. I take my role in helping them find security very seriously." And yet . . . Rachel.

"And what of their happiness?"

Etta paused, realizing that he'd been leading her. She took a breath and settled herself into this other topic in which she was well-versed. "It is the same thing."

"What is the same thing?"

"Happiness and security."

Mr. Firth laughed. "It is not the same thing."

"For a man, perhaps not. A woman comes into this world dependent on the men in her life—her father, her brothers, her sons. While most men do right by the women in their care, there is only one relationship in which she has any power—

that of her husband. A man who can provide for her and their children allows her to find her happiness within the circumstances he has power over in ways she never will. She must have absolute trust in his commitment to her so that her security is ensured."

Mr. Firth cocked his head to the side, looking at her closely. "So only a rich man can make a woman happy."

"Only a man with the ability to secure her future can make a woman happy."

"And love?"

"Will grow over time, if it will grow at all."

"You are a traditionalist, then," Mr. Firth said with a nod. "Marriage is a transaction."

"I am a realist, Mr. Firth. The world is such that women must depend on men, so a wise woman will choose a dependable man, thus ensuring her happiness."

"And perhaps love, if they are lucky."

Etta shrugged. "Love is not security."

"So then by your own definition, love is not happiness?"

She narrowed her eyes at him, unsure if they were being playful with one another or not. The tenets she was sharing were the foundation upon which she lived her life. "How on earth could something as fleeting and unreliable as love ever bring happiness?"

"It sounds as though you don't credit love as any asset in a good match."

"I don't."

He lifted his eyebrows. "You don't credit love at all?"

She shook her head. "Why would I?"

"Because love is . . . everything."

She snorted and looked out the window, feeling her past begin to burn in her stomach. "Love is nothing," she said under her breath.

She was unsure he'd heard her as the silence stretched and pulled between them. Brief flashes of memories associated with love moved through her mind . . . each memory ending in heartache that would not have been so sharp if she hadn't loved in the first place. Her first husband had courted her with fervor, only to distance himself once they were wed and turn cold when it became apparent that she would not be able to give him an heir. For the last two years of their marriage, he would not even dine with her. His death was painful because of the love she still held in her heart for him—enough to have kept her hopeful that one day he would realize what she had to offer, aside from children, and love her again. That day never came.

She entered her second marriage believing herself wiser in the ways of the heart. Timothy had not wanted additional children and so that did not work against her, and she believed love would grow between them in time. His children, however, were chaotic, and he was indulgent to the point where she had no respect for him, let alone love, which he knew and resented. She had learned to function as a supportive partner, and in public he had treated her with kindness, but behind closed doors he was increasingly cruel and impossible to please as each year passed. She never loved him, which made his death much easier to accept, and it solidified her belief in seeking security and nothing else. Had Timothy lived another twenty years, however, she'd have been content because he had the means to provide a life that gave her happiness and position. That was what she wanted for her charges—confidence in their place in the world.

"What if Rachel loves him?"

It took a moment for Etta to bring her thoughts back to the man sitting across from her in the bouncing carriage.

"She does not love him."

"She ran away with him," Mr. Firth reminded her. "She risks her entire reputation, family, and future to be with him."

"That is infatuation, desire, and ignorance—not love, though I can see how those things are easily confused with one another as they are all equally tenuous."

He smirked. She smirked back.

"But seriously, what if her feelings for him are strong? What if family, reputation, and future do not matter as much as how she feels?"

"Then she needs to be protected from herself," Etta said. "Those feelings will not last, to say nothing of the fact that she is a young woman with a fortune, which puts her at even more risk. She cannot know your son's intentions; therefore, she cannot trust her feelings either."

He held her eyes a moment across the carriage. "We are not talking about my son."

Etta paused a moment to review their exchange thus far. "Yes, we are, you began this line of conversation by asking if she loved him."

"Him, but not Reed. She is not with Reed."

Etta sighed dramatically and cast her eyes toward the carriage ceiling. "You make my point exactly."

"How so?"

She leaned forward slightly. "Amid your questions to me, you did not ask if I have children of my own because you know that I do not and do not wish to rub salt in the wound. A credit to your manners, to be sure, but I suspect that in your mind, you have determined that since I do not know what it is to have and love a husband or a child of my own, I cannot know what love is. I shall turn that on its head and state that because you are blinded by the love you feel for your son, you cannot imagine him behaving outside of the values you have tried to teach him. Love is both blind and blinding."

"And you are, therefore, the only one who can see any of this clearly." Mr. Firth waved his hand through the air. "Because you love no one."

She held his eyes, then turned back to her window. She did not expect him to understand, so why was she arguing?

"I have known great love in my life," Mr. Firth said.

She turned to look at him, a quick retort on her tongue about men and women loving differently due to the power of their positions, but he was looking out the window, his eyes far away from the landscape streaking outside of the glass. "I met my late wife when I was seventeen years old, and I knew that she would change my life forever. We could not marry, of course, but for the next six years, I did all I could to get ready for the day. When that day arrived . . . " He paused for a breath and Etta felt the change in the air. The sounds outside the carriage muted. "I don't even have the words to explain what it felt like to take her hand and step into a life together. I suppose I did offer security: a successful estate and responsibilities in the village that kept me grounded. But I do not believe that is what made us so happy together." He turned to look at her. "Each other's welfare was our top priority, and therefore we were both well cared for. That is what made us happy. Not the land and the comforts of our lifestyle; it was all about the love. Love was everything."

They stared at one another, and though Etta felt several points of argument arise, it felt wrong to make the counter.

"If Rachel loves him," Mr. Firth said, his voice soft, "you should find a way to help her have him, not convince her to turn against her heart."

Him again. Not Reed.

"Rachel is a child."

"I was seventeen when I met Laura, also a child. And I was absolutely right. I cannot imagine my path if someone had convinced me not to believe that what I felt was real. It would have been the tragedy of my life."

"And when she died?" Etta heard herself say before she realized she'd decided to say it. "Was it not the greatest tragedy of your life? Compounded by the love you had let yourself feel?"

He pulled back, the shock of her words showing on his face. She should apologize, she knew that she should, but she also knew that in a relatively short time, they were going to arrive at the house party in Luton and Reed would not be there and then Mr. Firth would know what his silly beliefs in conquering love could do. They could convince two young people to act on rash and ridiculous notions to the point where their futures were changed forever.

He turned to look out his window without responding. She turned to look out of hers.

Nine

ETTA HAD NOT THOUGHT TO eat before leaving London, and it was pushing three o'clock when they passed St. Mary's church in the village. Mr. Firth had leaned back on his cushions and put his hat over his eyes after their last exchange. She doubted he could sleep amid the rumblings of the carriage and believed he just didn't want to talk to her anymore. She couldn't blame him for that. The words she'd said kept echoing back to her—they'd been too harsh. They'd hurt him. Yet they had been the truth.

The carriage driver stopped to ask directions, rousing Mr. Firth, and then continued through the village before turning down a narrow drive. She straightened in her seat, trying to see ahead of them almost as though she expected Rachel to be here—which she did not. Her thoughts moved forward to what would happen next.

Mr. Firth would still help her once he realized that Reed had run off with Rachel, but would he be contemptable about it? Especially after what she'd said about love having cankered his children? And what if the grooms did not find the couple in their searches of the inns? The chances of being able to hide this indiscretion and preserve Rachel's reputation and prospects would be far more limited than they already were if she weren't found before nightfall.

Regardless of when they found Rachel—they would find her eventually—her foray in London was over. Even if they could hide what she'd done, Etta would not continue the sponsorship; in fact, she was unsure she'd ever sponsor another girl again. She had not protected Rachel from men who would take advantage, and she had not succeeded in helping her find the security she'd promised. That was the truest tragedy of this entire experience. She'd promised Rachel's parents to take care of their daughter, and it had all come to this.

"Mrs. Markshire."

The carriage was beginning to slow as Etta met his eyes.

"I apologize for what I said," Mr. Firth said.

She wasn't exactly sure what he was apologizing for but was grateful for the opportunity it afforded her. "As do I."

"And, um, if Reed is not here, I want you to know that I will do all that I can to make this right."

Etta just nodded, her heart in her throat as the carriage came to a full stop. Mr. Firth opened the door from the inside and stepped down, then put out his hand to help her. It put them in close proximity, like that first night when he'd held her wig in place—she was embarrassed to think of that again—and she inhaled the scent of his cologne that she'd noted that first night and in his bedroom earlier that day. It made her nervous to be noticing such things, and she let go of his hand as quickly as she could.

They ascended the front steps together. The door was opened before they knocked; likely, the staff had been alerted by the carriage wheels.

"May I help you?" a thick-set butler asked in precise tones.

"I am here to see a guest at the house party," Mr. Firth said. "Mr. Reed Firth."

"Very good, sir. Let me show you to the front parlor while I get him—I believe the men are playing games out on the back lawn."

Etta and Mr. Firth shared a look of equal confusion and curiosity. Did the butler's response mean that Reed was here? Or did the butler mean to defer the giving of information to the host?

They were shown to a large and well-appointed parlor. Mr. Firth went to the window and looked out on a garden of some sort while Etta sat. After only a few seconds she was too nervous to sit, so she stood and began to walk the room, taking in the décor without seeing any of it.

"What if he's not here?" Mr. Firth said quietly but loud enough for Etta to hear.

"We go to the rendezvous point with the grooms." She had little doubt this would be their course. Oh, how she hoped the grooms had caught up with them!

"What if they are... compromised?" Mr. Firth said. "Will we have them marry?"

"That is not my decision to make," Etta said, the butterflies in her stomach increasing to ridiculous proportions at the reminder that she would have to explain this to Nathan and his wife.

"Right," Mr. Firth said, taking a deep breath and then letting it out. "Reed did not even want to come to London. Would that I had listened."

Etta turned to look at Mr. Firth's back. "What?"

"I knew it would be additional security to Lydia to have him with her—she's had a difficult time since Laura's death. I knew she wasn't ready but feared she never would be if she did not start. I suppose I made her come as well—what a selfish man I am."

"You are not selfish for wanting her to find a match," Etta reassured him. "Is that why you did the first half of the Season in Manchester?"

Mr. Firth was silent for a long time. Perhaps a full minute, sparking Etta's curiosity all the more. There was a somberness about him that she had never seen before. "I chose Manchester. A woman I had interest in was there, and I wanted to explore the prospect of more than a letter-writing campaign between us. The feelings between us did not develop as I thought they might, so we came to London to try my hand there."

Etta blinked at his back silhouetted in the window and prickles of realization moved up and down her spine. "Your hand?"

She watched Mr. Firth's shoulders raise and lower as he took a deep breath and then let it out. "That's the funny thing about love," he said to the glass. "Once you've had it, life feels quite empty without it." He turned from the window and faced her. "It has been five years since Laura passed, and I have known for at least the last three that I was ready to love again, but my children were not. I decided it was time for all of us to move forward. It was easy to credit our coming to London—and Manchester, for that matter—to them, but it was a poor plan. Neither of them was ready—Reed hasn't expressed any interest in marriage at all."

Etta knew that her surprise was showing on her face. "But he has been so attentive to Rachel, and that first night you confronted me for having interfered."

"He knew so few people in London; Rachel was an important connection for both of them, based on our disadvantage in Town," Mr. Firth explained, no malice in his voice. "I feared that if he did not get your good opinion, both of their prospects would be affected." He raised a hand to his forehead and closed his eyes. "If I'd known that he might . . . that it was even a risk, I would not have done this. Not for—"

"Father?"

Mr. Firth, who was already facing the doorway, opened his eyes wide and dropped his hand from his forehead as he looked past Etta. Etta spun around and stared at the young man she'd been trying to keep away from Rachel.

"Mrs. Markshire?" Reed said with even more surprise, his demeanor returning to that of the awkward young man she'd observed with distrust so many times before. His hair was sweaty and his jacket was rumpled; there were bits of grass stuck to his wet boots. "What are you doing here? Is everything all right?"

Ten

"Jonathan Rigby," Etta said under her breath as she stared at the rug beneath her shoes. They were sitting around a tea tray that she had not yet touched despite her hunger. She looked up at Reed. "Are you certain?"

"Well, um, no," he glanced at his father, then back to her. "I'm not certain, but if I had to hazard a guess, it would be him. She talked about him all the time, and at the Carters' party, they were both gone for some time, then returned from separate entrances. We all suspected . . . something, and Rachel was broken up when he left London."

Etta thought back to the night Rachel had been so sad over dinner. She'd assumed it was because of Mr. Winfred's engagement, but it was within the same timeframe that Mr. Rigby had left London. Gracious. She'd had it all wrong.

"You should have told someone of their particular attentions to each other," Mr. Firth said, leaning forward with his elbows on his knees.

Reed laughed, then looked at Etta and sobered quickly. "That simply is not done. We are grown."

"Rachel is not," Etta interjected.

"With all due respect, ma'am, if she is grown enough to find a husband, she is grown enough to dally in the garden if she chooses."

"She does not know her own mind," Etta countered hotly, unimpressed with this boy's cheekiness.

Mr. Firth stood, interrupting the dialogue. "Well, we'd best start for the Straw Hen. If we leave now, we ought to arrive by nightfall."

Reed Firth also stood, and Etta followed suit. "Is there anything I can do to help?" Reed asked.

Mr. Firth and Etta exchanged glances. Mr. Firth turned back to his son and spoke. "Do not inform your friends of what's happened. A girl's reputation is a fragile thing."

"Of course," Reed said, nodding. He turned hesitantly to Etta. "Rachel is a good person, Mrs. Markshire, please do not be too angry with her."

"And Mr. Rigby?" Etta asked. "Should I be angry with him?"

Young Mr. Firth looked away, and the weight of the circumstances filled her with uncertainty and embarrassment. She had not known what was happening in her own household. She had accused an innocent young man, and his father had gone to great lengths to help her, only to have been right about his son's character all along.

She had been a complete fool.

Mr. Firth clapped his son on the back and excused him to return to his friends. As soon as he'd left the room, Mr. Firth picked up a plate and began to pile it high with items from the tray. Etta watched him, waiting for him to look at her with anger and righteous indignation for what she'd done.

"You might as well do the same," he said, adding two biscuits to his plate and nodding at the empty plate on the tray. "We won't have a meal until we reach the inn."

"You do not owe me anything, Mr. Firth, and I . . . I owe you a deep apology for accusing Reed and . . . all the things I said in the carriage. I am beyond humiliated."

"Apology accepted," he said. "Our grooms are gathering information, and we need to meet them at the inn."

She stared at him. "You'll continue to help me?" She really had no options if he chose not to—it was his carriage, his grooms, his plan.

He looked up at her and popped a pink macaroon into his mouth. He chewed twice, then waved a hand at the empty plate again, speaking with his mouth full. "Eat."

They were back in the carriage, Etta steeped in embarrassment and worry and Mr. Firth watching her, which she pretended not to notice.

"Tell me about your husbands," he said after the silence apparently proved too much for him.

She met his eyes. "Why?"

"We've hours yet to travel, the time will go faster if we have conversation. Besides, I told you about my late wife. It is only fair."

"You have good feelings for her, it likely feels nice to share them."

He smiled. "A happy aftereffect of having been in love, I suppose."

It was a thin reference to what she'd said about the woman's death causing pain only because he'd been in love with her, but she could hardly blame him for the jab. As the depth of his sacrifice for her situation became more real, her embarrassment for being so confrontational got stronger. Had she any right to deny him the information he was asking for now? She owed him a good deal more than that.

"I married Mr. Knight when I was nineteen years old, and we were married eight years before his death. I married Lord Camey two years later, and we were married twelve years. He passed eight years ago and left me well cared for."

"And they were not happy unions?"

He looked at her expectantly, eyebrows raised.

She argued with herself and decided to be more open than she might be otherwise. "I could not have children. I did not know this when I married, of course, but my husband was unable to forgive me for it, and whatever warmth was there died between us. My second husband gave me the security I needed, for which I will ever be grateful. But he was silly and indolent and increasingly . . . mean as the years went on. In regard to women finding happiness in security, however, I was happy."

"Yes, those sound like the marriages of a very happy woman."

She shrugged. "You asked the question, sir."

"That I did," he said, nodding. "So, twenty years of marriage, ten years of widowhood. I can only imagine which of those you prefer."

She nodded, then fiddled with the strings of her reticule.

"Have you ever been in love?"

"Mr. Firth," she said, feeling heat in her cheeks. "This is an inappropriate conversation."

"My apologies," he said with a nod. "But have you? I'm guessing you might have been in love with the first husband, probably not the second. Anyone in between?"

She let out a breath and gave him a pointed look, which he ignored.

Instead he leaned forward and put his elbows on his

knees, shortening the distance between them and causing her skin to warm with the ferocity of his attention.

"Have you thought to marry again?" he asked. "I would imagine that a woman of your countenance and mind would have had any number of suitors."

The compliment took her off guard but did not change her answer. "I have no need of marriage."

"But you have had suitors," he said as though this were a fact, which it was, though she would not confirm it. "You are a striking woman, as I'm sure you are aware, and your confidence and capability are . . . disarming, to say the least. Surely I am not the first man to have noticed that."

She swallowed. It had been a long time since she'd heard such a compliment, and she felt her heart soaking it in. "The people in my circle are aware of my disinterest in another match. There are plenty of other women to choose from."

"Have you taken lovers during your widowhood?"

If she were not in a carriage, she'd have stood and stormed from the room, but she was in a carriage—his carriage. She clenched her teeth together and turned to look out the window, aware of how hot her cheeks were and certain he noticed.

"I shall take that as a yes," he said.

She snapped back to face him and he laughed. "Or rather a no. Surely you miss a touch in the night, a knowing look from across the room."

She forced herself to hold his gaze, even as her mind went back to the conversation she'd had with Elizabeth not long ago and her acceptance of the attraction she felt toward Mr. Firth. There had been a few men over the years with whom she'd entertained a dalliance, though perhaps flirtation was a better definition. She'd not taken them to her bed, though she'd been tempted a time or two. It had never felt right to share such intimacies with someone she would not commit to, and she had been quite certain each time that she would not commit. There was no reason for her to give up her independence, and she had discarded the men who threatened it. In time, the connections that mattered were with her women friends, and that provided all the richness she needed.

Even if, at times, she did miss the touch in the dark and the knowing look from across the room. The realization she'd made with Elizabeth, that some part of her still longed to be loved, caused her to shift in her seat. She was forty-nine years old. Any chance of love had long since passed her, if, in fact, there had ever been a chance at all.

Mr. Firth was watching her so closely that she feared he could see every image in her head. "I have not taken lovers," he finally said, sitting back against the cushions and letting out a breath. He stretched his arms across the back of the carriage seat, giving the air of this exchange the feel of a casual conversation. Which it was not. At least for her.

"Please, Mr. Firth," she said, shaking her head and yet accepting her own shimmer of curiosity. She did not have these sorts of conversations with anyone, let alone a man. And this man in particular. This man whose words haunted her, this man whom she took particular notice of each time they were in shared company. This man who confounded and intrigued her.

"I do not feel it right if I am not committed," he continued. She swallowed her surprise at him having said the same thing she'd thought only moments before. "After Laura died, there were a number of women in the village who became quite attentive. I was not ready to marry again, however, and did not pursue any of the invitations."

"Do you regret that now?"

He shook his head. "No, it would not have been right. I

want equal intention when I do marry again. I want partnership. Devotion." He shrugged. "Love."

"You truly are a hopeless romantic," she teased in an attempt to lighten the mood.

He shrugged and put both of his palms up in a show of surrender. "Alas, it is true."

"And the woman you pursued in Manchester?"

He dropped his hands back to the seat. "A friend of Laura's, actually, from when they were girls in Devonshire. We began correspondence after the death of her husband two years ago. It was a friendship at first, with someone who understood loss and then last fall, it turned to something more. With Lydia and Reed masking my agenda . . . " He paused to let out a breath and shake his head. "I arranged to go to Manchester and see what might come of it. It wasn't the same in person as it was on paper." He looked up at her, eyebrows lifted. There were tiny shots of silver in those eyebrows, and she found herself wishing his hair was unbound as it had been that morning. Was it only that morning she'd confronted him in his home? "We gave it a solid try, but it just wasn't there, at least for me."

"What wasn't there? Love?" She heard the censure in her voice when she said it.

"Attraction," he said to clarify. "And not because she wasn't beautiful, she was, but there was just . . . " He rolled his hand through the air as though searching for the answer, then dropped it. "There just wasn't that feeling you get that makes you want to be closer. The feeling that makes you pretend to accidentally touch their shoulder or hold their hand a bit longer than necessary when you help them into the carriage."

She caught her breath and he looked at her quickly, then shifted uncomfortably and looked away, picking at something on the seat beside him.

She continued to stare at him, thinking of the times he had accidentally brushed her shoulder—the most recent time was when they were at the musical performance last night, but it had happened before. Each time he'd handed her into the carriage today, he held her hand a bit longer than necessary—and she hadn't necessarily wanted him to let go.

She looked at her skirts, thinking about all those times as well as her own awareness of him.

"Can you relate to that, Mrs. Markshire? In any small way?"

She looked at him and saw both the curiosity and anxiety in his eyes; of wanting to know and fearing the answer. "That sensation of fire you feel in their company that makes you wonder if you were ever to find yourself alone with them, what might transpire."

She blinked at him but did not look away. "I-I don't know," she finally said. "Sometimes a certain feeling can be interpreted as something else." Would that she'd explored those thoughts Elizabeth had shared. Perhaps then she would be better prepared for this moment.

"And what do you feel when you and I are together?"

Goodness, but he was bold. Yet here, in the relative safety of his carriage, it felt almost . . . normal for them to talk this way.

"Annoyance, mostly," she said.

He smiled. "And?"

"Curiosity," she admitted.

"About what?"

"Mr. Firth," she said, at a loss for words and transfixed by those eyes. He scooted forward on his seat, their knees nearly touching in the center of the carriage.

"Because I think that if both of us are feeling this . . . curiosity, we ought to explore it. See what else might be there.

I think that we are at a time in our lives when we should not put off such things."

She looked away then, overwhelmed and, frankly, confused. She felt so much when she was with him—but what exactly had she been feeling? She'd translated it as many things: concern for Rachel, an irritation at him for stepping into London, a threat to what she had been working so hard to do. The threat, however, had never been what she thought it was—the threat was that he upset her balance, upended her determination, made her want and feel what she worked so hard not to want and feel. She leaned back against the cushions, not having noticed that she'd leaned forward at one point toward him. Her mouth was dry and her heart was racing. Was this happening? Had he actually said these things?

"Women of a Certain Age do not expect to hear such things," she finally said after far too long a silence had rumbled between them.

"Beautiful, accomplished, and capable women of any age should absolutely expect to hear such things and feel such things."

He watched her a few more seconds, then scooted back on his own seat. "You should know that men of a certain age do not want games and side steps, Coletta. I find the direct route to be the most effective most of the time, and so, if you do not feel what I feel, it would be best for me if you would say so. I am well-versed in handling disappointment, so you need not protect me if I have overstepped and overstated. I would rather know sooner than later, if you don't mind. Perhaps we can talk of this some more later, after you've had some time to your thoughts."

She could think of no words but nodded after a few more moments had passed.

He smiled back at her in acknowledgement.

What, exactly, had she agreed to?

The sun was going down, causing the light inside the carriage to deepen into golden tones that fit the mood. Mr. Firth put his hat over his eyes—to give her privacy, she suspected. She turned to look out the window, a confusing array of emotions swirling in her chest, but a small and unexpected bubble of joy in her heart. She smiled, then glanced his direction to make sure he wasn't watching before giving in to the smile completely.

Eleven

IT WAS FULL DARK WHEN the carriage rattled past the road sign that read the Straw Hen Inn.

Etta felt as though she'd lived a lifetime in this carriage—Mr. Firth's bold confession had . . . changed something within her. Woken ideas and shown possibilities she had long since stopped entertaining. Even admitting to Elizabeth that she was attracted to him hadn't opened those vaults of thoughts and ideas. And talking about her marriages and her views of love with him—a topic she had never discussed with another person in all her life—made her feel so . . . herself. And yet so much a stranger at the same time.

Arriving at their destination pushed her thoughts to what would come next, however, and the slightly breathless feeling melted away in light of what awaited them. She felt a stab of guilt for having not thought of Rachel's predicament and not thought ahead to this moment. The words and the feelings still residing inside this carriage had taken over every thought and sense.

She had to shake her thoughts back to the here and now. The inn.

Rachel.

They would confer with the grooms and hear what they had learned. They would stay the night and make a plan for tomorrow. There were too many variables for her to guess what tomorrow would be like.

Had the grooms learned anything?

Was there any hope of overtaking the young couple before they reached Scotland?

What if Rachel did love him? Or think that she did? Was Etta as prepared to dismiss that as she'd been at the start of the day's journey?

"Everything will be all right," Mr. Firth said when the carriage stopped.

She smiled and nodded at him, hoping she looked brave.

He let himself out of the carriage, then reached for her hand and held it a bit longer than was necessary. They walked to the inn side by side, and she brushed his shoulder with her own not so accidentally. He turned to look at her and she held his eyes a moment, then faced forward again and swallowed. He opened the door to the inn, then put his hand on the small of her back when she passed him in the doorway. He did not remove it as he guided her inside and she did not want him to.

She blinked into the relative brightness of the room as her eyes adjusted and then felt his hand stiffen against her back. She became tense in response and then looked up to see Rachel standing from a table, her eyes red from crying. Five grooms sitting nearby stood as one, all of them looking at Etta and Mr. Firth. A woman, likely the innkeeper's wife, stood from where she'd been sitting beside Rachel and disappeared to some back room.

"Rachel?" Etta said in a breath.

Rachel hung her head, covered her face with her hands, and began to cry. Etta crossed the room and pulled Rachel into her chest, wrapping her arms around her and smoothing her hair. "It is all right," she said, echoing what Mr. Firth had told her. "Whatever has happened, it will be all right in the end, I promise it will."

It was hours before Etta let herself out of the room where she and Rachel were staying. The girl had cried and explained and cried some more. Finally, the innkeeper's wife had brought a tonic, which had settled Rachel's frantic mind and allowed her body to sleep. Etta had stayed, stroking her hair and humming a hymn until she was certain Rachel was asleep. She would sleep in that same room, but she needed a moment... perhaps she would walk in the coolness of the yard. Or stare into the dying fire downstairs in the parlor.

She let herself into the hall and was two steps from the room when the door across the hall opened, and Mr. Firth stood in the frame, his shirt open at the neck and hanging to the knees of his breeches. He stepped out to meet her in the hallway and reached out to touch her arm. "Is she all right?" he asked in a whisper.

Etta nodded. There was much to tell him and yet so little to say. Rachel had been a fool, Mr. Rigby had been a scoundrel, and though the worst had not happened, this would mark an unforgettable point in her life forever. Rachel had admitted that she hated London—had hated it from the start but put on a brave face for Etta and her parents' sakes. The continual comparisons to Beatrice had been painful, and though she'd managed to become friendly with the other girls, she was overwhelmed by the comparisons and competitiveness they all felt toward one another. Mr. Rigby's attention had overridden her better judgement at a time when she felt she could not handle London any longer.

"Mr. Rigby left her at an inn when she would not comply with his pursuit—she had thought they were going to watch the sunrise together and that she would be home before anyone noticed." Etta shook her head and raised a hand to her throbbing temple. "I am relieved, and yet she is heartbroken and embarrassed and has been so miserable all these months. I don't . . . " Her voice trembled. "I do not know what to do now."

When Mr. Firth's arms wrapped around her, she let him pull her close, much as she'd comforted Rachel upon their arrival. She turned her face to rest against his chest and closed her eyes, taking comfort in his presence and concern. He rubbed her back, kissed the top of her head, and rocked her gently for a time before releasing her. His arms remained around her waist and her hands rested on his arms.

"I am so very out of my element here, Mr. Firth," she whispered into the intimate space of this hallway. "I do not know what to do."

He reached up, brushing his thumb against her cheek. "Well first, you must begin to call me Wynn." He smiled. "And then for the next few hours, the only thing you need to do is sleep."

She nodded, the fatigue compounding at his reminder of just how very tired she was. He stepped back, his arms dropping from her waist but one hand capturing hers and holding tight. When he began leading her into his room, she did not resist. He closed the door, enveloping them in darkness as he led her to the bed.

"Wynn," she said, noting how easy it was to transition from the more formal address to his given name.

"You are going to sleep here," he said back, lifting her

onto the bed. "And I am going to hold you for a little while at least. You do not need to carry this by yourself, and you are safe with me, Etta. Let me be your partner in this, if only for tonight."

She felt no desire to argue. Receiving comfort was something she had little experience with, yet it felt like something in her soul had broken open, and a longing for this thing she did not know was aching within her. Wynn's arms came around her and pulled her back against his chest so that she could feel the rise and fall of his breathing. Their middle-aged bodies fit together perfectly, and she felt her anxieties fading into his embrace. Had it only been this morning that she'd sat across from him and said in six different ways that she did not need or want this? He kissed her neck, and she felt the heat travel through her body, but he did not kiss her again. "It is going to be all right, Etta," he whispered. She closed her eyes, settled into his arms, and chose to believe him.

Twelve

ETTA AWOKE THE NEXT MORNING in the bed with Rachel, who was turned toward the wall and curled up so small that she looked very much like the child she was. Etta had fallen asleep with Wynn's arms around her, feeling as safe and secure as she ever had, but she had a fleeting memory of him bringing her to this bed in the early hours of morning. She remembered a kiss to her forehead before hearing the creak of the hinges confirm his departure before she'd fallen back to sleep.

She stayed where she was in the morning light for a long time, enveloped by all that had happened. London and her life there felt so very far away, and she allowed herself to imagine a different life than the one she had worked so hard to build for herself. A shared life. A partnership. He hadn't offered such a thing, and it seemed preposterous that he would—but if he did, would she want it? Could she want it?

When a sheepish Rachel finally awoke, Etta was already dressed, wig in place and the hat with the single pheasant feather pinned upon it. She still did not know what to do, but the memory of Wynn's comfort helped her know how she wanted Rachel to feel—supported and optimistic. "Good morning, dearest," Etta said, sitting on the edge of the bed.

Rachel sat up, pulling her knees to her chest, still in yesterday's dress. Etta reached for Rachel's hand and gave it a squeeze.

"We have some decisions to make," Etta said softly, reining in her desire to be the one making those choices. "What do you want to do?"

"I do not want to return to London," Rachel said.

Etta nodded, having expected that. "We shall have to return long enough to still any gossip and pack your things. I'm sorry, I wish we could do differently, but the risk is too high for that."

"And then you shall send me home?"

"I'm not aware of any other options, my dear." If Etta had a place in the country where they could hide together, she might consider that, but she only had her home in London.

Rachel's chin trembled and she rested her head on her knees, staring at the bedcovers.

"Are you hungry?" Etta asked.

Rachel paused, as though having to think hard about the question, then nodded.

"Ready yourself and then meet me in the parlor."

Rachel agreed, and Etta let herself out of the room and down the stairs. She smiled when she saw Wynn stand from a table near the base of the stairs. A smattering of other patrons were seated in the dining area, so Etta nodded toward the yard and he followed her. The door to the inn closed behind him, and he took her hand, pulling her toward the stables behind the inn. As soon as they rounded the corner of the building, however, he stopped and pulled her toward him, stepping backward so that his back came against the wall of the inn. She thought he might kiss her, the energy between them so strong, but he Instead put his hands at her waist and looked over her face.

"Are you all right?"

She nodded, looking at his mouth.

"And Rachel?"

"She'll be down for breakfast in a few minutes. I dare not be gone long."

Wynn nodded. "I know a great deal has happened these last two days, and I want to apologize if anything I have said or done has been inappropriate or—"

She raised a finger to his lips, stopping the words she did not want to hear. So help her, if he apologized for last night . . . "Wynn," she said softly.

He could not speak with her finger against his lips, so he raised his eyebrows and kissed that finger.

She smiled. "You have been . . . unexpected, to be sure, and such a gift. I do not know exactly how to make sense of it, and—"

He put a finger to her lips, which made her smile—how silly they must look right now, each shushing the other. And then he moved his finger and inclined his head toward hers as she too moved her finger away from his mouth and made up the distance. It happened so fast, so naturally choreographed. She pressed her lips against his softly at first and then with greater intensity that he matched with fervor. His hand came to the back of her neck and her arms went around him as they both let everything else fall away for just a minute. The pleasure of his body pressed against hers and his mouth against her mouth was all-encompassing and primed her focus on him and only him. There were reasons not to lose herself in this, but for the moment she could not think of a single one.

When his grip softened and the passion stilled, she fell against his chest and let herself breathe in the lingering tendrils of the wanting and the being wanted. He wrapped his arms around her back and held her tightly, planting a kiss on the top of her head. This was not love—she would never believe that—but it was . . . something. She wanted more of whatever it was, and yet the responsibilities of life were stacking back into her conscious mind: what needed to be done and what could not be avoided. Exploring Mr. Wynn Firth moved down her to-do list rather quickly. A sad but unavoidable reality.

"Rachel," she breathed against his chest. Saying a hundred things in just one word.

"Yes," he replied, then pulled back so that they were looking at one another. "I would like us to continue this exchange later." He kissed her lightly, then pulled back so that he could look at her again. "But on the pressing topic of your niece, I have an idea."

Thirteen

AND SO IT WAS THAT Rachel returned to London for one long and uncomfortable week, which allowed them to attend a few events where they could pretend that all was well. With the help of her friends, Etta planted the seeds of information that supported the idea that Rachel had never planned to make a match her first Season and was going to Shrewsbury with her friend Lydia Firth for the duration of the summer.

The final London event they attended was a dinner party hosted by the Duchess of Monroe. Rachel had done a remarkable job of keeping her composure through these social events that she hated attending, but then, Etta had realized, she'd been pretending to enjoy them all Season long. Only knowing she was nearly done made it possible for her to endure the final days.

The Firths had managed an invitation as well—the duchess was good friends with Wynn's younger sister—and it took a great deal of focus for Etta not to get carried away with the shared looks from across the room. She felt irritated that the social protocols and need to keep gossip at bay prevented her from interacting with him the way she would like. Trappings and fripperies had never felt so confining and foolish.

As the evening transitioned from dinner to entertainment, she noticed Wynn making his way in her direction, and she subtly—she hoped—began to do the same. While they had not seen one another since the carriage ride back to London, Etta had thought of little else other than Rachel's situation and her own situation in regard to Mr. Wynn Firth.

They reached one another near a potted plant, somewhat removed from the crowd that mingled and laughed a short distance away. Each had a glass of wine and a careful expression.

"Mrs. Markshire," he said, bowing slightly.

"Mr. Firth," she replied, dipping the slightest curtsy.

They both turned out as though surveying the room.

"My carriage will come for Miss Johnson at eleven," he said as he took a sip of his wine.

"Very good, thank you," she said, also sipping her wine.

He brushed against her arm. She met his eye. Held it. "We never finished our . . . conversation from last week," she added.

"I was unsure if you wanted to revisit it."

"I have not stopped thinking about it."

"Neither have I."

They both sipped their wine again, hiding their smiles behind the rim of their glasses.

"If you came to Shrewsbury with your niece, we could find a great deal of time to discuss it further."

She turned her head fast to look at him—completely losing her public composure. He held her eyes. "Go to Shrewsbury?"

He nodded.

She stared.

He took a half step closer to her and lowered his voice. "What do you want your life to be, Etta? If this"—he waved the hand not holding his wine to indicate the well-appointed parlor and fashionable people—"is what you want your life to be, then you already have it. Is it what you want, or is it the only option you have had?"

She blinked at him. Was it?

"Mrs. Markshire?"

Etta turned forward and smiled politely at Lady Gwen—she'd asked Etta to reserve some time to discuss her charity lunch, and apparently that time was now. Etta looked at Wynn. "Can we speak more about this tomorrow?"

"Of course," he said, inclining his head. "I shall look forward to it."

It was after midnight when Etta and Rachel arrived home, and they'd discussed the final details of Rachel's journey in the carriage. Rachel's relief to be done with London was in equal measure with her excitement to go to Shrewsbury. It was remarkable to Etta that anyone could dislike London as Rachel did, and yet she had felt different here too since the Straw Hen. She'd come to realize how much of her life was about creating an impression on the people here and giving them no cause to judge her actions. That impression had been more important than Rachel when she really thought about it. It was an uncomfortable realization that stacked neatly upon other uncomfortable realizations she'd been avoiding for too long.

What did she want her life to be?

As she had the first night she'd encountered Wynn Firth, she watched her costume disassemble in the mirror: the dress, the petticoats, the hoops, the hair, the makeup. She asked Lowry to take down her hair, though it was not time to wash it, and then wet it herself in the basin before brushing it out and taking in the truth of who she was—the skin and the shape and the hair. Her skin. Her shape. Her hair.

"What do you want?" she asked the woman in the glass, then lifted her chin and turned her face from side to side. She was not put off by what she saw, only thoughtful and curious about whether this version of Etta Markshire could be enough.

For Wynn Firth.

For herself.

London had given her purpose and security, and by her own definition, that was happiness. But was it what she wanted? Could there be other ways to find happiness? Did she dare look?

Fourteen

LOWRY WAS UNABLE TO HIDE her surprise the next morning when Etta said she only wanted the small corset, which supported Etta's breasts but little else. She then asked to wear the lavender day dress with a round neckline, elbow-length sleeves, and a shape that barely hugged her figure at all. It was a dress Etta only ever wore on days she stayed home—of which there were few.

"I'd like natural hair today," Etta said after she was dressed, further confounding her maid. It took far longer for Lowry to style her hair than to pin on a wig, but Etta was pleased with the result. She waved off the pot of rouge Lowry held out to her, then changed her mind and added a very small amount to her cheeks and lips—far less than her usual toilet. She smiled at her reflection and tried to quell the butterflies in her stomach as she stood from the dressing table and thanked an uncomfortable Lowry before leaving the room.

She was in the parlor catching up on her correspondence when she heard the knock at the door just before eleven o'clock. She stepped to the doorway and watched as Wynn Firth came into the foyer, handing his hat to the butler. He looked up the stairs and saw her, paused, then smiled, causing those butterflies to rise back up in force.

"Might I have a word, Mr. Firth?" she asked from the doorway.

He nodded and she turned into the parlor, confident he would follow, which he did.

When she turned to face him, he was pulling the door closed—she hadn't quite expected that. Or his crossing the room to her in four steps and pulling her against him so quick and hard that she gasped. With one hand holding her uncorseted waist tight against him, he used the other hand to touch her hair, trace her jaw, and then run the backs of his fingers along the neckline of her dress.

"Wynn," she said with a nervous laugh, surprised at his forwardness but not displeased.

He leaned down and kissed her neck and her collarbone and she gasped again, then put her hands against his chest and pushed him back. "You're going to make me forget everything I planned to say."

He kept his arm around her waist. "This is . . . you. It is amazing."

"I feel half naked without my usual toilet."

"Mmm," he said, leaning in to plant another kiss at the hollow of her throat.

"Wynn," she said again, though there was a longing quality of her tone that surely was not supporting her objection.

"I'm sorry," he said, pulling back again. "What did you want to talk about?"

"Shrewsbury," she said.

"Come," he said simply, smiling. "Come with me to Shrewsbury. Build a life with me."

"I have lived most of my life in London, Wynn."

"Yes, with wigs and frames and fripperies. You don't need any of those things in Shrewsbury. You can be . . . this." He looked her up and down, then met her eyes. "If that is what you want."

She swallowed, then nodded, then kissed him to seal the promise.

She went to Shrewsbury.

Women of a Certain Age, you see, were allowed to change their mind and step into a new beginning with the wisdom of experience, the knowledge that things did work out, and the understanding of themselves being sufficient to give everything and lose nothing all at the same time.

JOSI S. KILPACK has written more than thirty novels, a cookbook, and several novellas. She is a four-time Whitney award winner, including Best Novel in 2015 and 2019, and has been a Utah Best of State winner for Fiction. Josi loves to bake, sleep, eat, read, travel, and watch TV—none of which she gets to do as much as she would like. She writes contemporary fiction under the pen name Jessica Pack.

Josi has four children and lives in Northern Utah. For more information about Josi, visit her at:

Website: www.josiskilpack.com or her
Blog: www.josikilpack.blogspot.com

A Most Unsuitable Suitor

Sarah M. Eden

One

London 1770

IN ADDITION TO A TITLE and an ancient estate, Julian, Lord Wesley, had inherited a reputation. The family's penchant for dissipation and spendthrift ways had finally caught up to them. However, as Julian was the only member of that family still living, he was the one enduring the consequences. The Wesley estate was in such dire straits that he'd needed to empty the family home in Sussex of nearly all its furnishings and sell them piece by piece to the highest bidders. He'd needed to rent the London home for the Season rather than live there himself, it being entailed and therefore unable to be sold. Between those two efforts, he wouldn't starve, but neither would he be breathing easily anytime soon.

"I've never before seen you grow tired of London so quickly." The observation was made by his best friend as the two of them sat in a quiet corner of their London club. He and Franklin Daubney had known each other since their school days. There was very little they didn't know about each other.

"I suppose I *have* lost some of my enthusiasm." Julian

had been nursing a glass of sherry for some time now. Their club was quiet. Most of the members were at gatherings of the *ton* or at their homes.

"I suspect my father wouldn't object if we sauntered out to the family seat." Franklin's family wasn't the collection of ne'er-do-wells Julian's was and, as a result, were still in possession of their home. Despite being a younger son, Franklin had a future to claim and an income enough to live on while he waited to take his place as the vicar of the family's parish. "My grandmother is there and would happily occupy all our time and attention for however long we're there."

"I don't think I'm as desperate as all that," Julian said with a laugh.

Far from offended, Franklin returned to his sherry, his ponderous expression growing a bit lopsided the longer they sipped their troubles away. "What we need is a diversion," he said after a moment.

"What I need is money," Julian insisted.

Franklin was undeterred. He rose from his chair and walked, almost in a straight line, to where the club's betting books were.

Julian shook his head. "Gambling is part of the reason I'm in this mess. I'm not going to place any foolhardy wager in an attempt to escape it."

"I wasn't going to suggest that you place wagers." Franklin dropped to his chair once more, setting the book on the table. "I thought we might amuse ourselves by seeing what ridiculous things *others* have wagered."

It was actually a good idea. There was no danger of making his already difficult circumstances worse. He might actually feel a little bit better about himself upon seeing how comparatively responsible he was than some of the gentlemen of Society. A number of their wagers were famous for how absurd and reckless they were.

Franklin flipped through pages until he came across one that he read aloud. "Lord Parcell predicts that his mare Copper will foal before Mr. Jameson's mare Honeysuckle does. Wagered amount: £50."

Julian shook his head. "£50 on the birth of a foal." It wasn't as risqué a wager as was often found in the betting book, but it was certainly frivolous.

Franklin flipped more pages over. "Oughtta—" He hiccupped. "Oughtta be one that'll make us laugh."

"Shame no one wagered that the respected Mr. Daubney would spend this evening at his club, getting deeper and deeper into his cups." Julian raised his glass, only a quarter full.

"Nonsense," Franklin insisted. "I'm not drunk, just tipsy enough to enjoy this more than I probably would otherwise." He turned another couple of pages, then read aloud. "Mr. Preston stakes £100 against the same amount pledged by Mr. Harrington that the Duke of York will declare himself a believer in the Cock Lane ghost before year's end."

Julian laughed lightly. A harmless wager but entertaining just the same. "What else is in there?"

Franklin turned more pages before stopping, his eyes pulling wide.

Julian leaned a bit closer. "What is it?"

"A wager involving you."

"Me?" That was ridiculous. Not since his schoolboy days had he involved himself in the placing of wagers.

Franklin read out loud. "A wager in the amount of £1000 pounds."

Julian swallowed hard. He knew he hadn't placed any bets, yet there was no reason for his friend to be inventing this wager.

"That Lady Charlotte Duchamps will be married by her

twenty-first birthday, else the placer of this bet, whose identity is recorded elsewhere, will pay Lord Wesley the forfeit declared above."

Julian was too shocked to even begin making sense of it. "Someone will pay me that exorbitant amount if Lady Charlotte doesn't marry by her twenty-first birthday?"

Franklin nodded.

Lady Charlotte was not unknown to either of them, though they were little more than bowing acquaintances. Furthermore, it was generally considered ungentlemanly to make a wager involving a lady. To go so far as to wager on a lady's matrimonial prospects was a significant breach of etiquette—no doubt the reason the placing of the bet remained anonymous in the public book.

But the bet *was* recorded there, which made it binding by the gentlemen's code. Someone whose identity Julian could not even begin to guess was obligated to pay him £1000 pounds if Lady Charlotte remained unwed.

"Do you happen to know how old Lady Charlotte is?" Franklin asked.

Julian shook his head even as he began to think out loud. "She is in London for the Season, and I'm reasonably certain this is her fourth." It was all he could offer with confidence in the solving of the mystery. After all, he was not well acquainted with her, which made the matter of this wager all the more strange. "If this is her fourth Season, and this wager is centered on her twenty-first birthday, I suspect that is the very birthday she is about to mark."

Julian knew he wasn't thinking as clearly as he would prefer, though he wasn't so sloshed as to be entirely without good judgement. "The year of her birth, I find, is of tremendous importance to me. £1000 important to me. Do you suppose there's a copy of Debrett's in the library here?" He motioned with his head in the direction of the club's extensive collection of volumes.

"One way to find out."

The two of them made their way toward the library. A quick search revealed the very volume they were searching for. Lady Charlotte was daughter of the Earl of Tarrant, and his family would most certainly be listed inside.

Franklin read out loud even as Julian himself scanned the words. "Lady Charlotte, born the 6 of June in the year 1749."

The two gentlemen slowly raised their gazes from the book and their eyes met each other's. Franklin's eyes were pulled wide. Julian's were as well.

"She turns twenty-one in a month," Julian said. "One month, and I do not recall seeing any announcements in the *Times* regarding an engagement."

"Neither do I," Franklin said.

Julian scratched his hairline, the powder long since dried and settled and making his scalp itch a bit. Hair powdering was not optional when one wished to look clean and put together. The effort helped hide the true state of his financial situation.

"A courtship can prove successful, leading to an engagement and even a wedding within four weeks," Julian acknowledged. "Though it would be a bit of a tight timeline, there's every chance she could be married before the 6th of June. It'd be a helpful thing if we knew a little more about how close she might be to an engagement."

"I do know Lady Charlotte, though vaguely," Franklin said. "My family hasn't the standing of hers—or *yours*. I am not always invited to the same gatherings your ilk are."

"My ilk." Julian shook his head, the impact of sherry rendering the movement a bit more clumsy than he would prefer. "People of 'my ilk' and of 'my birth' are not to be confused. I hope I am a better sort of fella than those whose shoes I'm called on to fill."

"Can't entirely make sense of that mix of words," Franklin said, "but if you're trying to say you're a decent fellow, I'll agree to that."

Julian blinked a few times, looking to focus his thoughts. "The betting book didn't say who it was that placed the wager?"

Franklin shook his head slowly. "But the gentleman's identity is recorded elsewhere."

That did happen now and then—someone placing a bet wished for their identity to be anonymous, and that information was kept quite confidential by those who oversaw such things at the club. The wagerer would be made to pay, should the forfeit be required of him. And he would be required to pay *Julian.* Pay him £1000. Such a sum would perhaps not go as far as it would have during his grandfather and great-grandfather's day, but to Julian, the Lord Wesley of 1770, it still constituted a much-needed windfall.

"Have you heard this wager talked about amongst the gentlemen?" he asked his friend.

Franklin shook his head and lowered his voice just as Julian had. "Wasn't made loudly or publicly, it seems. The placer of it must be watching to see if Lady Charlotte's leading anyone into the parson's mousetrap."

"And likely making an effort to see to it that she does," Julian acknowledged.

"The person placing it must know that you don't know that you stand to win such a sum."

Whoever the mystery gambler was must have also known Julian's financial situation. It would explain why he chose him to be the recipient of this wager. The unknown wagerer felt, in some ways, like an angel of mercy. Except he was an angel who was likely working quite hard to make certain he never had to pay the forfeit.

"It's a shame we don't know who the fellow is," Franklin said. "We could make any of his efforts to win this wager a little bit more difficult."

"We don't know who the bettor is, but we know who he's betting on." An idea began to form in Julian's head, one that, if not truly brilliant, was definitely risky. "We could pay a bit closer attention to what is happening in Lady Charlotte's life. If we discover any suitors getting a bit too close to success for our comfort, we can slow down their progress a bit."

"Would be unkind to spoil the lady's chances," Franklin objected.

"We don't have to outright say, 'Hey there, fellow, seems you ought to be sniffing out greener pastures.' We can simply make nuisances of ourselves, should any gazes grow too warm or words turn too poetic between Lady Charlotte and some gentleman."

"Nuisances?" Franklin looked increasingly committed to the idea that they had not fully formed yet.

"Nothing interferes with Cupid's arrows quite as much as awkwardness." Julian knew from experience, he having been remarkably awkward on more than one occasion in his time.

"We keep an eye on Lady Charlotte, and should things seem to be getting a bit romantic, we step up and offer an observation on indigestion or something?" Franklin looked a bit confused but still seemed every bit as determined to move forward.

"We can offer up whatever the moment requires," Julian said, "without causing anyone actual distress or humiliation, of course."

"Of course." Franklin offered a stiff nod.

Julian met his friend's eye once more. "We need only be ourselves for a few weeks. And if those few weeks should not bring a wedding for the Earl of Tarrant's daughter, then we can happily head to our respective homes. And mine might finally not have a hole in the roof."

Franklin raised a glass he was not actually holding. "To holeless roofs."

"And to four weeks of awkwardness." Julian clinked his imaginary glass against Franklin's.

A potentially helpful wager. Weeks of awkwardness.

London just got remarkably more interesting.

The Earl of Tarrant was responsible for the well-being of a widowed mother, an opinionated sister, a school-age son, and a daughter who'd had suitors aplenty but was, as yet, unmarried. Lady Charlotte, she of the lurking spinsterhood, recognized her father's difficult situation and she empathized. She also meant to look out for herself, just as she'd done during her previous London Seasons.

She knew enough of the world to have accepted that her eventual husband would be chosen by her father. She also knew enough of his temperament to know that he would not intentionally choose anyone who would make her truly miserable. He, however, was a man with a great deal on his mind, and had a tendency to rush headlong at somewhat ill-advised things once he'd made up his mind to do so, then become immediately too distracted by other responsibilities to reconsider his decision. And thus she had been quite carefully directing her own Seasons for years now.

"St. James's Park will be rather dull once you leave to become a very sophisticated married lady," Charlotte said to her dearest friend in all the world as the two of them continued their circuit of the very busy park.

Miss Louisa Selby was soon to be Mrs. Granville, something Louisa hadn't chosen for herself but thought a fine prospect just the same. Mr. Granville was not decades older than she, nor was he lacking in moral fiber or unkind to his future wife. Not all ladies could say as much about the gentlemen their families matched them with.

"I'll return next Season," Louisa said with a light laugh.

"But you will be terribly sophisticated."

Louisa adjusted her parasol. "You might very well be the same variety of 'sophisticated' by the end of this Season. Your father mentioned the possibility no fewer than three times during last evening's soiree."

In dry tones, Charlotte said, "I noticed."

"I daresay *Mr. Vernon* noticed as well." Louisa grinned rather unrepentantly.

Mr. Vernon was as harmless as he was unexceptional. He was also a kind person, and she'd found him to be perfectly agreeable.

"Mr. Vernon is a fine person," Charlotte said.

"Fine enough that, should your father choose him, you would be pleased with the arrangement?" Louisa's tone was teasing, but there was also an earnestness to the question.

"He would not be a terrible choice." Not her first choice nor necessarily the best choice, but not a terrible one. "Sir Duncan, on the other hand, *would* be a terrible choice."

"But an intriguing one," Louisa added with a laugh.

"His variety of intriguing is acceptable in an occasional dance partner, but in a life partner it would be precisely the wrong sort of exhausting."

The baronet himself rode past in the very next moment. He tipped his cocked hat to the two of them, his perfectly symmetrical smile filled with his characteristic confidence. Charlotte didn't think he was actually arrogant, at least not in a way that was hurtful to others. She wasn't certain Sir Duncan considered himself one of her suitors, and she didn't think her father thought of him that way.

"My mother is proving a bit tiring," Louisa said. "She is determined that my wedding will be impressive to even the most discerning in Society. I have attempted to explain to her that the most discerning in Society won't be in attendance."

"I beg your pardon." Charlotte pretended to be deeply offended.

Louisa laughed. "Oh, you simply must promise to visit me in Sussex after my wedding trip. I will miss you terribly if I have to wait until next Season to be granted your company again."

"Does Mr. Granville have a pianoforte in his fine Sussex home?" Charlotte knew perfectly well that he did—it had been a topic of discussion before—but she could not resist teasing her friend.

"He does, one obtained from Italy." Louisa was even more fond of music than Charlotte was. Enough so that Charlotte had teased her about the presence of an Italian pianoforte being the very reason Louisa was pleased at the prospect of marrying her intended.

"And will you be permitted to take your harp with you when you marry, or will that be required to remain at your parents' home?"

Louisa sighed with what sounded like relief. "The harp will go to Sussex with me."

"I am convinced, then." Charlotte nodded firmly. "I will visit your new home, but only with the promise that we spend an evening or two at our chosen instruments playing our favorite pieces."

"I am not above bribery."

They smiled broadly as they continued along the park path.

But Louisa's expression turned somber after a moment. "If your father does decide it is time for you to make a match, do you suppose he will choose someone who will still allow you to come visit me?"

Charlotte assumed a determined posture. "I am not entirely helpless in this. I can discourage and encourage where needed. Anyone who would refuse to allow me a jaunt to Sussex will find himself with decreasing opportunities to make an impression on my father."

"It is a shame you cannot be permitted to simply enjoy the remainder of your Season."

"Oh, I intend to enjoy it," Charlotte said. "After three and a half Seasons, I know what to expect and how to make the best of it. Predictability is a useful thing."

"And if something drastically unexpected happens?" Louisa pressed.

"'Drastically unexpected'?" Charlotte laughed once more. "I am expecting a perfectly pleasant and perhaps even slightly boring remainder of the Season. And that, my friend, is perfectly fine with me."

Two

CHARLOTTE WAS EXCESSIVELY FOND OF a musical evening. To spend an evening listening to those who had great skill on various instruments was a joy indeed. Unfortunately, Louisa would not be present at the gathering held the evening after their discussion in St. James's Park. The Selbys were a family of good standing, but the Bowens, who were hosting the musicale, were rather particular about whom they invited to their gatherings. It wasn't so much that they were arrogant or looked down on people who hadn't quite their social cachet, though that did factor a little into their decisions. The Bowens preferred their musical evenings be very small and intimate, and that narrowed their guest lists significantly.

It was, in terms of social standing, a point in Mr. Vernon's favor that he was amongst those invited to that evening's gathering. His inclusion would help Charlotte's father think more highly of him.

It was on her father's arm that she entered the grand music room at the Bowens' London home. Charlotte's mother had died many years earlier and her grandmother almost never came to Town. Her aunt, as far as she knew, had disliked London when she was a younger lady and there was absolutely no mistaking that she disliked it now. As such, it fell to Charlotte to undertake the role of the lady of their family in public. She had been trained from a young age to carry herself with dignity and to accept the drudgery that often accompanied this role but also to understand the importance of it. Not everything in life was fun, and not every obligation was a joy to fulfill. But she deeply liked her father, and having known a great many young ladies whose fathers did not treat them as kindly as hers, she thought herself quite fortunate.

They were greeted very warmly. Everyone employed a tone of sincere pleasure when in company with the Earl of Tarrant and Lady Charlotte Duchamps. There'd been a shift in that perception in the past three years. During her first Season, she had been appreciated only for her familial connections. Now, well into her fourth Season, she felt she was liked and respected and valued and welcomed for herself and considered to be a good addition to an evening's gathering.

Amongst those they paused to exchange words of greeting with were people of her father's generation and acquaintance as well as her own. There were a few gentlemen in the ranks that she did not wish her father to think too closely on the possibility of a connection with.

Her first Season had been one of both nervousness and joyousness. Father had not been anxious for an immediate match, so she'd been permitted to simply find her place in Society and make new friends and acquaintances. As she'd embarked on each successive Season, she'd had to temper her enjoyment with strategy. She did so again now.

Whenever her father would appear to be on the cusp of being pulled into a conversation with someone she didn't particularly wish to remain overly long in his thoughts, she would have to find a means of redirecting him without giving offense.

Much to her relief, that evening's navigations proved rather simple. She led her father away from Sir Duncan before conversation of any kind could occur. She offered an, "Oh, there is my dear friend, I must go speak with her," after a few words of greeting to Mr. Casper. No one would guess she was avoiding interactions as much as seeking them out. And when their circuit of the room brought them to Mr. Vernon, she breathed a sigh of relief. She could relax for a moment.

"I had hoped to see you here this evening," Father said once the expected words of greeting were exchanged.

"Were you?" Mr. Vernon echoed the very question that arose in Charlotte's mind. Perhaps her father had taken more of a liking to him than she'd realized.

"You told me at the soirée last evening that you had recently read *The Delicate Distress* and enjoyed it. I wanted to tell you that I found a copy of the first volume at the lending library, and I mean to begin it when I have the opportunity to do so."

"I'm pleased to hear it," Mr. Vernon said. "A good book is an enjoyable thing."

"It is, indeed," her father said.

"Indeed," Mr. Vernon echoed. He turned to Charlotte. "Have you read anything you have enjoyed lately, Lady Charlotte?"

"I have read a great many things over the past weeks and months. London has such a large selection of books."

"It does indeed," her father said.

"Indeed," Mr. Vernon repeated.

Conversations with Mr. Vernon often went this way. Discussions of perfectly acceptable topics consisting mostly of statements few people would disagree with, then expressions of agreement with those statements.

She would not be kept on the edge of her seat in her

interactions with him in the years to come, should her father select Mr. Vernon to be his future son-in-law, but time spent with him was at least easy and basically pleasant.

Mr. Vernon had an understanding of music and could carry a decent conversation on the topic. It was one of the things she actively liked about him. One could make peace with a marriage if one at least did not dislike one's spouse. But if there was something, anything, which a person truly liked in their intended, that was a reason for celebration.

It was in the midst of that thought that another gentleman arrived. She knew him, but only vaguely. They were what would be termed "bowing acquaintances." He was Lord Wesley, only a few years her senior and a baron. He was not known to be a rake or a wastrel or any of the other things young ladies were warned about. But there was something about him that made her shockingly aware of him whenever he was nearby. She never felt in danger or threatened in any way; it was more a matter of her heart pounding a bit more than usual and her insides responding by jumbling themselves in an attempt to make room for the pounding.

She knew, for reasons she could not make sense of, that her mind and heart found him intriguing. Her eyes seemed to struggle not to gaze on his slightly unruly hair with fascination. His locks were tied back and powdered, as all gentlemen's were, but not to the point that one could not tell that his wavy hair was a sumptuous and rich shade of brown. And to her shock, though whenever she did happen to see him, it was generally at a distance, she found herself unable to shake her curiosity about what that thick hair would look like left to hang loose.

Charlotte was fully aware that she was attracted to him. But she also knew enough of the world to realize that such a thing was rather ill-advised. Very few ladies were permitted much of a say in the choice of their future spouse, so it was best to keep one's heart whole and one's mind focused in more probable and sensible directions.

But there he was, with his distracting hair and a hint of bergamot wafting in the air around him, reminding her that he stood nearby.

"Forgive the interruption," he said after a quickly sketched bow to all of them. "I fear Lady Charlotte may have dropped her handkerchief, and I wish to return it to her before she finds herself in need of it." There was both kindness and a roguish twinkle in his deep-brown eyes, which, when combined with his fascinating hair, seemed to her a terribly unfair combination when one was attempting to keep one's head.

"I did not realize I had dropped it," Charlotte said. "I thank you."

She held out her hand. As if his eyes and hair and alluring scent weren't enough, the light brush of his fingers on her hand as he placed her handkerchief there, even through both their gloves, sent a shiver through her. Ladies of her station in life were told from childhood that marriage was a matter of business, yet gentlemen had the ability to upend them like this. It was yet another utterly unfair combination.

In an attempt to regain her composure, Charlotte dropped her eyes to her handkerchief. The shift in focus provided not only a distraction but also a new topic of conversation. "Please do not think that this will diminish my appreciation of your kindness, Lord Wesley, but this is not my handkerchief."

"Is it not?" He glanced at it himself. "I do believe those are your initials. That is, in fact, the reason I assumed it to be yours." He did not move to retrieve the handkerchief but did begin glancing about the room. "I can think of no one else here who shares your initials."

"True though that may be," she said, "it is still not mine."

"We had best all do what we can to find someone else who would embroider a handkerchief with a C and D."

But he did not go in search of such a person. He simply stood where he was, looking quite comfortable, while at the same time, somehow, making things a bit awkward.

"The evening promises to be a fine one," Mr. Vernon said. "The Bowens always arrange for the most talented of performers."

"They do indeed," Papa said.

"Indeed," Mr. Vernon added.

"Indeed," Lord Wesley repeated with emphasis. "I hope you will let us hover around your chair, Lady Charlotte. A great many of the gentlemen will be standing, and it is far more pleasant to be standing near someone one already knows."

Lord Wesley knew Charlotte but not overly well, which made his declaration both accurate and inaccurate. Mr. Vernon also didn't seem to know quite what to think. The four of them stood about in slightly uncomfortable silence. This was not likely helping Mr. Vernon make a positive impression on Charlotte's father. She knew he was not an ideal choice, but he was a good one. Perhaps there would be time at the interval or after the evening's performance was concluded for the guests to mingle.

Utilizing her skills for navigating away from uncomfortable situations, Charlotte offered a little bit of a curtsy to Lord Wesley before turning her attention to her father and Mr. Vernon. "I do believe the evening is set to begin soon enough. We ought to find a place to sit."

Before either of the gentlemen to whom she actually addressed the question could answer, Lord Wesley said, "Excellent suggestion, Lady Charlotte." Then he walked alongside them as they sought a place to sit.

In the end, they were situated with Charlotte seated and her father in the chair next to hers. Mr. Vernon stood to one side and Lord Wesley to the other directly behind her. It was not an unusual arrangement. Truth be told, it was quite unexceptional. Charlotte's only objection was that this arrangement would make it difficult for her to facilitate a direct conversation between her father and Mr. Vernon. Was it truly so much to ask that if she were required to accept an arranged marriage, then she might have some ability to influence the arrangement?

A soprano the Bowens had arranged to perform for the evening began the offering. She was remarkably talented, her voice rich and clear, and her presence as she performed was dramatic without being overpowering. A person could simply relax and enjoy. Or a person might, if she did not have Lord Wesley standing so nearby, smelling wonderful.

As the gathering applauded the end of the first selection, Mr. Vernon leaned forward a bit, enough to offer a quiet comment near Charlotte's ear. "How lovely it is to hear an Italian aria performed by an Italian speaker. The pronunciation is so much more precise."

"I especially liked the way she pronounced *languisce*," Lord Wesley said, leaning forward enough to whisper into her other ear. "*Languisce.*" He repeated the word a couple of times, his pronunciation a bit too precise.

"These settings offer such a nice alternative to hearing the same pieces that one hears performed in the large concert halls," Mr. Vernon observed.

"*Languisce*," Lord Wesley repeated again with the same ridiculous emphasis on every syllable.

Mr. Vernon looked confused, and well he might be. Charlotte felt a little confused herself. She didn't think Lord Wesley was actually so inept at social interactions. Either he was acting the part of being rude or . . . perhaps had indulged a bit too much in the offered beverages. The best way she could think of to describe his presence in that moment was awkward.

One glance at her father told her he was feeling the same thing. He shifted a bit on his chair, his brows pulled in uncertainty. This was not how she'd expected the night to go. Not terrible, not horrendous, just not what she'd expected.

"Do you suppose the entire evening will feature selections in Italian?" Mr. Vernon asked.

"Possibly," Lady Charlotte said. "Though I suspect she can perform in many languages."

"*Languisce*." And for reasons Charlotte could not begin to explain, she found herself struggling not to laugh.

As the evening wore on, it was all she could do not to toss the word out herself in the same ridiculous way, though he eventually stopped doing so himself. He offered comments now and then and always seemed to be hovering about, but her impression of him being mostly harmless did not change. He was handsome and likely could have been remarkably rakish if he'd chosen to be. But overall, he was acting odd, a bit lacking in the social graces, which was not the impression she'd ever had of him in the past.

Mr. Vernon, who had also remained stalwartly at her side, offered his farewells after the evening's performances had ended.

"I do hope we will see you again soon," Charlotte said to him.

"I would like that as well," Mr. Vernon said. He turned to her father and dipped a gracious bow. "Tell me of any books you find that you enjoy."

"I will," her father said.

A friendly interaction. A common interest. That was

promising. Whether or not Mr. Vernon made anything beyond a vague impression, she didn't know.

"And I hope we shall see each other again also," Lord Wesley said, executing a bow of his own.

"It is a possibility," was the extent of her father's response. He wasn't rude or truly dismissive, but there was a stiffness to his posture and his demeanor that was unexpected. As far as she knew, he and Lord Wesley had few interactions and no true history. Indeed, she didn't think she'd ever heard her father even mention him except for the occasional offhand comment made in passing, such as discussing who was present at a particular horse race or gentlemen's club or in attendance at Parliament. Yet she couldn't help but feel that her father was displeased with him beyond what could be explained by the strange evening they had just passed.

"Thank you for your company this evening, Lady Charlotte," Lord Wesley said. "It was a pleasure as always." His words of farewell, marked with kindness, went beyond the rote words of parting, but not in a way that was overly familiar. Indeed, if not for her father's stiff treatment of him, she might have felt as though they had, in some strange way, struck up something of a friendship during the awkward evening.

Why did he have to capture her attention so thoroughly when he was nearby? Where Mr. Vernon was a bit dull yet perfectly acceptable, Lord Wesley was acceptable and worryingly intriguing.

She couldn't manage to say anything as she watched him walk away. She didn't dare. He was not anywhere on the list of suitors she felt there was any chance of her father accepting. Her focus needed to be on whittling down that list to the few acceptable to her.

It was while watching him that her eyes fell on Sir

Duncan. She had managed to avoid him all that evening, only to see him out of the corner of her eye now. He, thankfully, was on his way out and she would not need to navigate through an interaction.

No matter the distracting hair and eyes and smile and scent and humor of her encounter with Lord Wesley, she needed to remain focused. If she was not careful to avoid distraction, she might find herself inextricably tied to someone like Sir Duncan.

Misery was a far worse outcome than boredom.

Three

FOR THE FIRST TIME IN recent memory, Julian had deeply enjoyed time spent at a Society function. He didn't consider himself unsociable or disinclined to like gatherings. He had found much in Society to keep his interest in the years since finishing his schooling. But during that Season, his first since completing his period of mourning for his grandfather, there'd not seemed to be a true place for him in London.

His family's reputation had brought him to the attention of those with whom he didn't care to keep company. And those whose company he felt he would have enjoyed kept their distance on account of his family's reputation. Perhaps it was not truly boredom he'd struggled with, but loneliness.

It was rather early the next morning when he ventured out on his reliable but aging horse. Keeping a horse was a costly indulgence, but he'd not yet been required to deprive himself of it.

The mornings were his favorite time to jaunt to Hyde Park. It wasn't nearly as busy as during the late afternoon and evening. During the morning hours, he could take advantage of the relative emptiness and undertake a risk of a ride at a more invigorating pace. Or, on those mornings when Franklin joined him there, enjoy a conversation without struggling to be heard over the crush of people and carriages.

Though a bit tired from having been out late, he rode alongside Franklin, discussing the events of the evening before.

"You stationed yourself behind her chair all evening?" Franklin repeated what Julian had just told him. "I believe the goal here is to distract from potential courtships, not accidentally entangle yourself in one."

Julian shook his head. "There is nothing in the arrangement that would have given anyone the impression that I was courting her or that she was hoping I was. If anything, people will be confused that I was present at the gathering at all."

"As confused as they would be if Lady Charlotte was actually giving thought to the possibility of a connection with Mr. Vernon?"

Julian shook his head. "There is a mismatched couple if ever I've seen one, and I have most certainly seen plenty."

They kept their horses to a very sedate walk, having undertaken a bit brisker walk earlier.

"Vernon is a decent sort, but he is something of a dullard." Julian winced a little at hearing himself make so judgmental an observation. He had been the recipient of misjudgment in his life, people deciding who and what he was based on his family. He didn't care to be the one doing that to others.

"I don't know her overly well"," Franklin said, "but what I do know of Lady Charlotte makes me think she is not herself a dullard."

"That is the impression I have as well. If anything, she seems to work very hard at keeping what appears to be an active mind calm and quiet enough to endure the tedium of sometimes overly sedate gatherings."

"What happened that you are not telling me about?" Franklin glanced away from the road at Julian.

"Nothing specific that I can point to," Julian acknowledged. "More an impression. I inserted myself into the very mundane conversations that Mr. Vernon continually introduced, making certain my comments were neither insulting nor arrogant nor truly disruptive. Our goal is, after all, awkwardness. I feel that I managed that." He hated that he was in need of £1000 enough to dictate his behavior to such an extent. But there was no point denying his finances were not such as would pass muster.

"What impact did your awkwardness have?" Franklin asked.

"Rather than simply sensing the clumsiness of my company, she seemed to realize rather quickly that there was something odd in my behavior. There was such a look of intelligence in her eyes, as if I were a very complicated puzzle that she was interested in and capable of solving. Now and then, when I would make odd comments, a flash of humor would cross her expression. Mr. Vernon never seemed to bring anything to her expression other than . . . boredom."

"You seem to have taken quite an interest in whether or not Lady Charlotte's future is a happy one."

Julian recognized the meddling tone Franklin was beginning to employ and thought it best to squelch such things quickly. "I know what it is to be made unhappy by one's family. And as someone has connected her fate with mine, I would feel a little bit guilty if that eventual outcome was in any way made less pleasant than it would otherwise be because of my behavior these next few weeks."

"Do you at least think last night's efforts were useful?" Franklin asked. "I mean in terms of delaying the possibility of a wedding in four weeks' time?"

Julian nodded. "There certainly were no opportunities for Mr. Vernon to have any more tender interactions with her. I can say with certainty that he did not further any suit he might have been pursuing while I was there last night."

Franklin nodded in obvious satisfaction. "Then, despite some setbacks, the evening was successful."

On the surface, Julian would agree. And yet . . . "I had the very real impression that Lord Tarrant has taken a significant dislike to me."

"Over the course of a single evening? Were you making yourself more obnoxious than you are admitting?"

Julian shook his head. "His demeanor was stiff and cold when I first arrived among them. It grew more so as the evening progressed. I believe he had decided to disapprove of me before he even knew I was going to be there."

"That seems unlikely," Franklin said, generous friend that he was. "I'm not saying it's impossible for anyone to take a dislike to you; you *are* obnoxious, after all."

"Then what is it you are saying, Franklin?" He pretended to be deeply offended by his friend's declaration.

"As near as I'm aware, you have had very few interactions with the earl, almost none. For him to take such a dislike to you when you are not even that well acquainted is odd indeed."

"If you ask me," Julian said, "everything about this mess I've managed to toss myself into is strange."

"Was Sir Duncan in attendance?" Franklin asked.

"He was, though I was spared the misery of actually speaking with him."

Franklin pointed with his chin toward Rotten Row. "You won't be able to avoid that misery this morning."

Sure enough, Sir Duncan himself was riding toward them. The man was not a cad or a rake in the truest sense of the word, and it would be difficult to accuse him rightfully of anything that actually robbed him of his status as a gentleman, but he was arrogant and thoughtless except in matters pertaining to his own enjoyment. He was unpleasant, but not cruel. He was the sort of person one avoided but wasn't truly afraid of. Unfortunately, he was also the very person who was about to undermine Julian's peaceful morning.

He came up even with them, his mount wearing the same expression of self-importance as its rider.

"I didn't realize you rose this early," Julian said. "Most who were up late last night are likely still in bed."

"That would explain why Mr. Daubney is here so bright-eyed. I do not believe the Barrows extended an invitation to you."

"How fortunate I am that the common folk are being admitted to the Brantleys' ball this evening." Franklin made the observation dryly but with no indication of actual hurt.

"Oh, are the two of you meaning to attend?" Sir Duncan managed to make the question seem almost like mockery.

"We will weigh our many invitations against each other and make a decision when the time comes." Julian steadfastly ignored the look of laughter in Franklin's eyes.

"If you cannot stay up that late," Sir Duncan said, "you might manage to drop in on an earlier gathering and preserve your energy for riding tomorrow, perhaps on two horses actually worth riding."

"I've no arguments with my choice of horseflesh," Julian said.

"Is this a horse?" Franklin asked in a tone of mock stupidity.

Sir Duncan must've been terribly distracted by what he was about to say. He neither looked annoyed by Franklin's dry humor nor did he offer any retorts of his own.

"Perhaps you would care to test your nags against my beast here. I paid a small fortune for him," Sir Duncan said. "I can't imagine either of you could say the same."

It was certainly meant to be both a reflection on their horses, which, truth be told, were perfectly acceptable, and on their relative poverty compared to himself. Julian had long since grown accustomed to financial inferiority; Sir Duncan pointing it out didn't bother him in the least. Franklin, whose family claimed a perfectly comfortable income, did not possess a pride so fragile that he felt the need to defend himself against such a comment from someone he cared so very little about.

"A race would be an excellent idea," Julian said. "To the end of Rotten Row?"

Sir Duncan appeared terribly pleased with himself. "I'll make certain to congratulate the both of you when you eventually arrive." He turned his horse in the direction they were meant to race. "I will allow one of you to give the signal to begin."

Julian met Franklin's eyes and could see they both had the same plan in mind.

"I'll give it," Julian said. "Steady. And . . . begin!"

So Duncan set his horse to run. Julian and Franklin did nothing. They watched Sir Duncan earnestly participate in a race that was not actually happening, then they slowly turned their horses around and continued their slow ambling ride through the park.

Many gentlemen would not have been able to withstand the taunting or resist the chance to prove themselves. Julian came from a family that was all but defined by horrid behavior, which had long ago scrubbed him of any unwarranted pride. Franklin came from a family of means but unexalted standing, which meant he likely never developed arrogance to begin with.

As they rode away from the spot of Sir Duncan's challenge, Julian realized that not too far distant, riding sidesaddle on a cream-colored mare beside her father who was on a nearly matching mount, was Lady Charlotte. And she was watching Julian with that same look of a narrow-eyed evaluation he'd seen the night before.

And suddenly his bit of racing trickery began to feel like a bit of cowardice. And that bothered him. Not that he didn't undertake the race, but that this lady might think he'd been afraid to do so. He, who seldom concerned himself with what a lady thought of him, found he rather deeply cared what this intriguing lady, connected to him by an anonymous wager and a bit of ridiculousness, thought about the person he was.

Four

THE HOSTS AND HOSTESSES OF Society were in two simultaneous competitions: who could host the most exclusive event and who could host the largest. The flow of people in and out of the ballroom at Mr. and Mrs. Brantley's stately London home indicated they sought to be crowned the victors in the latter contest.

"I can't remember the last time you looked pleased to be attending a crush." Franklin smiled at Julian. "Lady Charlotte is a good influence on you."

"I think you mean the prospect of winning a wager is a good influence on me," Julian said quietly.

"And is that the only reason you wore your green coat with the gold embroidery? You have told me more than once that you consider it your most fashionable."

Julian tipped his chin, turning his head a little to assume a humorous version of the posture of one fully aware that he was remarkably handsome. "The goal is to be distracting, is it not?"

"I believe your goal was to be annoyingly vexing. So, well done." Franklin was one of those rare and delightful people with whom a fellow could easily laugh and jest. With growing interest, Julian recalled how close to laughing Lady Charlotte had seemed to be during many moments of their previous interaction. His continued repetition of the word *languisce* had, at first, been meant to cause confusion, but upon seeing her amusement, he'd continued the farce, hoping to bring her a bit of enjoyment.

"Which direction ought we to turn?" Julian asked. "To the right, which will take us toward Sir Duncan or—"

"To the left," Franklin answered without hesitation.

Yes, it was a fine thing indeed to be able to laugh so easily with someone. And Franklin's advice proved remarkably sound. After weaving around a few clumps of people to their left, they came across Lady Charlotte herself, standing beside another young lady, seeming perfectly content with her surroundings and the evening's gathering.

"Lady Charlotte," Julian greeted with a bow.

She answered with a curtsy. "Lord Wesley. Are you acquainted with Miss Selby?"

"I have not had the pleasure of meeting her."

Introductions were made amongst all of them. But before anything else could be said, Sir Duncan arrived, looking quite pleased with himself.

"How unexpected to see you here," Sir Duncan said to Julian.

"I could not countenance missing the Brantleys' ball," Julian said quite casually. "Clearly many others share that opinion." He motioned to the large gathering.

"I thought your humiliation would have kept you away." Sir Duncan smiled a bit smugly.

"Humiliation?"

Sir Duncan looked at the ladies, then at a few others hovering about before smugly answering. "You made quite a pathetic showing for yourself in our horse race this morning."

"Horse race?" Julian looked to Franklin, certain to make his expression one of confusion. "I do not recall participating in a horse race this morning."

"Neither do I." Franklin clearly understood the tactic Julian had chosen without needing to be told what it was.

Sir Duncan was undeterred. "You are correct in that it was not much of a race." Again to the gathering, he said, "My horse is a far superior animal to either of theirs."

"When precisely was this race meant to have occurred?" Julian shook his head in a show of being perplexed. "No matter the outcome, I suspect I would remember having engaged in a race."

"Perhaps you were cup-shot," Sir Duncan said sharply. "That is an indulgence the Lords Wesley are rather known for."

Julian didn't let his hackles rise. "So I not only was part of a race I was not aware of, but I also overindulged to the extreme in alcohol that I did not have with me? Your story is growing ever stranger, sir."

"I rode with you this morning," Franklin said. "I can attest that you were not the least inebriated. Indeed, I have known you for more than half my life and have never once seen you fully foxed."

Sir Duncan's attempts at blackening Julian's name did not appear to be fully hitting their mark, something for which Julian was both grateful and surprised. His family's reputation was not pristine, and his avoidance of Society had not particularly endeared him to the *ton*.

"And I was riding in the park this morning with my father." Lady Charlotte unexpectedly entered the discussion. "I saw you, Sir Duncan, part ways with these two gentlemen. You went in opposite directions after having conversed for a few moments while on horseback. I cannot imagine what race you are alluding to, as I saw nothing of that nature occur."

"There was a race, I assure you." Sir Duncan spoke through tight teeth but kept his genteel air.

"Are you calling Lady Charlotte's honesty into question?" Julian asked quietly, slowly, and with emphasis. A gentleman did not speak so disparagingly of a lady in public.

Sir Duncan was quick to deny that possibility. All who were listening seemed to more or less accept his denial, though many eyed him with just enough doubt that no one with any degree of social prowess would pursue the previous line of discussion. Sir Duncan was quick to offer his apologies to Lady Charlotte, who insisted his comments had not been injurious in any way.

Sir Duncan was quick to depart. The crowd around them returned to their conversations as well.

"I've been curious since this morning about what did happen at Hyde Park," Lady Charlotte said quietly. "Though I was not dishonest in my description of what I saw, I am still not entirely convinced that what I saw wasn't itself something of a deception."

Julian allowed a grin. "It was a rather unusual situation," he acknowledged. "Sir Duncan was making a nuisance of himself and issued a challenge that he likely thought we were too proud to turn down. But as neither Mr. Daubney nor I had any desire to engage in a horse race this morning simply because Sir Duncan spoke ill of us, we didn't feel it necessary to take the bait."

"Did you tell him that?"

Julian pressed a hand dramatically to his heart. "And devastate the poor fragile man? Of course not. We're not heartless!"

A smile of pure amusement spread slowly across the lady's face. Julian, who had already been quite intrigued by her, found himself utterly mesmerized.

"I daresay he crowed quite loudly upon his victory for at least one or two seconds," Franklin said, pretending to be quite serious. "Until he realized he was in a race against himself and as such was both the victor and the loser."

Lady Charlotte's smile remained lovely and beautiful as ever, but something in her eyes had changed—not on account of Franklin or what he had said, neither did she seem to be responding to Julian in any way. Indeed, her attention had shifted to someone approaching from nearby.

Julian looked that way and saw Lord Tarrant approaching with Mr. Travers, whom Julian had known at Cambridge.

Greetings were exchanged. Mr. Travers did not smile but also did not seem particularly unhappy. He'd always been almost unfailingly somber but wasn't actually a gloomy person. He was simply extremely serious. That didn't appear to have changed.

"We are well met, Mr. Travers," Lady Charlotte said. "Was this a coincidence, or were you hoping to see us tonight?" The question wasn't quite flirtatious, but there was an earnestness to it that told Julian she wished for Mr. Travers to remain, to speak with them, to perhaps make a good impression.

It seemed Julian had quite easily discovered yet another possible suitor he was meant to distract. Blast it all, he would far rather stand about attempting to make Lady Charlotte smile again. He couldn't remember the last time a lady had captured his attention so quickly and so entirely. That made the connection between her and himself, found quite by accident in the betting book of his club, all the more strange.

In his momentary distraction he had missed the conversation continuing around him. Only by quick observation and deduction did he realize Mr. Travers had secured Lady Charlotte's hand for the next set. A failure already. Being seen dancing, especially two people who made a handsome couple—and he suspected these two would—might very well begin the sort of rumors Julian would rather delay. There'd be whispers and those whispers, once they reached the earl, might turn his thoughts to the idea of Lady Charlotte and Mr. Travers making a match.

Something very akin to panic began to slowly set in. It was the matter of £1000, he told himself. The money, not anything so ridiculous as jealousy or disappointment at not being the one to have secured her hand for a dance or having been outmaneuvered by someone who didn't even know they were engaged in battle.

Mr. Travers accompanied Lady Charlotte to their place amongst the dancers preparing to perform a minuet. Julian likely could have secured a partner, but he would feel blasted guilty asking a lady to dance, only to neglect her whilst attempting to prevent any degree of closeness to grow between another couple. The best thing he could do was position himself such that he could catch Lady Charlotte's eye now and then and make her curious as to what he was thinking. It was an odd approach but also the only one he thought might work, since distracting Mr. Travers seemed unlikely. The gentleman's focus was as unwavering as his solemnity.

Julian wandered a bit as the elegant dance was undertaken. A few times, he did indeed catch Lady Charlotte's eye. He would lift an eyebrow the tiniest bit and smile. Once, he let that smile turn a touch flirtatious, and Lady Charlotte blushed. Heaven help him, he liked that.

She was returned to her father not long before Julian's footsteps took him past the place where the earl and his daughter stood.

"You are a very skilled dancer, Lady Charlotte," he offered as he came up to her side.

"Though I risk sounding horribly arrogant, I have been told so before," she said.

"If Mr. Travers is one of those making that very accurate observation, I sincerely hope he did so in the most glowing terms," Julian said, exaggerating his words so she would know he was jesting.

Her smile reappeared in an instant. "His is not the most flowery of vocabularies nor the most animated of countenances, but he's a good gentleman, and I do enjoy his company."

"I'm pleased to hear it," Julian said, a remark which clearly surprised her. Why would it surprise her? He'd teased a little about her taciturn partner, but he didn't think he'd given any indication that he disliked Mr. Travers or wished Lady Charlotte to be unhappy. "I knew Mr. Travers at Cambridge, and I liked him then. Our dispositions are not overly similar but not so disparate that I am unable to see the goodness in him." It was an honest evaluation, one he was almost surprised to hear himself give. He was rewarded with a look of approval in her eyes, eyes he was beginning to realize were a most beguiling shade of golden brown.

"What do you suppose Mr. Travers would have to say about you?" Lady Charlotte asked. Many people who hinted at evaluations of his character did so with references to his father and grandfather and great-grandfather and any number of his family members who had been less than the people they ought to have been. Lady Charlotte seemed to be genuinely curious about Julian himself rather than yet another Lord Wesley.

"I would hope he would say that while I do sometimes jest when I ought to be a bit more serious, I am not a truly frivolous person, that I am good company, and that I am not entirely witless."

It was the earl who answered that declaration. "I've never known a Lord Wesley who could be described in glowing terms, and I have known several."

"You will forgive me, my lord," Julian answered, "I have also known several, yet I assure you I offered the description of myself with sincerity and honesty. Though one is inevitably influenced by the family and home one was raised in, each generation need not be an exact duplicate of the last."

The earl didn't seem to entirely appreciate the correction. He watched Julian with a silent air of disapproval, one that sent him back to his days in the nursery when his grandfather and father would take it in turns to scold and belittle him. He could feel that little boy he'd once been, shrinking and cowering and tucking himself away. But he was not a child any longer. The family that had so tormented him was gone. Many people had declared it a tragedy that he had lost everyone he was related to. For Julian it had been, to a large degree, a relief. He'd finally had some peace, and he'd been granted the opportunity to determine who he meant to be without constantly fighting the people his family had been.

Julian kept his posture and held his head aloft without tipping it at an arrogant angle. "I don't claim to be perfect, but neither will I allow myself to be painted with a brush that does not suit me." He turned to Lady Charlotte and dipped a gracious bow. "It has, as always, been a great pleasure to see you again."

"Does this mean you are leaving?" That she sounded disappointed at the possibility did his heart more good than she could have imagined, and far more than it ought.

"I suspect, my lady, my absence will be met with approval in this particular corner of the ballroom, and it is merely this area I mean to quit." He refrained from looking at her father, not wishing to further antagonize him. "I do hope you will allow those in attendance the pleasure of seeing you dance once more. Should my path cross yours again before the night is through, I would consider myself quite fortunate to be the recipient of another of your smiles."

A tiny bit of color touched her cheeks, visible beneath the powder most ladies and many gentlemen wore on their faces. "I'm pleased you don't mean to leave entirely."

Not knowing quite how to respond and feeling the glare of the earl burning a hole in his temple, Julian simply dipped his head and stepped away.

Fool, he castigated himself. *Distracting would-be suitors to buy yourself time to obtain a bit of money you desperately need is one thing. Finding yourself developing a tendre for the lady is another entirely.*

A fool indeed.

Five

CHARLOTTE'S FATHER HAD BEEN UNWELL for a few days, and thus she had not attended many gatherings. Fortunately, he was feeling well again in time for their at-home day. She felt certain both Mr. Vernon and Mr. Travers would be present, along with a great many others. Though she didn't like to think of herself as vain, she realized she had made a great many friends. Her standing, as well as her father's, had made her sought-after amongst those who wished to improve their own standing.

During her first Season, that had bothered her. She'd felt a bit dismissed and more than a bit overlooked. But having now completed several Seasons, she understood a little better the necessary dance they all undertook. Even those who would not naturally view people in the context of their rank, nor use them to improve their own standing, often had very little choice. So much about a person's future, especially when that person was a woman, depended on making the right connections at the right time with the right people. What she had originally seen as hurtful and mercenary she now understood for the act of survival that it actually was.

She didn't begrudge people those things that they needed to do in order to stay afloat. And she valued those whom she had a more personal connection with that much more, those with whom she had a truer friendship.

Louisa was one such person. She had visited whilst Father was unwell, offering Charlotte some much needed company and reassurance. He'd not been so unwell that Charlotte had actually been concerned about his survival. But her mother had died when she was quite young. She had a sister who had not lived past childhood. Her grandfather had passed away, as had one of her aunts and her only uncle. When her father was ill, she fretted a little.

Louisa was present again for the at-home, this time with her fiancé. The more Charlotte knew of Mr. Granville, the more she liked him and the happier she was for her friend. Arranged marriages did not always turn out well, but Charlotte had every reason to believe this one would. Indeed, watching them together, she could see they were genuinely pleased to be in each other's company.

When the match had first been arranged, there had been a great deal of discomfort between the two. Now the best way to describe their interactions was "sweet." There was a tender kindness between them that Charlotte had to admit she was a little envious of.

All of this flitted through her thoughts while she was seeing to her duties as hostess. Her father interacted easily with guests of all generations. Charlotte had heard that her grandmother and grandfather had been the same way, despite the fact that her grandmother no longer interacted with Society. Her aunt, Charlotte had been told, lacked that polish, and she now fully eschewed the social whirl. Charlotte suspected she fell somewhere between the two extremes. She got along well with people and enjoyed friendly interactions, but she also cherished quiet time to herself. She needed to find a means of deciding which of the gentlemen she was encouraging her father to take notice of was most likely to appreciate those contradictory needs in her.

Mr. Vernon and Mr. Travers arrived at the at-home at almost the exact same time. They eyed each other with misgiving, a good indication that they realized they were positioned to be rivals. Some ladies would have been flattered by that. For her part, Charlotte mostly felt tired. She had begun to recognize the exhaustion for what it was: a small but unshakable feeling of helplessness. She was trying so hard to influence the direction her life would take once her father set his mind to it, but there was really so little she could do.

Still, she reminded herself, Mr. Vernon and Mr. Travers weren't terrible options when compared to some of the others who had shown interest in her or who would, she would wager, jump at the opportunity to connect themselves with her family.

The two gentlemen offered their greetings and were invited to sit. Charlotte watched Father for his reaction. He seemed pleased to see them, which was a good sign. He also didn't seem to have a preference for one over the other.

Did *she*?

She'd been so busy making certain her father didn't set his sights on someone entirely objectionable that she'd not stopped to think whether she ought to be encouraging one over the other. Perhaps it would behoove her to focus her efforts. But that would require deciding where she wished to focus them, which was a significant part of her difficulty. They were unobjectionable and would likely not be unkind to her. But she had no tenderness for either of them, no preference.

"Lady Charlotte, you were missed last evening at the Carlisles' soiree." Mr. Vernon offered the observation with sincerity, something that was not always the case in Society.

"I was sad to miss it," she said. "As my father's health has begun to improve, I am hopeful that we will be present at those gatherings that are upcoming."

He nodded. "Indeed."

It was a very common interaction with him: pleasant conversation that was neither overly personal nor overly interesting. Would such an arrangement at least prove not *unhappy*? Was not being unhappy truly the most a lady could hope for?

A discouraging thought.

She turned to Mr. Travers. "When last we spoke, you were concerned with the well-being of one of your horses. I hope all has continued to be well on that front."

He hesitated. "Yes."

"You sound discouraged," she observed, hoping to offer empathetic encouragement.

He eyed her with apparent confusion. It was not uncommon to assume that when interacting with a very somber gentleman, he was more upset with a situation than he actually proved to be. She imagined, over time, either she would come to understand him better or she would learn to not press the matter of his distress. Not the most exciting prospect.

During her distraction, Mr. Travers had taken up a conversation with her father, one that seemed to carry the undertones of something of a budding friendship. Charlotte had encouraged her father to think well of him. In theory, she ought to be pleased to see this step forward. But in actuality, she was a little discouraged. Which made her realize she was a bit more inclined toward a match with Mr. Vernon. She would be bored, at times nearly out of her wits, but she would not spend the entirety of her marriage wishing for someone with a lighter disposition.

She needed to do more to encourage her father to think well of Mr. Vernon.

Just as she resolved to do so, Lord Wesley of all people stepped into the drawing room. His friend Mr. Daubney was with him. The two seemed a genuinely happy duo. That was not something she could say for the two gentlemen seated nearest her.

Lord Wesley smiled at the greeting she offered to him, and that smile set her heart fluttering a little. In her four years in London, only he had managed to do that to her. When he'd watched her as she danced the minuet, she'd not been able to prevent a blush of delight. He'd not watched her in a critical way or a possessive way, as far too many gentlemen did. He seemed to genuinely be interested in what she was doing and seemed to sincerely find her to be a graceful dancer. There was a softness in his eyes when he looked at her, mingled with the hint of laughter she so often saw there regardless of who he was speaking with. Charlotte liked that about him.

She'd known him as a very distant acquaintance until quite recently. And now she felt as if they had very suddenly become friends. Friends with a hint of something else, something she didn't dare define.

The two newest arrivals offered their greetings and their well-wishes to her father. There were no empty chairs near where she sat, and Mr. Vernon and Mr. Travers had not been present long enough that they were likely to make their departure soon. She assumed, with an inexplicable drop of her heart, that Lord Wesley would choose to sit elsewhere in the room and converse with others, perhaps Louisa and her fiancé. Mr. Daubney did precisely that. Lord Wesley, however, hovered awkwardly nearby.

He was handsome and entertaining and had shown himself to be witty, but he had also, at times, been socially clumsy. When Mr. Vernon would say something, he would respond in a way that leaned toward awkward. When Mr. Travers would speak, he would respond in a way that emphasized his easy manner and lightness of mood. The two gentlemen at her side were a bit flustered by it. Charlotte, however, found herself increasingly intrigued by this baron and his confusing behavior.

Why was it he so seldom participated in Society yet had of late done so with enthusiasm?

Her heart whispered that his return to social activity had something to do with her, that she had captured his interest. Perhaps a bit of his heart. But her more logical mind did not think so. He was not undertaking anything that would indicate he was courting her. More to the point, he was not "courting" her father. She had no other word for what was expected of gentlemen who wished to marry a lady, considering that a lady's eventual husband was almost without exception chosen by her parents and most especially by her father.

Her father disliked him; he'd made that clear. Indeed, he had mentioned it more than once. She wanted to believe that was owing to the reputation of Lord Wesley's family. Everyone knew the previous Lords Wesley had been, without exception, wastrels. But she'd never heard the same things said of him personally. And he had defended himself against her father's insinuation otherwise.

This gentleman was intriguing, which was not something she could say for either of the gentlemen she had been hoping her father would choose.

Oh heavens.

The intrigue she'd felt for him had changed and she'd not realized it. More than curious about him, she had developed something of a *tendre* for him. She, who suspected this Season would be her last before Father saw to it she was married, had, for the first time since being presented, lost a bit of her heart to someone, and it was someone she knew her father would never choose.

Six

JULIAN'S CARRIAGE RIDE TO THE theater two evenings later was particularly uncomfortable. The carriage was well sprung, and the driver took it at a sedate enough clip as to not toss Julian and Franklin about. Rather, Julian's discomfort arose from an examination of his actions in the time since discovering the wager involving himself.

They had first formulated their plan for interfering in any particularly serious courtships involving Lady Charlotte while a bit in their cups. That Julian had followed through with their plan once sober was the bit that bothered him.

There was no denying he needed the money. And as the wager was made very quietly and very privately and wasn't bandied about, it was unlikely to cause Lady Charlotte any true unhappiness.

But he still didn't like it.

If she truly wished to make a match with Mr. Vernon or Mr. Travers, what right had he to interfere? He didn't mean to prevent a connection, only delay it. He'd told himself that many times and he didn't entirely believe it. The idea of her marrying either of those two sat poorly on his mind. Neither were bad people, neither were ungentlemanly or uncouth or particularly obnoxious people. He just couldn't picture either of them being a truly good match for her. She was lively and interesting. She had shown herself to be in possession of wit and humor. She flitted about from group to group with an ease that spoke to one who enjoyed Society and understood it but was not unhealthily dependent upon its acceptance.

She deserved to be joyful, and he wanted that for her. He'd only truly come to know her over the last week and a half, building upon the vague acquaintance they'd had before, but already her happiness mattered to him.

And thus he was decidedly uncomfortable on his way to attend another Society event at which she might be present and at which he, if he were to continue his schemes, would be expected to interfere further.

His mind clearly along the same vein, Franklin asked, "Have you heard for certain if Vernon or Travers will be at the theater tonight?"

"I haven't," Julian said. "I suppose it is possible."

"Then you are not attending as part of this mission of yours?" Franklin pressed. "I would suggest you were attending simply for your own enjoyment of the theater, but you have not exactly been socially active these last few years."

"Careful there, you are tiptoeing terribly close to the same observation Sir Duncan made at the ball."

"If ever I say something that comes within a close approximation of that coxcomb, I certainly hope you will tell me."

Julian could smile a little despite his swirling thoughts.

"If you are not attending in order to interfere with a potential courtship and, if history is any indication, are likely not attending for your own amusement, then I fear I must press my question: *why* are you attending this evening? You do not appear to be particularly excited about it."

Why was he going? Without any true reason to believe Vernon or Travers would be present, his presence was hardly necessary. He had heard whispers that Lady Charlotte would be in attendance. And if he were being entirely honest, that had been a significant part of his motivation. But not the entirety of it. "I suppose some part of me is looking forward to an evening at the theater and amongst the glittering *ton*. And I assure you, I am as shocked by this change in myself as you are."

Franklin's smile was one of friendship and understanding. "Not shocked so much as I am relieved. When we met our first year at Cambridge, you were a much more active and social sort of person. I saw that drift away after your father's passing and your grandfather's continued slide into dissipation. I never could decide if you were retreating out of grief or embarrassment."

"Both, really. I did grieve my father's death, though he had caused me no end of sorrow. And I was embarrassed by the person my grandfather was, at the person so many assumed I would be as a member of our family. In the end it was easier not to go about very often. If nothing else, it quelled the rumors that I was going to be a frivolous gadabout who wasted all my time and diminished resources on pursuits of shallowness."

"But how were they ever to discover that you're different from the previous Lords Wesley if they never have a chance to meet you?" Franklin could at times be very philosophical. Over the course of their friendship that tendency had alternated between frustrating and helpful. In that moment, it was decidedly the latter.

"I think Lady Charlotte believes I'm not a terrible sort of fellow. Her father on the other hand . . . " He let the sentence dangle, knowing he didn't have to complete the thought for Franklin to understand what it was.

"Lady Charlotte likely never met your grandfather or father. She'll know of your family's reputation; everyone does. Her father, on the other hand, knew them both. It's possible he even knew your great-grandfather. It's more difficult to overcome an actual memory than a rumor."

"Maybe that's what I'm hoping to do tonight: begin substituting those memories of Lords Wesley gone by and replace them with more flattering whispers about the current title holder."

"You mean to accomplish this while acting as a deterrence to Lady Charlotte's matrimonial hopes?"

Hearing it spoken so bluntly gave him further pause.

"I've been contemplating abandoning that effort," he said hesitantly. "Her birthday is not so very far off, and I think it's already somewhat unlikely she will be married before the wager comes due."

"And if she does manage it? You cannot convince me you do not need the £1000."

"Oh, heaven knows I need it," he sighed. "But it feels . . . wrong. We don't even know who made the wager. It might be someone bent on embarrassing her, in which case I don't know that I want my name attached to it at all, and certainly don't want to be seen as assisting the effort. Even if it isn't likely to be widely known, it is terribly ungentlemanly to make a wager involving a lady. Though I didn't make the wager and certainly have nothing to do with the forfeit, I will be seen to benefit from it, which would make it very difficult for me to convincingly claim that I had nothing to do with it."

Franklin nodded. "Especially considering the family reputation we were only just discussing."

The weight in Julian's stomach increased. "If only I knew who made the wager to begin with, I could ask him to kindly call it off."

"Such a private wager will be far harder to get to the bottom of. And though the keeper of the books at our club knows the identity of those involved, he would not breach their confidence by revealing the details."

Julian shook his head. "I've thought about this over the last few days. Once Lady Charlotte's birthday arrives and the results are known, it's entirely possible the wager will be whispered about. Someone who would place such a wager cannot be entirely trusted to use discretion when crowing over or complaining about the outcome."

Franklin's brows pulled. "That eliminates one of the people I have suspected of being involved."

Julian met his friend's eye. "Who is that?"

"Though I would hope he was not this sort of person, I wondered about the Earl Tarrant. He, after all, as her father, is more aware than anyone if she is likely to make a match and how soon. And the animosity he seems to feel toward you could explain why he attached your name to something so ungentlemanly."

"The ungentlemanliness of the wager made me wonder about Sir Duncan. He does seem to show up a great deal where Lady Charlotte is, which could indicate he's keeping an eye on her."

Franklin nodded. "And either of the two gentlemen who seem to have been accepted as suitors could be behind it, though neither seem to have the disposition for it."

"If it is not one of those four, but rather someone who had randomly selected her as the focus of this wager, we are unlikely to identify the culprit."

"You will if you are awarded the forfeit. The one who made the bet would be required to pay you what he wagered."

It was possible the wagerer would make the payment anonymously, but £1000 was a great deal of money, more than most people would have on hand in coin or currency. It was more likely to be paid by a banknote, which would have the payee's signature. And there would be some requirement of proof to the other man involved that the wagerer had made good on his debt.

"Part of me very much wishes we had never stumbled across this wager in the first place," Julian said.

"Why only part of you?" Franklin asked.

"I've enjoyed coming to know Lady Charlotte. She's an enjoyable companion, interesting to talk with. She has a lovely smile, which a gentleman cannot help but appreciate. Further, she has a very good and keen sense of humor and seems to enjoy mine as well." He smiled to himself. "She was very quick to defend us when Sir Duncan gave a very unflattering version of our 'race.' Her kindness was not something I would ever have presumed to ask for, and I cannot say I deserved it, but I very much—" Realizing Franklin was studying him a bit too closely for comfort, Julian stopped abruptly. "What has you so ponderous?"

Franklin's expression turned as somber as those that came so naturally to Mr. Travers. "I believe, my friend, you are walking on thinner ice than you realize."

"What do you mean by that?"

"There's a great deal to like about Lady Charlotte Duchamps. But her father dislikes you, and he will no doubt select for her a gentleman of greater fortune than you can currently claim, as well as one without your family's reputation. And should she learn of this wager you are connected to, not to mention your efforts to thwart her, I cannot imagine it will improve her opinion of you."

"None of that is exactly a shocking revelation," Julian said, studying his friend as closely as he was being studied. "Why the sudden concern?"

"I don't think you realize the way you talk about her, Julian. You are walking on thin ice, my friend. So thin that I can already hear it cracking."

Julian would have pressed for a greater explanation, insisted his friend was overreacting, but he couldn't honestly argue. He had been intrigued by Lady Charlotte from the moment he'd begun this charade. That feeling of being intrigued had only grown. He knew he was nursing a partiality for her.

He needed to be very careful.

Their turn to alight and enter the theater arrived. They stepped inside to find it already overflowing with attendees. The corridor wrapped around, connecting the various boxes of the well-to-dos and upper class, and surged with silks and scented hair powder. The ladies' dresses were, thankfully, not as wide as they were at court, allowing for slightly more ease when walking more than one abreast. Julian told himself he wasn't watching for anyone in particular, but he knew his eyes were searching for Lady Charlotte.

He also told himself he would simply keep a distance should he see her, but the moment he did, his feet took him directly to her.

Julian and Franklin offered elegant bows, which were returned with a curtsy on her part and a bow from her father.

"A pleasure to see you again, Lord Wesley," Lady Charlotte said. "And a pleasure to see you, Mr. Daubney."

"The pleasure is all mine, I assure you," Julian answered, one of those rare moments at Society gatherings when the commonplace response was deeply meant.

Lord Tarrant eyed him with a narrowed gaze, his mouth pulled a bit tight.

"I do not mean to impose on your evening's enjoyment," Julian said to them both. "I know, were my father here, I would appreciate being able to enjoy his company without disruption."

The earl spoke for the first time. "Your father was not the sort that most people longed to keep company with."

"Father," Lady Charlotte whispered sharply. "That is not a kind thing to say."

"I thank you for your thoughtfulness, Lady Charlotte," Julian said. "I also must acknowledge your father's not wrong. But though there is much that I disapproved of in my late father's behavior, he was my father. A son is permitted to love his father even after knowing the person he was. Having lost him so young, I do envy those children who have time with their parents, however flawed, however frustrating, however much sorrow existed in their relationship. I know that my father deserves the unkind words that have been spoken of him, but I will say this one thing: he would never have begrudged anyone a moment for grieving a parent. He had a good enough heart for that." Julian sketched a quick bow to the earl, another to Lady Charlotte, then took a step to leave.

A soft and gentle hand on his arm stopped him. He glanced up to see Lady Charlotte taking a step closer. It was her kind touch that had halted his departure. "Please do not leave angry," she said softly.

"I am not angry with you, Lady Charlotte," he said. "I suspect I could never be."

The tiniest tilt of her lips accompanied her next question. "Is that a challenge, Lord Wesley?"

"Would you like it to be?"

She raised a single shoulder, her head dipping in that direction. It was so coy and playful a shrug. He couldn't help the smile spreading across his face, despite the rather insulting conversation he'd only just endured from her father.

"If we issue a challenge," he said, "I would rather it not

be whether or not you could make me angry, but how pleased I can make you."

"That is a challenge I will happily accept. But be warned, I would then be on my guard and choose to not be amused by anything you might say."

Oh, she was delightful.

He took her hand and raised it to his lips, pressing a kiss to her gloved fingertips. It was a fairly commonplace gesture, one employed between gentlemen and ladies, which could ultimately be either a show of affection or of absolutely no significance at all.

But as he reluctantly released her hand, he knew that simple kiss was, for him, neither a token of mere affection nor insignificant. His heart pounded, his mind spun, and hope bubbled around the possibility of her company. His hand remained warm, tingling where his fingers had touched hers.

He wasn't merely walking on thin ice; he had fallen through.

Seven

WHEN NOT PARTICIPATING IN THE social whirl, Charlotte found herself particularly fond of visiting the circulating library to which her family had a subscription. Books were a wonderful way to pass a quiet afternoon—something she was grateful her father appreciated as well, as it meant she was granted both access to books and time in which to enjoy them.

Two days after their most recent venture to the theater, she and her father made the short journey to the circulating library to select new volumes for their enjoyment. They made their way along one of the rows of books, at the end of which was a gathering of chairs placed at a cozy distance from a low-burning fire. The proprietor of this particular library took pride in creating a place where his patrons would linger.

Father found a volume that captured his interest, and Charlotte followed him to the chairs and the warm fireside to see him seated, meaning to search out a volume of her own once he was comfortable. But her father asked her to sit beside him.

"You are nearing the end of your fourth Season," he said.

She nodded, suspecting with a drop of her heart that she knew where this conversation was headed.

"I believe it is time you were settled and beginning the next chapter of your life."

Even anticipating the topic, she was still a little surprised. And unexpectedly nervous.

"Have you made arrangements already?" she asked.

Father shook his head. "Not yet, but . . . the Season is nearly over."

Making matches was far more difficult outside of the London Season. If her father didn't arrange a marriage for her soon, he'd likely struggle to do so until the *ton* gathered again the next year.

She had known this. It was the reason she had done what she could to turn her father's attention to gentlemen who were not objectionable. But the thought of being wed to either of them now didn't feel "unobjectionable." She felt something far nearer to dread.

Dread.

"I realize the Season is ending soon, but could we possibly delay this until after Louisa's wedding?" If she didn't know with certainty her friend would not mind Charlotte using her wedding as a means of delaying this monumental decision, she wouldn't have done so. But she needed time. Time to sort herself out. Time to determine how to best move forward. "I wish so much to celebrate with Louisa free of distractions."

He reached over and patted her hand. "Of course, dearest." He then turned his attention to his book and was quickly lost in his reading.

Until after Louisa's wedding. That was only a matter of days. She didn't think it likely her father could be put off again.

To her surprise and dismay, emotions rose in her chest, thickening in her throat. She was not an unfeeling person, neither did she require herself to keep her emotions tamped down. But she did not often find herself unable to maintain her composure in public.

Charlotte rose. "I will go find a volume for myself," she told her father, keeping her tone light.

Father nodded but kept his attention on his reading.

Charlotte tucked herself down the other row created by a different set of shelves, this one more to the back and out of sight of anyone wandering in. She breathed in and out, slowly, deliberately.

It is time you were settled and beginning the next chapter of your life.

Settled. It was about as promising and enthusiastic a description as she felt she could reasonably apply. But it wasn't what she wanted. Not any longer. She wanted to be able to think on her approaching nuptials with some degree of joy and happiness. Surely that wasn't so much to ask.

"Lady Charlotte?" A quiet voice spoke her name in a tone of concern and uncertainty.

Lord Wesley.

He joined her beside the shelves she had not even attempted to peruse. "I saw you and your father through the front windows and stepped inside to offer my greetings." He was watching her with such a look of tenderness that it nearly undid what little composure she'd managed to retain. "You're upset about something."

She shook her head. "Nothing I have any right to truly be upset about. It is expected and ordinary and . . ." She stopped at the break in her voice, swallowed against the burning in her throat. "I oughtn't complain."

"You aren't complaining, dear; you're crying." He brushed moisture from her cheek, moisture she hadn't even realized was there. "Please tell me what's upset you and what I can do."

She was not an inherently untrusting person, but neither was she one to spill all her troubles in another's ear. Yet she told him immediately and without hesitation. "My father has decided it is time I married, and he means to see that arranged and final before the end of the Season. I've known he would soon enough; I'd even guessed that this would be my last Season unattached. But facing the reality of it is proving rather dreadful, I'm afraid."

"Has he chosen someone awful?"

Charlotte shook her head. "Not that I know of. I've been trying to influence any list he might be forming in his mind in the hope that he would choose someone at least pleasant."

Lord Wesley offered her his handkerchief, and she dabbed at the tears that continued pooling on her lashes. "Your birthday is near to the end of the Season, is it not?"

An odd question. Odder still that he knew her birthdate. "Yes, it is."

"Is Lord Tarrant a gambler, by chance?"

Odder still. "Not beyond the ordinary. An occasional wager over cards or a small, harmless one between friends."

"You insisted it *was* possible for me to grow angry with you," Lord Wesley said. "I think it more likely that *you* are soon to become angry with *me.*"

Apprehension tiptoed over her. "Why do I get the impression you are not speaking in general terms?"

"There is a wager I recently learned of, and the mystery of who placed it has been plaguing me."

"You think my father might be the wagerer?" She didn't know whether to be intrigued or insulted. That would depend on what the wager was about, she supposed.

"Actually, no." That seemed to be a sudden realization. "Though, I had wondered."

"What is this wager?" How quickly she had been distracted from her previous difficult topic of worry.

He hesitated. That did not seem a good omen. "I must emphasize that I was surprised to hear of the wager and had nothing to do with it being made."

Decidedly *not* a good omen.

"A wager was recorded in the books at my club," he spoke quickly and quietly, all the while watching her with uncertainty, "which I discovered quite by accident and have not ever heard spoken about. An anonymous wagerer has staked £1000 on . . . " He took a breath, then pushed forward. "That you would be married by your twenty-first birthday."

It was decidedly unexpected. "That I would be married?"

Lord Wesley nodded.

"I suppose that is better than a wager being made that I would not be or would *never* be."

"You aren't offended that you were the subject of a wager?" Lord Wesley asked.

"Not offended, no. There is some annoyance mingled with my amusement, but I know perfectly well that gentlemen make odd wagers quite regularly." She found she could even smile a little. "And for someone to be so confident in my matrimonial prospects to place so large a wager, is—" *Oh.* "That is why you wondered if the wagerer was my father, because he would have that confidence because, heavens, he would be the one arranging that marriage."

"But that is also why I have dismissed him as the wagerer. I don't think he would make his own daughter the subject of so potentially embarrassing a wager, nor one he could force to play out in one way or another. He seems a man of greater integrity than that."

She also couldn't imagine her father doing something so questionable. "If you know who would be paid the forfeit, that would at least give you one half of the wagering duo."

"It usually would, but not in this instance."

"Why is that?"

"Because the one declared to be the recipient of the forfeit was not involved in the wager. Indeed, he was utterly shocked to discover his name in the betting books."

In a flash as sudden as the pop of an untrimmed candle wick, she understood what he was struggling to say. "You will receive £1000 if I am not married by my birthday?"

He looked embarrassed. "I didn't place the wager. I only learned of it by chance." He held his hands up in a show of frustration. "I haven't told anyone. Franklin knows, but he was there when we saw the wager in the book. I would never embarrass you that way. And I wouldn't wish to prevent you from being courted or treated with kindness or warmly accepted by the *ton* out of a wish to see the wager play out."

Another flash of understanding. "This is why you quite suddenly showed an interest in knowing me better. You were intrigued by the wager."

"Yes." But it emerged as a dangling sentence rather than a complete one.

"I would kindly request that you finish your confession, Lord Wesley."

With a look of utter misery, he said, "We were able to discover that your birthday was not terribly far distant, and neither of us had seen any announcements regarding an engagement. We thought that likely meant you were not on the very cusp of marriage. I am embarrassed to say we hatched a plan to discover if any gentlemen had made progress in capturing your interest or were at all positioned to make an engagement probable. If we did, I . . . I thought I might prove myself a bit of a thorn in the side of romance and delay things a little."

"Until my twenty-first birthday, you hoped."

He sighed even as he nodded. "Not enough to cause you

embarrassment or prevent an engagement if one were imminent, but perhaps manage to secure that £1000, if doing so without being a complete blackguard was possible."

"Are you in particular need of £1000?" she asked.

"I am, unfortunately. Your father's assessment of my family was not entirely without merit. I inherited more of a mess than I wish I had." A look of determination entered his eyes. "I never intended to hurt you, and I hope that I haven't. And I have long since abandoned the effort at being an unmitigated annoyance. But it was badly done of me, and I will understand if you find it unforgivable."

She swore he was holding his breath. Seldom had she seen a man look more miserably contrite.

"Do you think you could resume those efforts?"

His misery turned to shock. "*Resume* them?"

She nodded. "You found a means of delaying an engagement, and I would very much like to not find myself engaged any time soon. And if you are in a position to receive a much-needed windfall while doing me such a welcome favor, that would be a fine thing. Seems we would do well to combine our efforts."

"Then you aren't—You don't—You don't despise me for my interference?"

"Despise you?" She grinned. "Heavens, I am all but begging to join forces with you. I am in need of your unique skills."

His smile slowly returned, and she was beyond pleased to see it. "What skills would those be?"

"Your knack for being very conveniently annoying."

His smile turned to a grin, and she knew an answering one settled on her lips.

"My annoying nature is entirely at your disposal, Lady Charlotte."

 Eight

HAD JULIAN BEEN ASKED TO guess how Charlotte would respond to learning she was the subject of a wager, and that he had been causing her grief in service of that wager, he'd have declared without hesitation that she would be hurt and angry and likely denounce him to all and sundry whilst consigning him to the very devil. Instead, she'd declared her desire to help him continue his efforts.

Shocking. And humbling. He knew he didn't deserve her forbearance or forgiveness. He would, however, do all he could to help her avoid a marriage she didn't wish to enter into.

In the interest of that commitment, he hied himself to Charlotte's London house for another at-home, determined to make himself equally as bothersome as he had on his last attendance there, should Mr. Travers or Mr. Vernon be in attendance or should her father seem to be favoring another gentleman.

And it was, in fact, another gentleman whose path he crossed first upon entering the drawing room. Heaven help Charlotte if Sir Duncan was her father's choice. As Julian dipped a quick acknowledgement, he glanced around the room, looking for some indication that the haughty baronet had somehow found his way into the earl's good graces. But the earl was not present.

"I don't imagine any of us can say we are surprised to see you here, Lord Wesley." Sir Duncan looked back at the gathering. "He certainly seems determined to annoy Lady Charlotte with his near-constant presence."

"I would never presume to be your equal in that." Julian offered the veiled insult with a perfectly pleasant tone.

Sir Duncan's stormy expression told him the remark had been understood. The titters around the room told him it had also been overheard. Though Charlotte smiled in obvious enjoyment, she didn't laugh, keeping the composure required of a hostess.

Mrs. Baskins, the wife of another gentleman with whom he'd attended Cambridge, offered a word of greeting, as did the lady sitting beside her. Julian offered words of pleasure at being in company with another lady whom he knew through a mutual friend. He was not insincere in his greetings, but he was not entirely focused either. All his thoughts were on Charlotte. What a change the past weeks had wrought.

Standing in front of her at last, he bowed. "Lady Charlotte. Thank you for receiving me."

"Thank you for calling. I fear my father is feeling a touch unwell and will not be joining the gathering."

"I am sorry to hear that." He indicated a chair beside hers. "Might I be so bold as to request the honor of sitting so near you?"

"You certainly may." She smiled as he sat. "Mr. Daubney is not with you today. That is a rare thing."

"He is calling elsewhere. Miss Selby is not with you. That is also a rare thing."

Charlotte sighed, the sound a bit dramatic. "Alas, she is days from her wedding, and her time is consumed with the final details of that."

"Are you pleased for your friend?" he asked.

"I am. Mr. Granville is a fine gentleman, and they are genuinely happy in each other's company. I could not be more pleased for Louisa."

Did she have any expectation of being happy in the company of anyone her father was likely to choose? She deserved to be happy. She deserved to build a life with someone who valued her happiness.

Mrs. Baskins spoke into the momentary silence. "Many have remarked at how pleased we all are that you are going about more in Society, Lord Wesley. You have hardly done so these past few years."

Though he might have felt some castigation in her declaration, he chose to focus on her expression of delight at his presence. "I confess I had been avoiding the *ton*. Knowing how my predecessors had too often behaved, I feared being misjudged. I ought to have shown more faith in the discernment of Society."

Expressions of both empathy and reassurance echoed around the room. He was touched. After a lifetime of being assumed to be a mere copy of his reprobate father and scoundrel grandfather, he'd found it easier to tuck himself away and limit his interactions to Franklin and a select few others. Perhaps he'd been doing himself and his potential associates a disservice. Perhaps *he* had been the one to misjudge *them*.

"I hope you will continue to be more a part of the social whirl," Charlotte said.

He met her eye, feeling the pull to her growing with every encounter, every conversation, every glance. "I intend to be."

Her soft smile warmed him through. The thin ice Franklin had warned him about had melted entirely. Sink or swim, he was in deep.

The ladies who had called on Charlotte were, to a one, inviting and welcoming and kind. He didn't know if they treated him that way out of pity or civility toward a guest in a home in which they too were guests, or if they had honestly decided to think well of the current holder of a title that had for generations been attached to people who'd hardly lived worthy of it. But he realized, sitting there, that he had some ability to determine which reason took hold. By absenting himself from Society, he had robbed himself of any ability to influence how he was perceived. His return, however oddly brought about, had given him an opportunity.

As he was the last to arrive, he was also permitted to be the last to leave, though being a single gentleman calling on a single lady, he dared not remain for more than the briefest of moments after the last caller departed.

He offered his farewells at the door and made his way to the street. He had walked to the earl's fashionable home from his rented rooms and intended to return in the same manner. But mere steps away, he realized he'd lost his case of calling cards. It must have slipped from his pocket at some point, likely while seated in the drawing room.

His knock was answered quickly by the footman posted there.

"I believe I have lost my card case in the drawing room."

The footman, one young for his post, motioned Julian inside and toward the drawing room. Generally, servants would have undertaken the search themselves, but it wasn't a complete breach of etiquette. And the drawing room proved empty, which simplified the situation.

Julian returned to the chair he had been occupying and

found, wedged between the cushion and the frame, the case he was searching for. It had most certainly slipped from his pocket. He returned it there and made to leave.

But in that very moment, Charlotte stepped into the room, pulling the door closed. She hadn't looked at him yet and, he suspected, didn't know he was there. He couldn't imagine she would close the door otherwise.

"You had likely best open that again."

She startled a little at his voice, confirming his suspicions that he had gone unnoted. "Lord Wesley. I didn't realize you had returned."

"My card case fell from my pocket. I was retrieving it."

"Thank you for calling today." She moved to where he stood as she spoke. "Though my father wasn't present, offering no opportunity to distract him from his purpose, *I* enjoyed having you here."

He took her hand and held it gently. "I enjoyed being here. I've feared rejection from Society for so long that I have simply avoided nearly anything to do with the *ton*. Feeling welcome proved a delightful change."

"You will always be welcome with me," she said.

He kissed her hand, closing his eyes over the lingering gesture. "I suspect your father would not agree, neither would your eventual husband."

He felt her other hand brush against his cheek. Julian opened his eyes once more. She stood very close, watching him with the same tenderness he'd seen in her eyes again and again during that afternoon's call. "I think my father could be brought around to seeing you as you are rather than a mere extension of your family."

"I am far more determined that he be brought around to seeing you as a lady worthy of choosing her future and her happiness." He tucked their entwined hands between them. "I want that for you, Charlotte." She offered no objection at his use of her Christian name. "I want you to be happy."

"In this moment, Julian"—he smiled at hearing his name on her lips—"I am entirely happy."

He bent and pressed a light kiss to her lips, his heart pounding at the tender touch. He'd have kissed her further, longer, but knew their situation was precarious for so many reasons. Far sooner than he would have liked, he stepped back and released her hand, then slipped silently from the house once more.

The day of Louisa's wedding arrived. The ceremony was lovely. The bride was beautiful. The bride's dearest friend was . . . distracted.

Charlotte knew her father would soon be selecting a husband for her, and that husband would undoubtedly *not* be Julian. She'd hardly known him a fortnight earlier, yet her heart broke again and again as she thought of building a life with anyone else.

She had long told herself that her only unwavering requirements in a future husband were that he be kind to her and not an unpleasant person. Julian was, of course, both of those things, but he was also so much more. He had a keen sense of humor, humility enough to admit he'd been wrong and misguided in his efforts to forestall her possible nuptials. He had shown himself to be intelligent and quick-witted. His long-standing friendship with Mr. Daubney indicated he was loyal and did not abandon people when it might have otherwise been convenient to do so. Defending himself against her father's unflattering assessment, but managing the thing without being harsh or hurtful, showed compassion and patience, mingled with an unwillingness to be run roughshod over. That was a rare combination.

And he kissed wonderfully.

Charlotte fanned herself a bit as the carriage rolled back toward home after the wedding breakfast. The memory of Julian's lips pressed softly to hers flitted through her mind with shocking regularity, and every time it did, her cheeks heated. It had been a fleeting kiss, so brief and light that she'd have expected to be far less impressed than she actually was. Instead of disappointment at the briefness of the moment, she found herself longing for him to kiss her again.

"Mr. and Mrs. Selby seemed pleased," Father said from the other side of the carriage. "And well they might be. Mr. Granville is a respected gentleman with income enough. A fine catch for their daughter."

"And how fortunate the new Mrs. Granville is that she and her new husband are truly happy in each other's company," Charlotte added. "That is not always the case."

Father shook his head slowly. "No, it is not."

"Were you and Mother pleased with your marriage?" she asked. "I'm afraid I have very few memories of her, none of which answer that question."

He nodded. "We were, after a time."

After a time. It was not an enthusiastic answer nor was it encouraging in the moment. She could, "after a time," learn to be pleased with either of the gentlemen she had been hoping her father would choose. She could be content. It was all she had ever aimed for, all she'd felt herself able to require in a match.

But that felt utterly unsatisfying now.

She wanted someone who made her heart flutter. Someone who could, with a single kiss, make her blush for days. Someone who wanted her to be truly happy. Not merely pleased. Not merely content. Happy.

Loved.

"I hope Mr. Granville does not object to bringing his new wife back to Town for your wedding," Father said.

Charlotte swallowed. "*My* wedding?"

He didn't seem to take note of the tremor in her voice. "Wouldn't do to wait too long. The Season is nearly over now."

"You were kind to wait until after Louisa's wedding." It had, in fact, been a kindness on Father's part. How could she ask for another delay? Yet if he made his decision in the very near future, he would most certainly *not* choose the gentleman she could actually see herself happy with. "Marriage is not something one ought to rush into."

"Fortunately," Father said, "we have had four years."

"Does that mean you have chosen someone?"

He shook his head, and she breathed a little more easily. "I don't intend to propose to a gentleman on your behalf." He laughed a little. "But there are a couple of gentlemen who, I believe, are on the cusp of approaching me. And should they do so, I would eagerly move forward with a match between either of them and my darling daughter."

Should they do so. If Mr. Vernon or Mr. Travers asked for her hand, Father would accept. And she would be married almost before she knew what was happening.

Thank the heavens for Julian's offer to continue interrupting would-be suitors. A bit of awkwardness would, she desperately hoped, go a long way toward preventing what would undoubtedly be a disaster.

Nine

JULIAN ARRIVED AT LORD AND Lady Fischer's soiree feeling surprisingly excited. Yes, a great deal of that was owing to the fact that he was absolutely certain Charlotte would be there, but that was not the entirety of it. He had, under her influence, come to truly enjoy the time he was spending in Society. Charlotte had welcomed him and liked him and, to his delighted shock, had forgiven him. She had opened the door and he was finally ready to step through it.

Franklin was not in attendance that night, as he was spending the evening with his family. Julian never truly envied his friend those familial connections, mostly because his own family had been such a source of misery. But he did miss family, just as he'd told Lord Tarrant. His father had been an objectively dreadful person, but Julian sometimes wished he were still nearby, wished he were still present, were still alive. It was a difficult thing being so alone.

Perhaps someday Julian would have a family of his own and a life filled with love instead of loneliness. His mind immediately conjured an image of his estate, set to rights, Charlotte there with him, their children completing the idyllic image. He didn't think it such an outlandish fantasy. She had kissed him, after all. And though it had been painfully brief, he had reason to believe she might feel for him what he felt for her.

But marriage, in their circles, was not the stuff of fantasies. It was approached logically, with an eye to connections and building family fortunes.

He was titled and had an estate and income, yes. But that estate was in a degree of disrepair, which was a bit of a drain on his income to the point that a wager of £1000 had been more than he'd been able to ignore. Add to that the fact that he was a Lord Wesley and that Charlotte's father knew enough of the family history to look unfailingly askance at Julian as a result, and only the tiniest thread of hope remained.

Still, he entered the grand drawing room of Lord and Lady Fischer's home with his head held high. He was greeted kindly, something which happened nearly everywhere he went the past week or so. He couldn't say for certain if it was the reception he would have received if not for Charlotte accepting him so readily and warmly. Whatever the exact reason, he was choosing to be grateful. Unfortunately, in the midst of the kind greetings came Sir Duncan. His presence seldom improved a situation.

The gentleman's attention, though, was not on Julian, but rather on Charlotte herself. The earl stood nearby. With her father present, it was not Julian's place to intercede. But Charlotte looked more than a little annoyed. If he wasn't mistaken, she was also a bit miserable. His role that night was meant to be utilizing his knack for being a bit ridiculous in order to slow the efforts of would-be suitors. Sir Duncan wasn't a suitor, but he could be thwarted the same way.

Julian sauntered to where they were and placed himself in the gathering.

"You have left all of the gentlemen of London wondering how long it will be before you follow your friend and marry as well," Sir Duncan was saying.

"The gentlemen of London may simply have to learn to be patient," Charlotte said. She managed a casual and friendly tone, but Julian recognized the frustration and tension in her gaze. Her father seemed oblivious to it.

"You could not be so cruel," Sir Duncan said, his tone teasing as well but with enough snap to the words to render them more demanding than friendly.

Julian had harbored some suspicion that Sir Duncan might be the one who had made the bet regarding Charlotte's marriage prospects. And he sneered enough at Julian when they were in company to add weight to the theory.

The earl was not moving to intervene, and Sir Duncan did not seem likely to abandon the subject or walk away. Julian was unwilling to leave Charlotte to deal with the blackguard herself.

"Is the theme of this evening's soiree 'Badgering Ladies on the Subject of Marriage'?" Julian asked, watching Sir Duncan with wide eyes and a look of feigned innocence. "I am afraid I have arrived with absolutely no experience in that area."

"I have badgered no one," Sir Duncan insisted, ruffling up on the spot.

Julian was not so easily distracted from his awkward aim. "Are we calling it something different? 'Pestering,' perhaps? 'Making Oneself a Nuisance in the Presence of'?" Julian turned overly innocent eyes on Charlotte. "Am I meant to be annoying you right now?"

She smiled broadly. "If that is what you are attempting, Lord Wesley, I fear you are failing. I find myself delighted with your company."

He looked to Sir Duncan once more. "My apologies, but it appears you will be required to undertake all of the pestering this evening. I am clearly quite unable to make myself irritating."

Sir Duncan was not amused, but many others gathered around were.

"Are you inferring that I am mistreating Lady Charlotte?" Sir Duncan demanded, nostrils flaring with vexation.

"I was *implying*," Julian corrected. "You were *inferring*." He looked to Charlotte once more. "Is incorrect word usage part of the evening's entertainment? I fear I will be unskilled at that as well."

Charlotte smiled at him. How had he lived twenty-five years without that smile? How could he be expected to live even one more without seeing it?

Sir Duncan looked to the earl. "This soiree seems to have attracted people unworthy of your daughter's company. I will happily call up my carriage to take us elsewhere."

"Now you are implying that you have the right to dictate where I and my daughter spend our time." The earl spoke very matter-of-factly, but there was no mistaking that he did not, at least in that moment, approve of Sir Duncan. Perhaps Julian had helped solidify that opinion. "I would suggest you leave off the suppositions for the remainder of the night."

The discomfort in Sir Duncan's posture promised a hasty departure, which he almost immediately undertook. That was one less person Charlotte's father might attempt to match her with.

The earl indicated Julian should walk with him and his daughter. He didn't object.

"Your father and grandfather were a lot of things, Lord Wesley, but they were not empty-headed. I suspect you are not as well."

"I would like to think I'm not," Julian answered.

"Then why act the part?"

The earl had realized Julian was playacting. Had he from the very beginning, at the musicale?

To be safe, Julian kept his explanation to that evening's performance. "Sir Duncan was making your daughter unhappy. Dispatching him without having to resort to calling him out seemed my best option."

"Would you have called him out?" Charlotte asked him.

"He would have deserved it," Julian acknowledged. "But I am not in a position to so formally take up the cause of defending you in that way. Presuming to do so would only make the situation even worse than it was."

Her gaze on him turned soft. "Are you always so mindful of the impact you have on others?"

"I try to be," he said, "but I fall short more often than I wish I did."

"I think we all do," Lady Charlotte said.

Julian shook his head. "You are endlessly kind and patient. You show people consideration and—"

He stopped short, realizing the earl was watching him a bit too closely for comfort. The gentleman did not approve of him. Drawing undue notice would likely make that even more true.

"I suppose I *am* making a nuisance of myself now." He offered a quick dip of his head. "I do know how to make myself scarce, and I can do so if you would prefer."

"Please don't," Charlotte said. Her eyes darted to her father, and she kept her expression one of almost neutrality. "Sir Duncan will not pester me if you are nearby, and I would greatly appreciate an evening-long reprieve."

His affection for her must have been written on every corner of his face. But what could he do? He'd lost his heart to her so utterly that hiding the state of his affections felt impossible.

"If your father will permit me to enjoy your company for a time longer, I would be honored to do so."

The earl was studying him again, and it was not an overly comfortable examination. Julian had promised Charlotte awkwardness, but he hadn't fully anticipated feeling ill at ease himself.

Mr. Travers arrived in that moment. He was received warmly and eagerly by Lord Tarrant. Charlotte watched the new arrival with misgiving. Not fear or distaste, neither with the actual misery she'd shown with Sir Duncan. But this suitor, one who'd seemed to gain her father's favor, had certainly not won her good opinion.

Time for weaponized awkwardness.

"Tonight's soiree involves pestering people," Julian told Mr. Travers. "And word misusage. Isn't that exciting?"

Mr. Travers's brows drew in confusion. "I beg your pardon?"

"A bit of revelry," Julian explained. "Of humor. Diversion."

"Is not the soiree itself the diversion?" Mr. Travers asked quite somberly.

"Soirees can contain diversions as well," Charlotte replied.

"That seems like a great deal of . . . merriment." That Mr. Travers didn't care for the idea couldn't have been more obvious.

"Do you not like merriment?" Charlotte pressed.

"It has its place, I suppose."

Her expression fell.

Julian eyed her father, hoping he noticed. Hoping he cared. The earl gave no indication one way or the other.

"Life needs a bit of lightness," Julian said. "What a drudgery it would be otherwise."

Charlotte looked to her father, holding his gaze earnestly. "That would be drudgery. It truly would."

The earl pulled Charlotte's arm through his. "Lightness is not a failing," he assured her.

"For some people, Father, it is a *necessity*."

He patted her hand and nodded. "It is a pleasure to have seen you again, Mr. Travers. Lord Wesley." To his daughter, he said, "Let us find a place to sit."

As she walked away on her father's arm, Charlotte looked back at Julian, gratitude in her expression.

He bowed, grateful to have helped and heartbroken to watch her walk away.

Ten

"Why did you not tell me Mr. Travers was not to your liking?" Charlotte's father posed the question over breakfast the next morning, quite without warning.

"He was never to my *dis*liking," she said, picking at her toast. "He would be kind to me and . . . most young ladies would consider themselves fortunate simply to have avoided unkindness. I had not set my sights much higher than that."

"But you *have* set them on Mr. Vernon?" Her father was sharp. He always had been. She ought to have realized he hadn't been unaware of her efforts.

"He is a good person," Charlotte acknowledged. "And he would—"

"Not be unkind?" Father finished for her. "And that is what you were hoping for."

"I know enough of the world to understand why marriages are contracted, and that the hearts and hopes of those being matched are seldom the topmost consideration. I was attempting to at least avoid misery."

He looked as though she'd wounded his feelings. "Do you believe I would choose someone who would make you actually miserable?"

"I hoped not, but it has happened before. It has happened in *our* family. Aunt Tottie was so displeased with your father's choice that she fled London and has steadfastly refused to return ever since."

"I would never treat you the way he treated her," Father insisted. "I wish to see you settled as you ought to be, looked out for, cared for, with someone dependable and reliable."

"Would it be so terrible if that person also had a tenderness for me and I for him?" she asked quietly.

He studied her. "You speak as though you already have someone in mind."

Truth be told, she did. But she couldn't imagine her father was ready for *that* confession. "Are you absolutely determined to see me wed by the end of the Season? The speed with which we are approaching this makes it difficult for me to believe that the outcome will be a good one."

He was clearly empathetic to her concerns, but he did not seem convinced by her arguments. "Even the daughter of an earl runs out of time, dear. Four Seasons is more than most are granted before being seen as a spinster. I would not wish for you to miss out on your opportunity for something more than what your aunt Tottie currently claims."

"But I do sometimes wonder if I would be more discontented in a marriage that I did not like than I would be if I were unmarried entirely."

Again, he seemed to understand why she would feel that way but did not give any indication he was softening to her line of thinking.

"You seemed satisfied with Mr. Vernon and Mr. Travers until Lord Wesley began interfering." Father took a sip of his tea.

"I did not realize until coming to know Lord Wesley better that I could enjoy someone's company as much as I enjoy his."

Father set his cup down with a bit of a clang. "He is not suitable."

"In what way is he not suitable?" She kept her tone conciliatory but also firm. "He has, on many occasions, stood my champion. He is not arrogant like Sir Duncan, and he is able and willing to quell that haughtiness without making the situation worse. He has a title and an estate. We have seen for ourselves that he is making inroads in Society and is being well received."

Father rose and paced away. "His title does him no credit. His predecessors were spendthrifts, and it is known that his estate is in disrepair and his finances do not bear scrutiny."

"But none of those things are reflections on *his* character," Charlotte insisted. "That he is not a copy of his grandfather or father or any of the other members of his family whose behavior has colored your assumptions about him ought to be a mark in his favor."

"Even if he proved, in time, to be the very opposite of the family who raised him, I cannot consider myself a good father if I resigned you to a life spent in a house in disrepair and an insufficient and unstable income."

"I do have a dowry," she reminded him.

He grew more resolved. "That is not its purpose."

Its purpose was not to secure her happiness. Was it any wonder she hadn't been certain her father would choose to accept a suitor who brought her happiness?

"If Lord Wesley were to obtain £1000 through means other than my dowry and set his estate to rights, would that satisfy you?"

Her father's mouth turned a bit in pondering. "Do you suspect he is soon to be the recipient of such a sum?"

She squared her shoulders. "If I have any say in the matter, yes."

"Where would this £1000 be coming from?"

"Believe me, Father, if I knew the answer to that, we would be having a very different conversation." She rose, smoothing the front of her morning gown. "One thousand pounds is a significant amount of money, and by the 6th of June, he will be in possession of it. Please give me until then to prove to you that he is worthy of your consideration, that he is the good and kind and considerate gentleman I have found him to be."

Father didn't agree, but neither did he immediately object. Hoping that meant he was at least considering, she excused herself and left the breakfast room, only allowing herself to breathe once she reached her bedchamber.

She had until her birthday. A mere week.

Julian received a summons from the Earl of Tarrant to meet him at their club. They were members of the same one but had never interacted there in the past. The difference in their ages and Julian's hesitation to reenter Society had more or less guaranteed that.

The earl was in a quiet corner in the library when Julian arrived. He was invited to sit with the gentleman and did so.

"Is there a reason, Lord Wesley, why my daughter is convinced that you will be the recipient of £1000 on her birthday?"

Without losing his composure in the least, Julian turned the question around. "Is there a reason the convergence of those two things *specifically* has struck you so entirely?"

Lord Tarrant released a breath as he nodded slowly and ponderously. "Let me tell you a story, and we will see if we can't answer each other's questions that way." He entwined his fingers and set his woven hands on his lap. "There is a wager on the books of this club, one that declares that should Lady Charlotte Duchamps *not* be married by her twenty-first birthday, the anonymous wagerer will pay Lord Wesley a sum of £1000."

Good heavens. Was Lord Tarrant the one who had placed the wager after all?

"This wager was recorded twenty years ago."

Julian's eyes pulled wide. Someone had bet against Charlotte's matrimonial prospects while she was still an infant?

"My sister, Tottie, still went about Society at the time, though she'd had two unsuccessful Seasons and had given every indication that she did not intend to undertake a third. She was the recipient of a lot of unkindness on the matter, not the least of which came from our father. He arranged, by the end of her final Season, for her to marry a man with whom she would have been miserable. Utterly and entirely."

Julian listened closely, unsure of the connection between past and present but hoping to understand better so he could help more, so Charlotte might not be as mistreated as it seemed her aunt Tottie had been.

"I would like to believe our father would have been kinder in his choice had he not felt desperate to see her married quickly," Lord Tarrant said. "She was turning twenty-one soon, and that was not a milestone he felt he could . . . afford to reach with her still unwed."

Afford. The pieces were suddenly falling firmly into place. "What is your sister's Christian name, Lord Tarrant?"

"Charlotte."

That would make her *Lady Charlotte Duchamps*, just like her niece. The wager had been placed twenty years ago, when she would have likely been nearly twenty-one years old. And there had been a Lord Wesley at that time who would not have minded being connected to a wager that was potentially harmful to a lady.

"I was horrified when I learned of the wager," Lord Tarrant said. "I love my sister, and she did not deserve to have her name bandied about. Upon discovering our father had placed the wager and was willing to throw away her happiness in order to win it, I was more angry than I ever remember being with him. Tottie fled London to avoid the match being forced on her, and she has never returned. She has never trusted anyone enough to do so, not even me, unfortunately."

"Then the inconsiderate wager is not a recent one and does not involve the current Lady Charlotte or Lord Wesley?"

The earl shook his head. "It is not and does not. *That* Lady Charlotte was ruined by the wager. *That* Lord Wesley received his £1000 and lost it the next day on a horse race."

"I can understand why you despise my family so much."

"Mine was not entirely innocent in the matter," Lord Tarrant generously added. His shoulders squared a moment later. "What was it you did when you learned of the wager?"

It would be hypocritical of him to be dishonest with the gentleman after he'd been so forthcoming. "At first I hoped to delay any suitors from successfully pressing their suit. Delay, you understand, not prevent or discourage. But then I discovered that the gentlemen who were closest to success were unlikely to be a good match for her. She didn't smile when they were nearby or seem delighted to spot their arrival. She didn't seem to miss them when they left. And nothing in her interaction with them gave me the least reason to think Lady Charlotte would actually be happy if married to either one of them, and I couldn't bear that thought."

The earl watched him in silence.

"The wager quickly slipped quite low on my list of concerns. She deserves to be happy every bit as much as your sister did. I need those £1000; I'll not deny that. But I would give up every penny I do have if it meant she didn't have to flee London and hide herself away for the rest of her life. She deserves better."

"Do you?" the earl pressed.

"Life has dealt me an unfair hand, and there is little I can do about that. Unless, of course, someone else places an irresponsible wager and makes me the recipient of another fortune." He tried to smile, but the expression slipped away almost immediately.

Charlotte was not the focus of the insulting wager, which he was grateful for. And this conversation might very well save her from an unhappy match, which set his mind at ease. But he now had no hope whatsoever of obtaining the money he needed to undo the damage his grandfather had done. And that ended what little chance he had of building a life with the lady he'd come to love.

He stood even as his heart dropped to his feet. "Perhaps making certain Lady Charlotte is treated with greater respect and consideration than your sister was, will allow us to atone in some small way for the treatment Lady Tottie experienced at the hands of our predecessors."

Julian left the earl to ponder that. He, himself, couldn't manage any thought beyond the unshakable realization that happiness had been within his grasp—and he'd lost it.

Eleven

JULIAN FELT IT BEST TO make certain Charlotte understood the reality of their situation. He'd not begun their interaction on a foundation of candor, and he regretted that. The presentation of his calling card at her London residence was answered by the butler with instructions from Lady Charlotte that he be shown to the back garden. It was a reasonable way for her to receive him despite both of them being unwed and unrelated to each other.

He made his way there and found Charlotte standing amongst the honeysuckle and climbing roses. Her eyes lit as he approached. He imagined his did as well despite having arrived to deliver unfortunate news.

"Charlotte." Her name emerged softer than he'd intended, but his heart was heavy.

"You seem upset."

He took gentle hold of her hand, grateful they had enough privacy to allow the gesture while also being enough in public to avoid scandal. "I feel like we've had this conversation before."

"We have, though it was you who comforted me at the lending library when I was upset."

"I fear, though I know you will try, that there will be little comfort to be had once I tell you the source of my distress." He set his other hand atop hers, cradling it between both of his. "I have learned that the wager we were depending upon to delay your nuptials and set my finances to rights is, in actuality, an old one involving a different Lady Charlotte and a different Lord Wesley. There is no forfeit to be had."

A string of expressions passed over her features as she sorted out what he had revealed. "My aunt Tottie?" she finally guessed aloud.

He nodded. "And my grandfather."

Charlotte pressed her free hand to her heart. "Poor Tottie."

Julian set their entwined hands against *his* heart. "I will do all I can to continue helping you to avoid whatever unwanted matches your father might press on you, of course."

"Any match my father might press on me would be unwanted." She sighed. "He's already told me that he considers you unsuitable."

He raised her hand to his lips and kissed it gently. "I cannot say that I blame him, and I wish I knew how to change his mind."

"So do I." She closed the distance between them and leaned against him.

Julian set his arms around her. He likely would never be granted the opportunity again. How quickly he'd fallen in love with her. And how quickly that had fallen apart. He kissed her temple, closing his eyes in a vain attempt to prolong the moment.

Fate seemed inclined to undermine them: footsteps sounded on the path nearby.

Charlotte slipped back and out of his arms, looking as disappointed as he felt.

It was the earl who came into sight a moment later, and he didn't appear the least surprised to see them there. Perhaps this location was not as private as he'd thought, despite the climbing roses and honeysuckle creating a bit of seclusion.

"Lord Wesley," the earl said as he walked past, "I thought I might find you here."

"Did you?" He had not indicated any intention to come to this house after his time spent at the club.

"I am not so oblivious as some might think." Lord Tarrant sat on the bench tucked among the honeysuckle. "Come sit with me, Charlotte."

She did so. Julian, not having been dismissed, remained nearby.

"I had the opportunity while at my club this morning to undertake a very enlightening conversation," the earl said, "but also to peruse the betting books while I was there."

Charlotte looked up at Julian, confused and concerned. He wished he had some reassurance to offer.

"I have discovered, Lord Wesley, why it is you did not realize the wager you stumbled across was not a current one." The earl threaded his fingers on his lap just as he'd done during their earlier conversation. "The wager was not dated, neither was it marked as fulfilled."

"I *had* thought it odd that, after only a half a glass of sherry, I was left so inebriated that I couldn't comprehend what I was reading, yet somehow remembered in great detail what I had read."

With a lift of his eyebrow, Lord Tarrant said, "Perhaps you should keep to champagne."

Julian laughed lightly. "That is likely very good advice."

The earl seemed both surprised and pleased by that response.

"Were you able to have the wager marked complete?" Julian asked.

"I can't. Only the one who placed it and the one to whom the forfeit was to be paid can have it officially declared completed."

That *was* a difficulty. "Both of those gentlemen are dead."

The earl nodded. "But their heirs are not."

"*We* are their heirs." Julian knew the earl realized that. There must have been more to it. "Could we not declare in their steads?"

The earl shook his head. "To do so, we would need to have some proof that our predecessors did as they pledged. But I am certain my father did not record the payment he made, as he would have been ashamed of the entire thing. And considering how quickly your grandfather lost what he was paid, I don't imagine he recorded it either."

"Likely not."

"I cannot imagine any of this is legally binding," Charlotte said.

"Yet," her father said, "it is still binding in a very real way. The existence of the wager does not reflect well on either of our families. To be believed to be delinquent in the payment of it only makes the situation worse."

She squared her shoulders. "If you think I will allow myself to be forced into an unwanted match so that your gentlemanly obligation can be met—"

Both Julian and the earl were quick to insist they would not countenance such a thing. That her father was not thinking of subjecting his daughter to such an unkindness set Julian's mind a bit at ease.

"What is it you mean to do, Father?"

"I mean, in one weeks' time, to pay Lord Wesley £1000."

Julian shook his head. "That is hardly necessary."

The earl rose once more, moving to stand in front of Julian. "I have spent much of the weeks since your arrival in our lives determined to believe that you were exactly like your father and his. I ought to have been doing more to show that *I* was not like *mine.*" He looked Julian fully in the eye. "You rose to my sister's defense despite not knowing her. You pleaded for my daughter's happiness, even knowing you were unlikely to secure your own. And even now, when you found yourself in a position to receive a much-needed windfall, you objected to what you felt was an unwarranted burden on me. You have led me to rethink a great many things."

"Your daughter has led me to do the same. She is a remarkable person."

"Yes, she is." He smiled quickly at his daughter. "And she seems to think very highly of you."

Charlotte was watching Julian, her gaze uncertain but tender, gentle.

"Do you suppose, Lord Tarrant, that in light of Lady Charlotte's approval, I might be permitted to call here now and then? Perhaps join you some mornings when you ride in the park?"

Lord Tarrant dipped his head. "I would appreciate the opportunity to learn for myself if you are worthy of the good opinion that she has bestowed upon you."

Charlotte rose and stood at Julian's side, facing the earl. "You have seen his good character for yourself, Father. You've only just said as much."

"As your father, I will require repeated proof," he said. "But I am not unwilling to allow him to provide it."

Taking Julian's arm with eagerness, Charlotte said, "You will soon have the money you need to set your estate to rights. At last you will be able to shed the burdens your family has left you with, and not merely the monetary ones."

He set his hand on hers. "And I hope you have at last been able to shed some of the neglect of your own happiness you had resigned yourself to."

The earl cleared his throat, pulling their attention back to him. "I am going to take a turn about the garden. That ought to grant you about five minutes of privacy." On that declaration, he did precisely as he said he would.

The moment they were alone, Charlotte threw her arms around his neck, something to which he did not object in the least.

"Father will come around to accepting you, I know he will."

Julian held her close. "I suspect you are correct, though it still feels like a miracle."

"I have never been more grateful for a wager in all my life."

He bent nearer, his lips a hair's breadth from hers. "Neither have I, my dear. Neither have I."

They had five minutes of time together and they did not waste a moment of it. They kissed each other, held each other, declared their great fortune and their love. A wager had brought their paths to cross, but the love that had grown between them would keep them together. Always.

Photograph © Annalisa Rosenvall

Sarah M. Eden is the *USA Today* bestselling author of multiple historical romances, including Foreword Review's 2013 "IndieFab Book of the Year" gold medal winner for Best Romance, *Longing for Home*, and two-time Whitney Award Winner *Longing for Home: Hope Springs*. Combining her obsession with history and affinity for tender love stories, Sarah loves crafting witty characters and heartfelt romances. She has thrice served as the Master of Ceremonies for the Storymakers Writers Conference and acted as the Writer in Residence at the Northwest Writers Retreat. Sarah is represented by Pam Pho at D4EO Literary Agency.

Visit Sarah at www.sarahmeden.com

www.ingramcontent.com/pod-product-compliance
Lightning Source LLC
LaVergne TN
LVHW021800060526
838201LV00058B/3181